What Love Demands

by

Renata North

What Love Demands

Cover Art by *The Wild Rose Press, Inc.*

The Wild Rose Press, Inc.
PO Box 708
Adams Basin, NY 14410-0708
Visit us at www.thewildrosepress.com

Publishing History
First Edition, 2023
Trade Paperback ISBN 978-1-5092-4930-5
Digital ISBN 978-1-5092-4931-2

Published in the United States of America

In an instant, they were riding double, the heat of Jim's body warming her. At first, she was desperately clumsy riding partnered. Clumsy until she yielded to Jim's unspoken command. The more she relaxed and attuned to Jim's cues, the more gracefully they rode.

She'd tried to convince herself that Robert wouldn't mind. However, Jim's strong arms were about her, his firm thighs braced hers, his chest rose and fell against her back, and his body rocked her to the mare's rhythm. Even the scent of him, a mix of smoke, sweat, and raw, masculine sex, enveloped her. His breath, warm against her temple, carried the faintest sweetness of liquor.

He'd be a fearsome match against any foe and Cora felt safe against the night but not safe with herself. As she sensed Jim's arousal, a heat rose within her, and they were pulled into a mystical dance. As they approached Brucedale, Jim slowed them to a walk, but the spell didn't break. His hot breath upon her, he nuzzled her ear, softly kissed her neck and collar bone, grazed her skin with his stubble. Her skin sizzled under the touch of his lips. She had to stop him. It was madness.

Dedication

To Andy

Chapter 1

1874, Southwestern Ontario, Canada

Cora closed the screen door for the last time. While the sensible citizens of Maryville took shelter, she ignored the gathering storm and focused on her errand. Rumbles of thunder warned the cows to lie low in their pastures, dogs to cower under porches, and women to snatch laundry from clotheslines and hurry their children indoors. Gusts of wind twisted branches, rattled gates, and lifted the hat of any man who failed to shelter behind a sturdy wall. As the clouds thickened, Cora gripped her leather satchel and hurried on her journey to Aunt Jenny's cottage.

If Cora and her father, Dr. John Patton, meant to make an early start the next day, she had to restock the herbs that evening. Mr. Tucker needed liverwort for his jaundice, and she'd promised Betsy Meyer she'd bring feverfew to relieve her spells. There was a plentiful supply of any herb created by God in the cottage garden. The west wind whistled in the trees and the townhall bell tolled. She quickened her pace to a jog.

As the bell rang a fourth and final time, the winds shrieked a warning, loud as a steam locomotive. Cora saw a tall, young man further up the street. He was broad-shouldered from a summer of heavy work, judging by his clothing. He crossed Main Street and dashed, two steps at a time, onto the stonework porch of St. Andrew's Presbyterian Church.

The wind pulled Cora's skirt and bonnet and loosened her auburn hair from the practical, braided bun she wore while working. If she ran, she'd just make it to Aunt Jenny's before the storm.

In the splinter of an instant, a bolt of lightning lit an ancient maple, splitting its trunk with a deafening crack. The man turned toward the source of the noise and yelled, "Run!" His voice barely carried over the storm. He descended the steps as Cora approached, rain lashing her face and stinging her eyes. "Come on," he called. "It'll be safe in the church. Hurry!"

The man extended his hand. Cora didn't need a hand. She was quite capable of taking herself up the stairs. She raced by him, though he gained the porch and reached for the brass door handle before her.

"In here," he urged. "We'll be safe in here." They ducked inside, Cora entering the narthex first, the man pulling the door closed and latching it behind them.

"Thank God it was unlocked." He leaned against its oak panels. He wasn't out of breath, but he paused to collect himself all the same.

"Yes, thank God indeed," said Cora. Her "indeed" sounded like a rebuke, as if reminding him not to take the Lord's name in vain. She corrected herself with a nod and a shy "Thank you," wiped the rain from her eyes, and looked up at him, her vision adjusting to the gloom. His face was at once familiar yet…different. A mischievous boy's face had squared into the chiseled features of a grown man, dark brows over deep-set eyes, strong jaw, peach fuzz transformed into bristle, lopsided smile. Jimmy…Jimmy Sinclair. Notorious class clown and ne'er do-well.

"Cora?" Jimmy's baritone carried over the howl of the wind. "Cora. For God's sake. What were you doing out in a storm like this?"

"I could ask you the same thing, Jimmy," Cora tried to tuck locks of wayward hair under her bonnet.

"I was headed to the store for nails and wire to mend a fence."

"And it couldn't wait," finished Cora.

"No, it couldn't wait. But you—"

"My errand couldn't wait either." Though Cora wondered if it should have.

The wind howled through the belfry and caught the church bells, raising a cacophony of discordant notes. Jimmy looked up, a shadow of worry knitting his brow. Then, he flashed a smile. Pure Jimmy. He was always quick with a smile after he'd tied an unsuspecting girl's braid to her chair or carved a heart with the names of a mismatched and thoroughly embarrassed boy and girl on the beech tree at the school gate.

That smile, now a grin of even, white teeth, lips curled, ready to tease, his deep, fake-serious voice over the wind. "Say, Cora. When this lets up, do you think we'll start a rumor when we're seen leaving church together?"

Brazen. So brazen. Cora remembered his schoolyard taunts. *Freckle Face. Polka Dot.* The worst was *Spotsy.*

"You should be so lucky for people to think so, Jimmy Sinclair," she replied evenly.

"I'm 'Jim' now," he laughed. "Or 'James'. But you may call me 'Mr. Sinclair', Miss Polka Dot."

"Jimmy," Cora retaliated. He kept his silly grin. No wonder he'd been kicked out of college. She'd wipe that smirk off his face. "How's law school?" she asked, sweet as honey.

Success. The smile vanished. "I guess you didn't hear. I had to leave. McGill was great and I learned a lot, but Dad needed me on the farm." He shuffled his feet and hastened to change the subject. "That's some wind."

Obviously. Only the profoundly deaf wouldn't hear the roar of this storm. Anyway, so what if she'd touched a nerve.

He seemed to misinterpret her silence as borne of fear, and he spoke earnestly. "Though I was only twelve at the time, I helped install the roof here. Fetching dropped hammers, gathering nails, stuff like that. The building will hold. It's good and sturdy, Cora."

She didn't doubt it. The solid, red brick church was the pride of Maryville. For the past decade, the congregation gathered in its oaken pews every Sunday, hymns filling the nave, heads bowed as Reverend Cameron intoned solemn prayers and soporific sermons.

Jim continued, "When the storm lets up, there'll be a bit of work to do. Bound to be some branches down. That old maple's likely blocking the road."

"It was a grand old tree," she said, accepting Jimmy's tacit offer of peace. "Everyone will miss it come fall."

She stood awkwardly beside him, reluctant to express her fear of the damage they might find when they eventually emerged from the church. They shared this sanctuary and a truce of sorts, but Cora wasn't ready to forgive him entirely. Through school, Jimmy Sinclair had been Cora's nemesis. Too clever for his own good, scoring laughs at her expense, disrupting lessons with sly questions and remarks, especially if the teacher was inexperienced and struggled to keep order. Cora had not forgotten the time in fourth grade when Jimmy stole her skipping rope and convinced his friends to tie her to the flagpole like Joan of Arc. She freed herself from the clumsy knots and ran after him brandishing the rope like a whip only to be caught by Miss Brady and punished for horseplay. Jimmy never confessed that he was the instigator.

And now they waited in damp shadow, neither speaking, only listening to the wind. A tall, muscular, dark-haired man and a wild-haired, green-eyed woman with freckles speckling her cheeks and nose, both twenty-two, each wary of the other. At least that's how Cora felt. If Jimmy teased her again, she'd match his wit and more.

At last, the wind diminished to a whisper. Jimmy turned the latch, pushed the door open, and bowed theatrically. "After you, Miss Polka Dot."

Cora objected to the nickname as she stepped over the threshold, then abruptly stilled her tongue. She didn't know what to say. She had no words for what she saw on the other side of the door.

****

In the dimness, that sacred dimness common to unlit churches and haylofts, he'd glanced sideways at Cora. She stood smartly, back straight, shoulders square, chin up as if standing sentry at a castle door, clutching her satchel as though he might steal it. The messy curls tumbling from under her bonnet over her forehead and graceful neck were at odds with her prim attitude. She never could take a joke. She giggled with her girlfriends when they skated on the millpond or picnicked on the riverbank, but she wouldn't laugh for him. She had expressive, ocean green eyes, freckles sprinkled over her skin like cinnamon on cream, and a wide smile, but not for him. Never for him. While her friends laughed at his antics, she pursed her lips and stared daggers with those startling eyes.

Cora didn't behave as if afraid. If anything, she seemed irritated by the inconvenience of waiting out danger with him for company. He sought to reassure her anyway, though in honesty he was reassuring himself that the roof and windows would hold. If Jim had known what lay on the other side of the doorway, he'd have gone through before her, ladies first be damned, though that wouldn't have spared Cora the awful truth.

She saw the damage first, though he was by her side in an instant. Across the street, the new plate glass window at Beck's Dry Goods had shattered into a million shards. Papers littered the street. Shop signs dangled over doorways and overturned barrels rolled in slow arcs. The smell of wood smoke permeated the air. Beyond the fallen maple, to the east up Main Street, smoke billowed in a remnant breeze. Was it Doc Patton and Cora's house? They had a wooden house. It mustn't be. It was.

Cora ran home, unaware he was with her. By the time they crossed Silver Creek and gained the eastern boundary of Maryville, the Patton house had transformed into a funeral pyre. Patrick O'Mallory, first on the scene, said the good doctor hadn't escaped his collapsed home before the wind whipped flames from the stove into a blaze that made rescue impossible. Cora, still clutching her satchel like a life preserver, stared into the fire and Jim stared at Cora. Forlorn, beautiful Cora. He wouldn't touch her. He couldn't touch her. He longed to comfort her, to offer what solace he could, but such a gesture was forbidden him. There was nothing Jim could do or say to make things better.

Having rushed to Brockett's Mills, the fire brigade failed to appear. The O'Mallory boys came through the orchard with buckets of water, though teacups would've served their futile purpose equally as well. The newspaper man, Robert Helston, stood apart from the small crowd gathering around Cora. Kate O'Mallory encircled Cora's shoulder with a plump arm and folded her into a consoling embrace. Cora's shoulders shook. Kate rocked the grief-stricken girl in her arms and whispered in her ear. The crowd parted for Jenny Patton. Weird Jenny Patton whose eyes pierced through the rampart of any half-truth, façade, or lie, and peered into the soul of the person behind it. Jenny strode to Cora and Kate and held them both.

A man spoke. "It's a terrible thing, isn't it? What an unspeakable tragedy for the girl. She's so young to be without her father. She'll be utterly bereft and vulnerable, I'm sure."

Helston, the newspaper man. His pretentious turns of phrase gave him away. Jim turned to face him eye to eye, crossed his arms, and nodded once.

Undeterred by Jim's wordless response, Helston leaned in. "It was only a frame house. One is somewhat surprised that a physician, even John Patton, humble country medic, wouldn't have been able to afford brick or stone."

Jim shrugged. If he were a hound, the fur on the back of his neck would stand on end in the company of this man.

"It's a most dreadful day for the citizens of

Maryville, isn't it, James?"

"Jim."

"Of course. Jim. Mr. Jim Sinclair. I shall run an article on how the stalwart citizens of Maryville endured the tempest of the century."

"Good idea," said Jim, hoping Helston would pursue his inquiries elsewhere.

"Where were you when the storm unleashed its fury, Jim?"

"Downtown."

"My word. That area is badly damaged. And where, may I ask, did you shelter?"

"In St. Andrew's." Jim tipped his cap with a flick of his finger. "Pardon me, Mr. Helston. I'd best head home for an axe to help clear the damage." Without a further word, he did just that.

Chapter 2

"Where do you think you're going?"

Cora stopped short at the side door of Aunt Jenny's cottage and went to the sitting room from whence the drill sergeant voice had issued. Jenny sat on her small, embroidered sofa by the window. Early morning sunshine cast shadows in the lines of her face. She looked as if she'd aged a decade in the night.

"I'm going to see Mr. Tucker and Betsy Meyer," Cora replied. "They both prefer early visits, and they need—"

"Nothing," Jenny said sharply. "They need nothing. Really, Cora. No one expects to see you today. No. I correct myself: no one wants to see you today. Your father isn't even buried yet. Folks will be mortified if you show up on their doorsteps. They won't know what to say to you. You think you're helping them, but they'll feel terrible for you and try to help you. Save everyone the fuss and stay here. Please. Hang your satchel and bonnet back on the coat rack."

Cora reluctantly obeyed Jenny's order, protesting all the while. "But what about Mr. Tucker? He was so yellow at my last visit and—"

"Yes. Yellow as a lemon. So what? Our elixir can't compete with the flask of brandy he keeps in his pocket, and you'll have him blubbering like a big, fat, yellow baby when he sees you." Jenny hugged herself, hung her head, and mock-sobbed, "Poor Cora Patton, an orphan. It's ever so tragic…tragic! And poor Doc Patton, burnt up like a forgotten piece of toast. Imagine…"

"And Betsy Meyer. Betsy needs me."

"Like the Pope needs a harem."

"Aunt Jenny!" Cora laughed despite herself. "Betsy gets those awful headaches, and your herbal mixture really helps her."

"So would a brisk constitutional and a plate of creamed spinach. The cause of Betsy's problem is Miss Betsy Meyer herself. She's not sick; she's spoiled." Jenny's voice rose with exasperation, then she gently implored, "Really, my dear. Sit down."

"I can't, Aunt Jenny," Cora confessed. "I can't be still. When I'm still, all I can think about is the tornado and that horrible fire. How Father asked me to remain at home, but I left anyway. And now he's gone."

"It's a good thing you have your own mind and did leave the house."

Cora shrugged away the platitude. "Don't you see, Aunt Jenny? That was Father's last memory of me. Doing what I wanted instead of what he asked of me."

Jenny patted the cushion next to her, and Cora collapsed onto it.

"I should think your father's last memory was one of admiration for his only daughter. Of you running bravely into the storm to fetch medicine for the sick," Jenny said softly.

"He was all alone."

"And maybe that brought him peace because you were spared."

"But I might have saved him."

"Or you might have died."

Cora tried to swallow her tears. Crying served no practical purpose; it was self-indulgent. The Patton family shared an ethic of simple service to others conducted with stoic fortitude. They didn't give in to self-pity.

Jenny shared Cora's distaste for sorrowful display, but she pulled her niece close, took a snow-white handkerchief from her sleeve and gave it to her anyway. Cora was relieved that Jenny said nothing when her tears came. Aunt and niece sat slumped together for several minutes, their sadness expressed in wordless, miserable companionship. So still was the room that a blue jay landed on the south windowsill to feed on the corn kernels Jenny had left there. The bird's eager pecking reminded Cora that life continued outside the cottage walls. For instance, people were cleaning up and making repairs in the aftermath of the storm.

Cora straightened and said hesitantly, "Shall I write a list? Of things we need to do?"

"Okay." Jenny smiled and punched Cora's shoulder affectionately.

Cora walked across the oval rug to the walnut bureau to find writing materials, relieved to busy her hands. She found a bottle of ink and shook it only to discover it empty.

Jenny said, "I have a full bottle of ink—no—*we* have a full bottle of ink in the top drawer, next to the pens. Now it seems to me that you are rather without many necessities. Let's begin with 'Things Cora Needs,' and then we'll plan for your father's wake."

Cora was scarcely seated with pen in hand, when the first of an army of condolence callers rattled the brass knocker on Jenny's front door to deliver a freshly baked pie and a jug of cider.

****

The noonday sun conjured waves of shimmering heat on the butcher shop roof where Jim Sinclair and Tom O'Mallory knelt, replacing cedar shingles that had blown away in the storm. Jim wiped sweat from his forehead, dried his palm on his trousers, and gripped his hammer. As he positioned a shingle at the eave with his left hand, he spotted Miss Betsy Meyer holding a parasol and a basket on the street below. Jim ducked behind the pile of shingles between Tom and him.

Tom sat back on his haunches and with an impish grin, regarded Jim from the corner of his eye. Then he peered over the eave, waved, and called cheerfully, "Good day, Miss Meyer. It's a fine day for a pretty girl to enjoy a stroll, isn't it?"

Betsy tipped her parasol back and looked up, a golden frame of ringlets around her pale face, her frock a confection of ribbons and flounces. "Why, thank you, Tom. Hello to you too, Jim," she called back with a curtsy. "Indeed, it is a fine day, though it's ever so hot."

Jim emerged from behind the shingles as if surrendering his position in battle and nodded his greeting.

Betsy batted her eye lashes coquettishly and her voice rose an octave if a note. "I do believe that gratitude is in order, Jim. I heard you cleared away the old maple last night, after you heroically attempted to save Dr. Patton's life."

"You heard incorrectly, Betsy," said Jim. "Patrick O'Mallory arrived at the house first and Tom and his brothers tried to put out the fire. And Mrs. O'Mallory took Jenny Patton and Cora away from the fire."

Betsy smiled thinly at Tom to credit him and his family and looked back to Jim. "I'm taking a spice cake to Cora and Jenny," she said in a noble tone.

"They'll appreciate your visit," said Jim.

"What a tragedy for them," Betsy continued. "Two defenseless ladies, living without the protection and guidance of a man. However will they manage?"

"The Patton ladies are capable of managing themselves," Jim said, seizing the opportunity to talk about Cora.

"You can't mean that," Betsy protested.

"I do mean it. Cora and Jenny show up, day and night, to care for anyone who needs them. They deliver nearly all the babies in Maryville. It's terrible to lose a brother and a father, but they'll cope."

"What about the role of the male head of the household in enforcing moral standards?" Betsy asked rhetorically, batting her eye lashes again.

Not caring if he were rude, Jim shrugged as if to say, what about it?

Betsy clarified, "Do you think that Jenny Patton will see that Cora doesn't fall into any, um, compromising situations?"

Jim flashed a wicked smile. "Compromising situations? With Cora? A man should be so lucky."

At once, Betsy stamped her foot. "May I remind you that you are speaking to a lady," she snapped. "Good day, Mr. Sinclair."

Betsy shifted her basket on her forearm, tilted her parasol to block her view of Jim and Tom, and stalked off in the shadow of the eaves.

Tom sat back and laughed. And laughed.

Jim put some nails in his pocket, returned to his row

of shingles, and scowled at Tom. "I don't see what you find so funny."

"*Compromising situations.*" Tom slapped his own knee to stop his laughter. "As you so aptly stated, lucky is the man who finds himself in a compromising situation with any of the pretty belles of Maryville including Cora and Betsy."

As Jim resumed his task, Tom said, "Can I ask you something?"

"Shoot."

"Why *don't* you pursue Betsy Meyer?"

"I think a better question is, 'why don't *you* pursue Betsy Meyer?'" Jim deflected.

"That's bloody obvious," said Tom.

Jim pretended it wasn't with another shrug.

"Since the heat is making you soft in the head, Jim, I'll spell out the particulars. Her father will only allow an upstanding Protestant, preferably a Lutheran, to court his precious daughter, though any literate member of the Orange Lodge who scrubs behind his ears will do. I admit, I'm handsome, strong, intelligent, and humble. A perfect specimen of a man, am I. However, the Meyers have a peculiar view of me and my kind. They call us 'Dirty Irish Catholics'. Now you, on the other hand, are a Presbyterian—"

Jim swung his hammer hard and drove a nail through a shingle to punctuate his irritation.

"And although you're an imperfect candidate for Betsy's hand, you're likely good enough, especially if you go back to school," Tom prattled. "Even the blind can see that Betsy adores you. Her father adores her. And I've observed that the Meyer *pater familias* makes sure Betsy gets what she wants. Also consider that, financially, you'd marry up."

Jim struck another nail and shook his head. "No way. I have absolutely no interest in courting Betsy Meyer."

"It was only a suggestion."

"And I have a suggestion for you."

Tom raised a brow in curiosity.

"Turn away from thy popery, Tom, and you may court her," said Jim.

Tom rubbed his chin. "Hmm, convert, marry Betsy, and join you in hell or remain obedient to the One True Faith…"

"Life is filled with hard choices," said Jim.

"I might consider the very eligible but probably less choosy Cora Patton to—"

"She's too good for the likes of you," Jim interrupted.

Tom laughed again as they both returned to work.

****

Cora was surprised to greet a dewy-faced, pink-cheeked Betsy at the front door. The girl seldom left the Meyer mansion, and when she did venture abroad, she was usually conveyed in a carriage.

"Oh, don't look so shocked, Cora," Betsy scolded. "Mummy is helping Mrs. Brockett to organize an emergency charity bazaar and Daddy is occupied at the bank today so I came by myself to offer our sympathy. They'll be along later."

"Well, thank you, Betsy," said Cora. "Your visit is a comfort to Aunt Jenny and me. You'll have a rest and a cup of tea with us, I hope."

Betsy agreed she would and presently all were seated in the sitting room.

"This cake is delicious," said Jenny, who'd snuck a piece in the kitchen and was already jabbing her fork into another slice. Cora marveled at her aunt's appetite given their loss.

"Thank you," said Betsy. "Anna Mae said she used her Dutch grandmother's recipe. It was ever so heavy on my arm. Perhaps it's too buttery?"

"Not at all, not at all," Jenny mumbled through a mouthful of cake. "It's perfect."

"Everyone is being so kind," remarked Cora. "I was supposed to visit you today and you came to us instead."

"It's the least I can do. One must overcome one's frailties at a time like this and think of others."

"We haven't been out to survey the damage yet," said Cora.

"It's mostly fallen trees, broken windows, and missing shingles," said Betsy. "Jim Sinclair was repairing the butcher shop roof when I walked by. Roof repair is such dangerous, heroic work."

"Fixing a roof that is practically flat is neither heroic nor dangerous," said Cora.

Jenny shot Cora a fierce glare. "No doubt everyone is pitching in to put Maryville to rights. Jim Sinclair included."

"We must all do our part," Betsy agreed, brightening. "Which reminds me. Mummy and I were discussing your circumstances, and we realized that I have some frocks I seldom wear, and we thought you might like to have them."

"I couldn't," said Cora.

Jenny broke in, spewing crumbs. "Yes, you could." She addressed Betsy directly. "That's very kind of you, Betsy. Cora is grateful to receive your gift."

Betsy said, "We're close in size. You'll have to tighten your corset a good deal more, Cora, and have the hems shortened, of course."

"Fortunately, Cora's a skilled seamstress," said Jenny.

Cora sipped her tea and imagined herself attending the sick in a flouncy, pink gown with an enormous bustle. Transforming Betsy's frocks into sensible clothing would be a rigorous test of skill.

Betsy said, "I even have a black dress from Grandmother's passing which—oh, I'm so sorry. That was insensitive."

"Not at all," Cora said. "Aunt Jenny's right. I appreciate your generosity."

Cora was reaching for the teapot to refresh Betsy's cup, when they heard pounding at the front door.

"Someone is eager to express sympathy," said Jenny. "Or panic, judging by that racket. Cora, you'd better—"

Cora was already hastening to the door. She found Archie Cameron, age eight, standing on the porch with a note.

Archie delivered his message in a breathless tumble of words. "Father told me to fetch you, Miss Patton. Mama was standing too close to the window when the storm came, and the wind broke the window and the glass went into her skin, right through her clothes, and Father tried to pick out all the glass, but now her arm is red and puffy."

"Is that what the note says?" asked Cora.

"Yes." Eyes big with worry, Archie nodded.

Jenny appeared behind Cora, handed her satchel and bonnet to her, and said, "Go on, Cora. I can receive visitors myself. This doesn't sound like something that should wait."

Chapter 3

The next day, Cora rose early. The sky was turning from navy to deep purple as she threw a shawl about her shoulders, slipped out of the cottage, and walked the familiar route to her former home. She half expected to see a diaphanous outline of the white, gable roofed house that'd sat in modest dignity on the hillside between the O'Mallory and the Finney farms only two days prior. However, as she crossed the stone bridge over Silver Creek, she saw that the house was indeed gone.

There wasn't even a ghost of a house. There was only a flame-wounded pear tree beside heaps of charred timbers, no longer smoldering yet still warm, still emitting an odor of smoke. Cora preferred to confront reality alone. A parade of curious sightseers, drawn to the wreckage of Doc Patton's house like ants to a puddle of syrup, would fall into formation when morning chores were finished. By then she'd be long gone.

Cora circled the ruins, picking her way over debris in the dim light. Here and there foundation stones jutted through burnt planks. The O'Mallory boys had scooped Father's skeletal remains into a muslin bag and put them into a pine coffin, a macabre memento in a gigantic locket, now awaiting burial in the St. Andrew's graveyard. The whole business of death and mourning was numbingly surreal. She should feel terrible, yet all she had was an aching hollowness, a vacuum accompanied by a dread of what might fill it.

Cora leaned against the granite and limestone retaining wall that kept the hillside from spilling onto the lane. Only two days ago, in the blue light of dawn, she scribbled a list of patients that Father should see, then prepared his breakfast. As on any other day, he ate as if attacking a tedious yet necessary chore and departed, unaware that he'd eaten the last meal he would ever take at that table. A table with a wobbly leg that neither of them had gotten around to fixing. They didn't have to fix it now. Or rather, *she* didn't have to fix it, for Father was dead.

Dead and with Jesus in heaven, according to Reverend Cameron. Despite being a member of St. Andrew's Church, Father hadn't been a believer so meeting Jesus would certainly surprise him. Her too, truth be told.

Father had combusted into smoke and ash and charcoal. That was the plain truth of it. All she had of him were memories, lessons, and a shared belief that rationality and hard work were better servants than superstition and magical thinking. These immaterial gifts were icy cold comfort. She drew her shawl over her shoulders and folded her arms into its woolen embrace. Tears welled, tumbled from her eyes, soothed the ragged gap in her being. She let herself cry.

Beyond the orchard, a rooster crowed. Mauve smudges of cloud appeared in the eastern sky. Day followed night and the earth kept turning regardless of whom awoke upon it. Father was gone and she was not. Neither was Aunt Jenny. "Good-bye Father," Cora whispered.

It was time to make breakfast.

****

As Cora trudged down Main Street, Jim crossed the bridge and went up the lane in long strides. He set down his lunch pail and a rolled-up canvass sheet and dumped his tools from a burlap sack onto the retaining wall. Crowbar, hatchet, hammer, shovel—durable, efficient tools in capable hands. Yesterday the wreckage had been too hot to handle. Today there was only a lingering warmth.

In its current state, Doc Patton's house attracted gawkers and gossips. Cora would be hurt if she knew the site of her family's tragedy had turned into a Pompeii-style tourist attraction. Jim set to work, burying broken dishes, prying apart boards, removing nails, and after an hour and a half, all that was left of the ruined house was a tidy pile of charred lumber. He threw a canvass tarp over the pile and anchored it with loose, loaf-sized foundation stones. After he put his tools back in the bag, he surveyed his work.

Better. Those seeking a vicarious emotional thrill would be disappointed in their visit to the Patton's empty lot. Jim picked up his sack of tools and lunch pail and headed across town to the heavily damaged silo at Brockett's Millworks. Isaac Brockett paid well for an honest day's work.

****

After a long day of toil, Jim and Tom sat at the bar of the Shamrock and Thistle sharing the latest copy of the *Trumpet* and sipping what remained of their ale in an economizing manner, as Jim put it.

"Economizing?" Tom laughed. "You mean skin flinting."

"I prefer the term 'thrifty'. It's the highest value of

my people and the foundation for the first commandment of the Presbyterian Church: 'Thou shalt not squander thy precious shekels on intoxicating beverages.' I mustn't violate my moral code, so you have to buy the next round, my dear Papist."

Kelly, the barkeep, waved a beefy hand over the bar. "If yous didn't amuse me, I'd demand you buy another pint to claim this prime real estate within the tavern."

"Okay, okay," agreed Tom. "Another round, Kelly. And your opinion on this article if you please."

"What, in Helston's rag?"

"The same."

Tom pushed the newspaper across the bar and Kelly picked it up, extended his arms, squinted at the column of print, and read:

Tornado Ravages Maryville, 1 Deceased

Maryville was devastated by a tornado on Monday last. The town's oldest citizen, Mr. Iain MacTavish, declared the storm the worst he had ever witnessed in his ninety-two years. The merciless twister tore trees from their roots, broke windows, overturned wagons, and derailed a locomotive and tender as if they were mere toys. The terror commenced at four o'clock in the afternoon, beginning at Brockett's Millworks, where the roof was severed from the granary in the manner of a lid from a pot. The destruction continued on its hellish eastbound path through Main Street and across Silver Creek, culminating in a flattened corn crop in the back field of the O'Mallory farm. The demonic dervish ignited three fires, including a conflagration at Doctor John Patton's residence. Alas, Maryville's only physician lost his mortal life in the unbeatable blaze…

"That's enough for me." Kelly pushed the paper

back to Tom and reached for two clean tankards. "The bugger leads with the destruction at Brockett's Mill where nary a soul perished and leaves the bit about Doc Patton till damn near last. Mind, your cornfield was notable enough to get a mention, Tom."

Jim said, "You make a strong point on the coverage, Kelly. Makes you think: what isn't in Helston's paper but matters to the town."

Kelly spoke as he filled the tankards. "I reckon Helston covered most of the basics but neglected to mention the salt of the earth folks, the unschooled ones who don't buy papers. People who didn't lose much but didn't have much in the first place. Like those Gypsies down by the tracks. Their wagon blew over and the horse with it. Poor beast broke its leg and had to be shot. The Gypsies ain't going anywhere now. A whole family of 'em, granny down to a babe in arms, stranded in Maryville."

"I hope they weren't hurt," said Tom, accepting a frothy tankard.

"No, they were fine 'cause Jenkins let them wait out the storm in the station," replied Kelly.

"Decent fellow," said Jim. "A disaster is a test of character. There are those who help others, and those who help only themselves." He took a sip from his second tankard.

"Aren't you the wise philosopher today," said Tom. "You're the bleeding Socrates of Maryville."

"But he ain't wrong, Tom. Take Cora Patton," said Kelly.

"I'd love to," said Tom, eliciting an elbow jab in the ribs from Jim. "Hey, not fair. You can joke about Cora but she's off-limits for me?"

"That's right." Jim's frown betrayed a current of seriousness under the play-battle gesture.

"Lads, lads. There shall be no quarrelling in the S 'n T. This here's a tavern of peace."

"I turn the other cheek as Our Lord and Savior taught. What about Cora Patton?" asked Tom.

"Only that she's an example to us all," replied Kelly. "I saw her rushing up the street yesterday with young Master Cameron. She was wearing the same dress as on Monday night. Likely off to help someone who needed her, even though she just lost her daddy."

"She's not one to sit out work," agreed Tom. "And she probably won't have a moment's rest till Maryville finds another doctor."

"Her aunt's the same way. Unnerving lady, that Jenny Patton. The way she seems to read your mind and say exactly what you're thinking, yet she's just who you'd want at your bedside if you were sick," said Kelly.

"I'd rather have the maiden Cora watching over me," said Tom, risking another jab.

Jim drank deeply from his tankard.

"You're awful quiet." Tom looked at Jim through narrowed eyes. "And your ale's going down awful fast too, for a self-proclaimed skin flint."

"Just thinking," Jim mumbled.

"Now I see. You're thinking about Cora Patton." Tom winked at Kelly.

Jim didn't deny it.

Tom continued. "Seems to me she's out of bounds, Jim. A girl like that demands a high standard of man. The kind of fellow who doesn't patronize taverns."

Kelly broke in. "I protest, Tom. This here's a respectable establishment."

"Or get booted from law school," Tom finished.

"I'm going back to McGill," Jim said gravely. "It's only a question of coming up with the money."

Tom raised an eyebrow and took a gulp of ale.

Jim said, "If that's what it takes to gain her respect."

"Get under her petticoat," teased Tom.

"No. Gain her respect. I only want that. Nothing more." Jim plunked his tankard onto the bar.

"Guess that means you're leaving all the other girls for me?" Tom asked.

"They're not mine to leave," Jim said, tiring of the conversation. He dug into his pocket, set some coins on the bar, and spoke directly to the barkeep. "Thanks Kelly. Be sure to send Tom on his way in good time so he's fit for work tomorrow."

"Bloody sanctimonious Presbyterian," Tom squawked as Jim left the tavern.

Chapter 4

Jenny and Cora peered at Charles Tucker over a desk cluttered with documents, ledgers, and sticky glasses and mugs, Jenny with curiosity and Cora with concern.

Tucker wept. "I knew John for decades. Decades! I cannot think of a more tireless, self-sacrificing servant of the people than he. Maryville has suffered a profound loss. I can't believe he's gone. Gone! Such a remarkable man. Truly remarkable." Tears tracked over Tucker's florid cheeks.

Jenny passed Tucker a handkerchief and he blew his bulbous nose rather like a bugle, thought Cora. His skin was the color of an autumn elm leaf, and Cora smelled the faint odor of alcohol about him. Tucker tried to give the handkerchief back to Jenny, but she suggested he keep it in case more tears should flow.

"Forgive me. Forgive me! I weep while your eyes are dry yet yours is the far greater loss," said Tucker. "Did I remember to extend my condolences to you both?"

"Yes, you did," Jenny replied with a kind smile. "Thank you."

"And offer you refreshment?"

"Yes, you remembered, Mr. Tucker. You've only to read us John's will," said Jenny.

"Quite right. Well…well, it's short. Very short.

Brief in all respects. As a solicitor, I encourage brevity when I assist in the drafting of one's last will and testament, and John complied fully with my recommendation. Fully. Now where were we…"

"The will," said Jenny.

"Yes, yes." With tremulous hands, Tucker unfolded a yellowed sheet of paper, cleared his throat, and squinted through wire rim glasses at the words before him. "Yes. Here it is. 'I leave my house, its contents, and the land it sits upon to my daughter, Cora Jane Patton, and the remainder of my estate to my sister, Jennifer Anne Patton, and my daughter, Cora Jane Patton, to be divided equally between them'." Tucker turned the document toward Jenny and Cora, presumably so they could admire its simplicity themselves. "Along with the customary preamble, the 'legalese' if you will, that's it. Only that. Quite simple really. Yes, there it is."

"As far as we're aware, the tornado destroyed everything John owned," said Jenny. "Unless he had some money saved?"

"No. No, I'm afraid there is nothing besides a small sum in the bank. John donated every spare penny he earned to the orphanage in Brucedale. What's it called? The Christian Home for…for…"

"The Protestant Home for Little Wanderers," said Jenny.

"That's it. That's it. Quite so. John supported the orphanage enthusiastically but paid himself begrudgingly. Or not at all, actually."

"I realize it's unlikely, but did he have any insurance?" asked Jenny.

"No. No. He told me he considered insurance an extravagance. He couldn't see the point of it, really. He was a very capable physician, Miss Patton, but rather less competent in financial matters."

"So, there's nothing," confirmed Jenny.

"Aside from the land upon which his house once sat, no, I suppose there isn't. I'm sorry."

"Not at all," Cora said. "Aunt Jenny and I aren't surprised by Father's estate."

"But if anyone deserves to be wealthy, it's you, Cora. And you also, Miss Patton. I am so sorry that John left you in a state of penury."

"Penury, Mr. Tucker?" Jenny questioned. "Surely that's an overstatement. I own my home, and I keep a fine garden and a flock of Rhode Island reds. We have our vocation. Cora and I are really quite comfortable."

"I'm so glad to hear you say that. So glad. If there's anything I can do…as two maiden ladies, alone, utterly alone, in this cruel world, if you need anything at all…"

"Only tell us how you are," Cora demanded. "The truth. No sugar-coating."

"The truth? Well, yes, the truth. In truth I've become somewhat muddled. Since the twister, I've been under such strain, with clients and insurance claims and legal matters and so forth, and I've fallen into certain, well, insalubrious habits. Dipsomania, I'm afraid. So, there it is. My cards lie plainly upon the table. Oh dear. I fear I shall weep again."

"The handkerchief, Mr. Tucker," prompted Jenny.

After he'd mopped his eyes and nose, Cora said, "I know this sounds odd, Mr. Tucker, but patients with liver conditions feel much better if they acidify and move their bowels. A lot. Several times a day."

"Oh my. That does sound odd. Very odd," Tucker concurred. "And inconvenient. Most inconvenient."

"But it's something you must do if you are to feel better," said Cora.

Jenny drew a bottle of a syrupy potion from Cora's satchel and placed it on the desk. "Cut back on strong drink and mix a tablespoon of this elixir into your tea morning, noon, and night."

"The instructions are on the bottle in case you forget them," Cora added. She looked at Tucker with the wide, innocent eyes of a child one would hate to disappoint, and Tucker responded as she hoped.

"Yes. Yes, I believe I am fully capable of following your instructions, Cora. Fully capable. Three times a day, you say. And no brandy. At least, not too much. Now what have I forgotten?"

"Nothing," said Jenny. "Be well, Mr. Tucker."

****

"Now what have I forgotten?" mimicked Cora. "Oh, I remember now. My checkbook, my checkbook! For weeks and weeks I've forgotten. Now what is it I'm forgetting?"

"Mr. Tucker will remember to pay us eventually," said Jenny as she looped her arm under Cora's and they strolled down Main Street. "And when he does, he'll be grateful we didn't embarrass him."

"I suppose."

"Trust me. Trust me!" Jenny mimicked in return.

Cora sighed. "I guess a tiny part of me is disappointed that Father didn't leave us on a stronger footing and I'm blaming poor Mr. Tucker for it. I mean, it's admirable to care for orphans and all, and yet—"

"And yet, a small legacy would've been welcome," said Jenny.

"Yes."

"Your father thought he had plenty of time to see you married and secure. When he woke up last Monday, he had no inkling that it was his last day on earth."

"Donating heavily to the orphanage was noble but wasn't it also irresponsible, Aunt Jenny?"

"Your mother came from Brucedale. I suppose he was paying her tribute."

"So, Father was romantic and impractical."

"I don't know, Cora. It's not as if he left you with nothing. He saw to your education. You have skills and knowledge beyond your years and you've your very practical father to thank for that."

Cora's face burned with shame at her ingratitude to Father and her jealousy of the forlorn children who slept in a yellow brick dormitory without parents to comfort them. Father was gone scarcely more than a week and she'd already found fault in his earthly deeds. She even blamed him for dying, as if believing that if sorrow wouldn't bring him back, anger might.

Jenny squeezed her arm and said, "You were furious with your mother for dying when you were little. A part of us holds to childish notions that someone must be to blame, even those we mourn, when terrible things happen. These feelings will pass, Cora."

They travelled in pensive silence from the clamor of Maryville's commercial district into a residential area of stately houses, broad lawns, and floral borders. The first chrysanthemums and asters heralded chilly mornings of dewy apples and flocking geese.

"I never tire of walking here," Cora said as she admired the ornate Queen Anne façade of the Meyers' home. Late-blooming roses decorated the porch trellis and scented the air.

"Perhaps one day you'll live in this neighborhood. In a mansion," said Jenny.

"You sound like a Gypsy woman, predicting my future with a crystal ball and dregs in a teacup."

"Oh," Jenny cackled. "This young lass has a thrilling future with a dashing prince proposing on bended knee, an extravagant wedding, and a half dozen, golden-haired children. Three sets of twins."

"I'll take the dashing prince."

"Oh, my silly lass. You don't get to choose, for it is fated. Children follow marriage as dawn follows night," said Jenny, still in character.

They walked by Robert Helston's house, a well-proportioned, symmetrical Georgian with tasteful shrubbery and a flag-stoned semicircular lane. Cora always thought of Eliza when she found herself near this grand house, and of Mr. Helston, distraught for weeks after his wife's death in childbirth, and still alone three years on having never found a woman who was Eliza's equal, or so Cora supposed.

"Really, Aunt Jenny. Do you think I'll marry someday?"

"Someday?" said Jenny, breaking character. "You're twenty-two, Cora. I think you'll marry soon."

"But I'm in mourning." Cora waved her lacy, black sleeve in a graceful arc as if she were a tragic heroine in a travelling show.

"You won't be mourning forever. Before long you'll be thoroughly tired of me and wishing for a home of your own." Jenny cackled and rubbed her hands together. "Mark my words, dear Cora: soon a handsome, dark man will sweep you into his arms and teach you more about life than you ever imagined. It's foretold in the stars."

Cora took a lingering glance at the Helston home. If she ever married, she hoped her husband would love her as much as Robert had loved Eliza. He had been a model husband.

As the grand homes gave way to the modest housing and kitchen gardens of salaried workers and tradesmen, Cora and Jenny's conversation turned to practical matters.

"I'll check on Mrs. Cameron tomorrow," said Cora. "Reverend Cameron will want an answer on holding a memorial service for Father."

"I don't know what to say," Jenny said wistfully. "We held the wake for a respectful three days. On the other hand, his patients want to honor him."

"Father disliked fancy ceremonies. He would've been horrified by the idea of a grand service and all the flattery."

"Funerals are for the living, Cora."

"Well, we're living, and I'd rather not. A formal service will only make us sadder."

"What if we ask Reverend Cameron to pay your father a short tribute at the end of the regular Sunday service, nothing fancy, but a chance for folks to bid adieu together?"

Cora was about to agree when a bridled and saddled gray horse cantered by without its rider.

"We may be setting a bone shortly," Jenny predicted.

"Then again, maybe not," Cora said, spotting a hatless, muddy clothed Jimmy Sinclair running toward them.

Jimmy paused on the street and flashed his boyish grin. He bowed first to Jenny, then to Cora, and said breathlessly, "Good day, Miss Patton and Miss Patton. Has Buttercup, my noble yet nervous steed, passed this way?"

"Yes," laughed Jenny, pointing. "She went that way."

"Thank you, kind lady." He bowed again before sprinting off.

When he was beyond earshot, Jenny took Cora's arm again. "Now there's an eligible bachelor for you." Cora began to protest, but Jenny spoke over her. "He has his eye on you, and he has a bright future. He stopped chasing after his horse just so he could speak to you."

"He spoke to you, Aunt Jenny. Not to me." Cora yanked her arm free from Jenny's grip.

"Cora, a young man does not pause in his pursuit of a valuable animal to talk to a middle-aged crone. That handsome smile was for you and only you."

"Handsome is as handsome does," Cora sniffed.

"Indeed," said Jenny. "Jim has his faults, but he cares about his fellow man. Lord knows, his family isn't well off, yet he refused to accept any payment for repairing old Mrs. Smith's shed."

"She's a widow."

"She could afford to pay him something. A token toward his tuition at least."

"McGill Law School doesn't want the likes of Jimmy Sinclair. Betsy Meyer told me he was expelled for dressing the statue of the college founder in an old ballgown and tiara, among other stupid, disrespectful pranks."

"Do you really believe that?" Jenny sighed with impatience. "I rather expect he was a welcome breath of fresh air in the dry and dusty halls of law school, and he simply ran out of money."

"Can we drop this?"

"As you wish." Jenny's clipped words ended all conversation.

For the remainder of their homebound journey, Cora mentally enumerated the reasons why she would hold Jimmy Sinclair in contempt forever.

****

And there the naughty girl stood, saddle askew, munching on wormy apples under a tree on a lane that led into the rolling hills north of town. Maybe Buttercup's diet was the problem. She never refused a snack. Maybe she hated the saddle and misbehaved because the cinch strap bothered her belly.

Jim jogged up the lane toward the mare to unbuckle the strap, fix her saddle, and walk her home. They could sort out their differences in the safety of the corral. As Jim neared his large, gray horse, he saw a man on a sleek, black horse riding down the lane. Jim whispered to Buttercup and gripped her bridle so she wouldn't startle.

Helston halted a few lengths away. "Well, if it isn't James Sinclair," he called in greeting. "Trouble with your horse?" He looked pointedly at Buttercup's sideways saddle.

"Nothing we can't manage between us," Jim replied. Even if he needed help—and he didn't—Helston was the last person he'd ask. Judging by the lather on his horse, Helston had ridden hard, yet he looked as if he'd just left the barbershop. It wasn't reasonable, but Jim didn't trust a man who dressed like a dandy for a solo ride in the hills.

"The mare looks sound enough, if you can keep her away from the apples. She's bound to suffer a bout of

34

colic at the rate she's eating."

Helston was right, though Jim wouldn't admit it. "She has a cast-iron belly." Jim tightened his hold on Buttercup's bridle so she wouldn't snatch another apple from the ground.

"I'd venture she'd make a decent jumper with proper training." Helston rubbed his chin, as if he were in a boardroom signaling his intention to make a fair offer. "A well-run stable with a competent trainer, basic veterinary care."

"She's not for sale."

"Whoa. Whoa. Mr. Sinclair. I merely meant to compliment you for being in possession of such a fine animal."

"In that case, Helston, thank you," said Jim.

"However, now that you mention it, I believe we could make an arrangement. A win-win deal. My motive is not to offend. I prefer to be frank."

"As I said—"

"Listen, Sinclair. I'm aware of your impecunious situation. Through no fault of your own, you struggle, impoverished and burdened by the shortcomings of others."

"My father—"

"I'm not casting aspersions upon your father, however derelict he may be. I'm referring to the lack of charity shown you by the august educators at McGill. Now if I may—"

Jim shrugged.

"You've informed me that your mare is not for sale. However, if you were pragmatic, dare I say shrewd, you'd sell her to me, and I'd grant you riding privileges. You'd have the value of your horse and ride her too, in the manner of the consumption of the proverbial gateau." Helston chuckled at his own joke. "At the very least, the mare is worth a term of tuition."

"She's priceless," said Jim. "And because of that, she's not for sale."

"You'd throw away your future, a prospect of success, for an animal who doesn't return your affection?" Helston sneered at Buttercup's saddle.

"If that's how you see it," replied Jim.

"Well then," Helston smiled. "The offer stands, should you change your mind. Good day, Sinclair."

With spurs to his sides and the snap of the crop, Helston's gelding set off at a gallop and Jim and Buttercup regained the solitude of the lane.

Jim stroked Buttercup's neck and she shivered happily. Her summer coat felt like velvet under his hand. "Helston didn't even ask your name," muttered Jim. "You're stubborn, Buttercup, but you needn't worry. I'd never sell you. Especially to the likes of him."

Chapter 5

Hot and hazy August slipped into industrious September and a glorious autumn of crystalline skies and gaudy foliage. One afternoon late in the month, Cora was planting spring bulbs when Robert Helston sauntered up the lane.

"We could never keep the squirrels from digging up our tulip bulbs," Mr. Helston commented as he approached.

"Dried pepper flakes sprinkled all around. That's the secret to keeping squirrels away." Cora pushed her trowel into the soil and stood. "How are you, Mr. Helston?"

"Robert," he corrected, smiling in return. "I'm fine, but I'm afraid I've been terribly remiss in not calling sooner. I think of you and your aunt often, and well, I'm finally presenting myself to offer my sympathy. How are you, Cora?"

"Fine as well," she replied, sensing a disadvantage. Mr. Helston—Robert—cut a dashing figure in his well-tailored suit, top hat, and polished boots and she was wearing one of Aunt Jenny's old dresses, a faded brown calico. She'd bound her hair in a kerchief, and she suspected she'd left a smudge on her cheek where she'd brushed a fly away with a dirty hand. "If I knew you were coming—"

"But you didn't. I apologize for my unexpected

visit." He smiled again.

She hadn't noticed before how blue his eyes were, as azure as the sky. He doffed his hat revealing thick, wavy, dark brown hair with the first hint of gray at his temples. The effect of his bearing, speech, and attire was that of a confident, urbane man in the prime of his power and Cora felt an unfamiliar pull, as if she were a planet and he the sun.

"I'm…I'm afraid Aunt Jenny isn't home to receive you. She went to Brucedale today." Cora's voice wavered, and she glanced up the street reflexively, watching in vain for her elder. But why? For rescue? Robert Helston was simply a man, a gentleman, who thought to express his sympathy.

"Cora," he said, redirecting her attention to him.

She realized by the way he said her name, the way he drew out the syllables and held her in his gaze when he pronounced them, that he didn't care about seeing Aunt Jenny. He nodded subtly, almost imperceptibly at the porch, and she found herself asking, "Do you have time for a glass of cordial, Mr. Helston?"

"Robert," he reminded her. "I'd be delighted, Cora." Her name again. "If you're not occupied." Those blue eyes.

"I've only the gardening to do, Robert," she said, testing the sound of his Christian name on her tongue and finding it pleasing. "It's a lovely afternoon. We can sit on the porch."

"I'd love nothing more."

Of course he wouldn't want more. He was a gentleman. He and Cora moved in different social orbits and couldn't reasonably be paired, yet if neighbors noticed her welcoming Robert Helston inside the cottage, alone, the news would be scandalous dry kindling for the voracious fires of town gossip. Cora led Robert to the porch and saw him seated while she fetched the refreshment.

Indoors, she paused at the washbasin to wash away the garden from her face and hands. After a swift glance in the looking glass, she decided to fix her hair too. She shook her hair from the kerchief, brushed it, and pinned it into a loose chignon. The dress would have to do, and anyway, brown set off her auburn tresses and green eyes. She placed two tall glasses of rosy sweetness on a china tray, took a deep breath, and returned to the porch.

Robert stood, and his eyes alighted on the tray, or then again, perhaps not. Was he looking at her bosom? No. Absolutely not. He was a gentleman, he'd walked a good distance, and he was probably thirsty. He praised Aunt Jenny's raspberry cordial as the best he'd tasted, though Cora was too giddy to enjoy it properly, and he spoke of his gratitude to the late Dr. John Patton and to Cora, "her father's equal in moral character". Cora protested and fought an inexplicable urge to giggle like a schoolgirl. She was swept into Robert's sea of eloquence, charm, and sophistication as the afternoon passed in convivial conversation.

The sun hid behind the trees and shadows lengthened. Shivering, Cora crossed her arms against the chill.

"You're freezing cold, Cora, and I'm utterly thoughtless," said Robert. "I'd love nothing more than to wrap you in a blanket and converse with you all night, but I really must release you from your obligation to entertain me."

"Well, if you must go," Cora said as they both stood.

"Thank you for visiting, Robert."

He bowed and donned his hat. "I'm only sorry that I didn't pay you a visit sooner, my darling," he said as he departed.

My darling. Had he really said it? As Cora washed the cordial glasses, she reenacted the afternoon on her mind's stage, as if the memory of Robert's visit was a favorite, oft recited piece of poetry. She had never felt so…respected? No, that was too weak a word. Appreciated. Robert had appreciated her as a woman, not as an obedient pupil, or a faithful daughter, or a compassionate helper.

The hall clock struck seven, and Aunt Jenny would soon be home. Cora struggled to mind the stove fire and prepare supper, even cutting her finger with the paring knife as her thoughts darted here and there. For the first time in weeks, she thought of matters beyond the miseries of illness and death. Robert Helston was not her beau, but a girl could dream, couldn't she?

****

"How are the orphans progressing in their lessons?" Cora plowed mashed potato into furrows with her fork.

Jenny swallowed and cut another bite of ham from the thick slab on her plate. "Reasonably well given the chaos in their young lives. The headmistress said your father was in full agreement with her program of prioritizing routine and stability when the children arrive and delaying formal lessons until they've adjusted. She's wise and understands the children's needs."

Cora chewed without tasting and listened without hearing. The journey to the orphanage was important to Aunt Jenny but all Cora could think of was Robert. She forced herself to pay attention.

"If you could only see their innocent faces, Cora. I wish we could match your father's level of financial support, but we have less to contribute because patients will never pay us what they paid him."

"He went to medical school and trained us," said Cora. "He was our senior, professionally."

"And he was a man," said Jenny. "Even if you graduated from college, assuming one would accept you, you'd have to work twice as hard to be deemed half as competent as a male doctor."

"Well, I'm happy being a midwife and you know medicines and bone setting better than most doctors and druggists."

"Be that as it may, we're as apt to be paid in cheese and butter as in actual money and we won't be able to help the Little Wanderers the way your father did." Jenny spooned a second dollop of mustard onto her ham. "How was your day?"

"Fine."

"Fine?"

"Yes. Fine."

"You don't seem fine to me. In fact, you seem scattered."

"I'm fine," Cora protested.

"Did you spread the straw on the strawberry beds and finish planting the bulbs?"

"Um…"

"Um," Jenny mocked. "Cora, what is going on? You're acting very strangely this evening."

"No, I'm not."

"Yes, you are. You're sitting there, pushing food around your plate with your mind anywhere but here in this kitchen. If you didn't finish those small chores and no one needed you, what did you do all day?" Even in dim lamplight, Jenny's eyes flashed with irritation.

"Um…" Cora examined the salt cellar as if it were a rare artifact.

"Hello? Hello? Is anyone home?" Jenny knocked on the table and cocked her head to peer at Cora's face.

Though Cora wished she could keep her delicious secret locked in her heart, there was nothing for it but to tell Aunt Jenny about Robert's visit. "Rob…Mr. Helston came to offer us his condolences," she stammered.

"Today? More than a month after your father's passing?" Jenny squawked. "His timing was awfully convenient."

"He had no way to know that I'd be alone."

"Cora, I saw Mr. Helston when I was walking up Railway Avenue near the station this morning. He knew I wouldn't be home."

"Oh."

"Oh indeed. And you didn't finish the gardening. How long did he stay, pray tell?"

"He was here most of the afternoon. On the porch, I might add. A respectable visit."

"If you say so."

"I do."

"Cora, if I were you, I'd be careful."

"Careful of what?" Cora plunked the salt cellar back on the table. "Mr. Helston is a gentleman, not a scoundrel, and I'm not a gullible little girl. I'm twenty-two and quite capable of receiving a routine condolence call, outdoors in the light of day, I might add."

Jenny forked another piece of ham into her mouth and chewed it aggressively. She reminded Cora of a tigress.

Only last week, Aunt Jenny sang Jimmy Sinclair's praises and now she was reacting as if Robert had scandalously and secretly ravished her precious, only niece. Cora was bewildered by Aunt Jenny's obvious displeasure. Cora rose from the table and took her dishes to the washbasin. She poured herself a glass of water from the pitcher and drank it in gulps, swallowing the bitterness that rose in her throat.

Tonight was not the night to discuss the matter further. After that delightful afternoon, Cora felt she knew Robert better than her aunt ever would. Whatever Aunt Jenny's misgivings, they were entirely unwarranted. Cora washed the supper dishes in silence, and with a muttered "Good night," went to bed as the clock struck half past eight. Even if Robert had deliberately planned his visit to find her alone, she didn't feel that he'd tricked her. Quite the contrary. This was thrilling proof that he came to see her, Miss Cora Jane Patton, for reasons beyond an obligatory condolence call, and her heart raced with the possibility of seeing him alone again.

Chapter 6

On the first Sunday morning of October, the people of Maryville crowded into St. Andrew's Presbyterian Church to pay their respects to the late Dr. John Patton. Though Reverend Cameron had promised to deliver a modestly short, ecumenical tribute and prayer, he now expounded, with no hint of imminent conclusion, on the mercies of heaven that would welcome the righteous and the horrors of hell that would punish the wicked upon their deaths. The Pattons customarily occupied a pew at the rear of the nave, but today they shared the Camerons' pew at the front, next to Agnes, young Archie, and the twins who wiggled like trout in a net. Cora had worried the service would deepen her sorrow but though she was sad, she was also bored. She crossed her legs this way then that, checked she'd marked the correct page in her hymnal for the final hymn a dozen times or more, and played a covert game of peekaboo with the little girls much to Jenny's disapproval which was expressed with withering sideways glances and elbow nudges to Cora's ribs.

Cora was unaware that farther back, two men endured the drone of Reverend Cameron's sermon by fixing their eyes upon her and permitting their thoughts to range beyond matters of religion, mortality, and loss.

****

With long legs straying into the aisle, Jim Sinclair

was wedged into the fourth-row pew, next to a family of visiting Methodists. Jim observed the game of peekaboo with delight. Cora was beautiful, yes, but he was more fascinated by her disregard for churchly comportment and her playful alliance with the frustrated twins. If only she were meanly proper, he could stop loving her. Instead, she behaved in a manner that made him love her even more. He'd trade the attention of every other girl in Maryville if he could gain Cora's trust and respect.

The little girls began to push and pull at each other. Cora folded a starched handkerchief into the form of a bird and passed it to the twins who mangled it and made a new game of trying to restore it to avian form. Sunlight played upon Cora's auburn hair, stray tresses shining against her slender neck and the collar of her black caped dress. The plainness of her attire set off her beauty rather than diminishing it. She was not the sort of girl to be swept off her feet by flattering overtures. A man would win her heart by his deeds if he won it at all.

Finally Reverend Cameron raised his arms in benediction and the service was over. Jim's stomach flipped with the possibility of speaking to Cora. He waited at the end of the pew as the Methodists shuffled by and up the center aisle. One by one, the rows emptied, and Cora approached. Jim would've spoken, but her eyes lit with recognition of someone behind him, someone at the rear of the church, and she smiled broadly. He turned.

It was Robert Helston, hat in hand, pinstriped suit, a cravat and starched collar round his thick neck. Due to the ease of a sedentary life, he was incubating a sizable paunch. Cora practically jogged to his side, and he steered her through the doorway with a soft hand on her back.

Jim felt as forlorn as a motherless calf tethered to a fence in a storm, barely aware of Jenny Patton's sympathetic hand on his arm. As he delivered his condolences to her, Jenny peered back, her sharp eyes acknowledging the riptide of humiliation that had unmoored him. He had to get out, breathe fresh air, and clear his mind of the troubling sight of Cora with Helston.

****

Cora spotted Robert at the back of the church, arms open to receive her, sorrow and all. His somber, well-tailored clothing and erect bearing conveyed a solidity that Cora craved. She restrained herself from dashing up the aisle. He smiled at her, blue eyes a'twinkle and it felt natural to fall in beside him and leave church together, his comforting hand warm upon her back even through the fabric of her clothing.

"Are you quite all right, my darling?" His voice was low and only she could hear him.

"Yes."

It was true. She was all right. When her period of mourning ended, wouldn't Father have wanted her to find happiness with a man who equaled him in character and far exceeded him in wealth and power?

In a daze, Cora received the requisite condolences from the other worshippers and descended the porch steps. If only she could have a moment alone with Robert, some conversation that she could cling to after they had to part.

"Good day, Mr. Helston." Jenny's greeting was as disruptive as an alarm bell. "I do hope you'll excuse Cora and me. We really must be going."

Before Robert could respond, Cora felt Jenny's arm

slip and tighten under her own and she was wordlessly commanded away.

****

Jim unhitched Buttercup and swung himself onto her back, his athleticism belying the clumsiness he felt within. Evidently Cora believed he had nothing to offer her aside from juvenile foolishness and that Helston was a suitable match. Perhaps she wasn't wrong. The Sinclair's impoverishment had torn him away from a bright future in Law and he was as poor as a church mouse, his only asset a stubborn, gray mare.

Against his better judgement, Jim rode round the building, circled back onto Main Steet, and halted at the edge of the lawn where Buttercup could steal grass by the mouthful. Helston was at Cora's elbow as she spoke to Reverend Cameron. With handshakes and subdued smiles, they descended the porch steps, leaving Jenny with the cleric and a small circle of well-wishers. Other mourners tried to intercept Cora on the sidewalk, but Helston fended them off with his blocky body. The dramatic scene was brief yet cruelly informative. Cora was putty in Helston's hands.

In a moment, Jenny broke away from the group on the porch and sidled up to the pair, her movement casually purposeful. Helston stiffened, bowed formally to her, and turned to join his mother and aunt. Cora frowned, but she allowed Jenny to link an arm with her own and guide her down the sidewalk.

Jim wasn't hungry for the post-church meal his grandmother always laid out. He'd rather run Buttercup through the cold, clear air of the countryside until they were both exhausted and he could think rationally. As he clicked his tongue to prompt the mare into motion, he caught sight of Betsy Meyer, Helen Jones, and Adeline Brockett waving to him. He politely lifted his hand in response. The trio of giggling friends beckoned him, but he shook his head and rode away.

****

Cora hid her fury as best she could, which meant she didn't hide it at all. She responded in clipped tones to Jenny's comments on the weather and the thoroughness of Reverend Cameron's eulogy as they walked briskly in the crisp autumn air.

"Thorough? That's charitable," said Cora.

"If you'd peer past Reverend Cameron's verbiage, you'd see his good intentions," said Jenny. "He respected your father, and he honored him with the best sermon he could offer. I found the service touching."

Cora huffed dismissively and kicked some fallen leaves.

"Really, Cora. Today of all days, you should be remembering your father, following his example, and behaving decently and kindly," said Jenny.

"I am kind," Cora protested.

"Not to Jim Sinclair you weren't. You ignored him. I'd say you were cruel."

Cora shuffled her feet through a drift of leaves and said nothing.

"Jim is a hardworking, honest young man who—"

"Oh, enough about Jimmy Sinclair," Cora interrupted.

"Then let's talk about Robert Helston, shall we? After you gave Jim the cold shoulder, you practically threw yourself at Mr. Helston and he seemed very eager to catch you."

Cora's face burned. "I didn't throw myself at him.

He waited for me. Which is natural when two adults are friends and one of them is bereaved."

"Friends," Jenny snorted. "Cora, you have nothing in common with that man. You are just twenty-two, and he's well into his fourth decade."

"He's only thirty. He's not an old man."

"If I may continue, he is worldly and pampered and he hasn't put in a hard day's toil in his life."

"He owns newspapers, Aunt Jenny, and railway stock. Just because he doesn't shovel manure doesn't mean he doesn't work hard. You can't judge a man harshly for being refined and enjoying life's luxuries."

"Life's luxuries? Cora, he wouldn't survive a day in Jim Sinclair's boots."

"Oh. So now we're back to Jimmy Sinclair."

"No, we're not." Jenny halted abruptly and turned to Cora. "I didn't want to mention this, but I've noticed that Mr. Helston has roving eyes. He often looks where he shouldn't. He assesses women as if he were choosing a joint of meat at the butcher shop."

"Aunt Jenny!"

"Cora, I'm telling you that he may be unsuitable."

"*May* be," Cora repeated. "The operative word being 'may'. If you look at him objectively, you will find that Robert is quite suitable."

"I'm trying to do just that. Yes, he's handsome and rich and well-spoken. But something is missing. He seems…I don't know…calculating. As if he's hiding something. As soon as you're out of mourning, he'll wish to court you. Please don't be dazzled by gifts and flattery and be blind to his faults. Tread carefully. Promise me you'll tread carefully."

Cora softened her voice. "First, Aunt Jenny, I have

no idea if Robert intends to court me." She ignored Jenny's eye roll. "But if he does, I shall consider myself lucky. And I'll be sensible. You know I will."

Jenny responded by throwing her arm around Cora's shoulder and squeezing her tightly. "Any man who would win your heart is very lucky. Remember that, Cora. You have choices."

For the remainder of their journey, they walked in amicable, quiet companionship. Cora's fingers tingled with the memory of how Robert had clasped her hands in his warm grip and how his blue eyes seemed to sparkle with joy at the sight of her. If she lifted her fingers to her face, she could smell a trace of his soap, a masculine scent of cedar and sandalwood. She wouldn't speak of this to Aunt Jenny.

Chapter 7

Cora yawned with exhaustion as she attended the sick bed of Betsy Meyer on a gloomy morning in mid-October. She only wanted to take herself home after the delivery of Hilda Beck's healthy son, but she'd promised Betsy a visit and she kept her word. Her patient lay propped on a nest of satin and velveteen pillows with a cool cloth over her forehead. Cora drew a footstool to the bedside, set her satchel within convenient reach on the floor, and settled herself beside Betsy. Mrs. Meyer, angular, tall, and nervous as a thoroughbred, stood at the foot of the bed, ready to spring forth at her daughter's merest hint of need.

"It's all right, Mummy," Betsy whispered hoarsely. "Cora's here now."

"Well, if you're sure," Mrs. Meyer said tentatively, her forehead furrowed in anxious lines.

"I am. You may go."

Mrs. Meyer spoke to Cora. "If you don't mind, on your way out, if I could have a word."

Over Betsy's weak objection, Cora said, "Of course, Mrs. Meyer."

"I shall be in the parlor," said Mrs. Meyer as she left the room.

Cora took up Betsy's hand and felt the measure of her pulse at her wrist. She had a strong, steady beat with a fast pace typical of people who didn't take exercise.

Betsy's skin was warm and dry, and her nailbeds were a healthy pink. Cora kept her silence and, with a nod, bid Betsy speak.

"It's my head again," Betsy complained. "It feels ever so achy and heavy, like it's stuffed with wet wool. Your feverfew tea helps a little, but I think I need something stronger."

"Well, you have willow bark tincture for times like this," said Cora.

"Mummy has been mixing it into my tea, but it isn't working. I wonder if I should have something stronger. For bad days like today. Perhaps I should try laudanum?"

"Laudanum is very strong and very dangerous, Betsy. Sometimes people use too much and go to sleep, never to wake again. Others fall into needing it so badly they'll do anything to get it. I'd only ever use laudanum for someone who was very painfully injured…or dying."

Betsy sighed heavily, then pulled the cloth from her forehead with exasperation. "Perhaps I am dying," she moaned.

"Perhaps you're not," countered Cora. "Besides your headache, are you having any other symptoms?"

Betsy conceded that apart from minor dyspepsia, she had none.

"When this spell passes, you should get up and get dressed," Cora counseled. "Stick to a routine, regular healthy meals and a daily constitutional, even if you don't feel like it."

"You always say that," Betsy muttered as she rolled onto her side, turning her back to Cora.

"It's my best advice," Cora said gently as she took the handle of her satchel and stood.

"Wait. Don't go," Betsy cried, sensing Cora's

intention. "There is more wrong with me. A lot more."

Cora sat down, composing her face to hide her fatigue and irritation.

"Are you listening?" Betsy asked.

"Yes. Go on," Cora replied to Betsy's back.

Betsy's words spilled forth in a stream of angst. "My thoughts race around like a merry-go-round, repeating in circles, and I can't stop them. Sometimes I feel like I'm turning into a lunatic. If I stay here in my room, I feel safe, but it doesn't feel right anymore. I know I'm getting older. I should be getting on in life, but I'm stuck. Most girls we went to school with are either married or engaged."

"You're only twenty-one, Betsy. You're hardly an old maid. On the contrary, you're a beautiful young lady. If you rejoin society, you'll meet the right gentleman in due course."

"That's precisely the trouble." Betsy flopped over to face Cora again. "I've met him. In fact, I've known him nearly all my life, but he doesn't fancy me. When I go out, I try to look my prettiest in case we should meet by chance, on the street or in a shop. When I do see him, he's polite. Well, he's not always polite, sometimes he's rude, but that makes me want him even more. I might as well be turned out like a scarecrow for the attention he pays me."

Cora ran through a mental list of Maryville's eligible bachelors to guess who it was Betsy fancied. Potential suitor to a spoilt only daughter, the gentleman would have to pass muster with Mr. Meyer, which drastically shortened the list.

Betsy smiled weakly through her tears. "Can you guess his name?"

Cora shook her head.

"I'll give you a hint," Betsy said, brightening.

"Okay," Cora agreed. She was in no mood to play a guessing game but heartened by Betsy's emotional shift.

Betsy giggled, "He's a Capricorn. That's the sign of the goat and it means he's ambitious."

Cora shrugged.

"If he crosses your threshold at New Year with a piece of shortbread, he brings good luck to your home…if you're Scottish."

"So, he's dark-haired," said Cora, warming to the game. "Um…I still don't know."

"He isn't wealthy."

"So not Mr. Helston," said Cora, secretly relieved.

"No, of course not him. Mr. Helston won't find a new wife in Maryville. No one in this town is good enough for him," Betsy sneered sarcastically. "Well, come on, Cora. Guess again."

"I have no idea," admitted Cora.

"It's Jim Sinclair."

"Jimmy Sinclair?" Cora echoed with surprise. "But he's a—"

"Dream," Betsy finished with a far-away look in her eyes. "A diamond in the rough. He has his faults. He's darkly tanned, he forgets to shave, and he drinks at the Shamrock and Thistle. And he runs around with that silly Irish fellow."

"Tom O'Mallory."

"Yes, him. But otherwise, Jim is a genuine gentleman who's down on his luck. When he finishes law school, he'll make the perfect husband. He's ever so handsome and rugged and strong and funny." Betsy's voice softened wistfully. "Trouble is, he doesn't realize

I'd make the perfect wife."

"You're lovesick," Cora said flatly.

"I'm afraid so. Whenever I see him and he doesn't love me back, I wind up here, in my bedroom, in despair. It's lunacy."

Inexperienced in matters of the heart, Cora was at a loss for any advice that would remedy Betsy's conundrum. After all, she was falling in love herself, though she hoped her love would not be unrequited. If Robert chose not to court her, she'd feel very much as Betsy evidently felt: emotionally devastated. Strategies such as distraction with a hobby or bromides such as the existence of plenty of other fish were not helpful. One didn't fall out of love with one man, even an obnoxious rogue like Jimmy Sinclair, and fall into love with another man at will.

Betsy said, "I feel a tiny bit better for telling you, Cora."

Cora nodded, acknowledging her patient's turmoil. "Even if you don't feel like it, you should still stick to a wholesome routine," she said gently. "You know what you need to do: fresh air, vegetables."

"Yes, Mother. I'll try." Betsy's smile verged to a smirk. "Speaking of mothers, you won't speak of this matter to mine, will you?"

Cora shook her head. "Not if you don't want me to. But I will warn her, sternly, not to give you laudanum. Okay?"

"Okay," Betsy sighed. "By the way, you're just my age—"

"I'm twenty-two."

"And you don't have a beau."

"Not yet."

"Who do you fancy?"

Cora laughed. "That, my dear Betsy, is a secret."

Betsy propped herself up on her elbows and exclaimed, "So you do like someone!"

"I won't confirm it or deny it." Cora picked up her satchel and took her leave before Betsy's mood turned sour again.

Chapter 8

A bitter north wind painted the windowpanes in lacy patterns of frost. The cottage was cozy and snug with a lively fire in the stove and a pot of tea at the ready, though Jenny had taken to wrapping herself in an eccentric, sleeved quilt of her own design in case of errant drafts. In the sitting room, aunt and niece poured over knitting patterns and planned ambitious projects to use the skeins of yarn that a grateful employee of the woolen mill had given them for helping him tend his motherless children when they were ill with mumps.

"The heavy yarn will knit nicely into a shawl or cape," said Jenny. "And we can use the fine yarn for stockings and mittens. What do you think of this pattern?"

"That's as fashionable as a cape from Paris, Aunt Jenny. I suppose we needn't rush to knit pretty things though." Cora ran her fingers through a luxuriant, worsted yarn. "This shade of blue is lovely and it's a good weight for a cape, but the color isn't appropriate for mourning."

Jenny removed her reading glasses and turned to Cora. "Young lady. How long do you think you ought to mope about the cottage in that dreadful black crepe?"

"I thought I should follow what is customary. At least into the new year."

"Whatever for?"

Cora felt as if she were being quizzed by a schoolteacher. "Because it shows my respect for Father?"

"And do you think your father would have thought it necessary?"

"Well, I suppose not. He wasn't one to stand on ceremony or appreciate grandiose gestures."

"Quite right. Casting off black for brighter colors doesn't mean you've forgotten him, and youth is fleeting," Jenny said magnanimously. "Perhaps you should dress in cheerful colors again and go to balls."

Cora laughed. "Go to balls? Aunt Jenny, we live in Maryville, population two thousand, not Paris."

"You know what I mean."

"But what will people say if I shorten my mourning? What about Mrs. Brockett, and Mrs. Meyer, and all the ladies at St. Andrew's?"

"Who cares what they think?" Jenny shrugged. "I don't. Let the old scolds wag their bitter tongues. You'll be infamous for two minutes. Then, some other imaginary scandal will arise to attract their disapproval and poof! You'll become the toast of the town in your royal blue cape. You look positively radiant in blue."

"I do adore it." Cora held a strand of soft yarn against her wrist, testing the shade against her skin.

"Which is fortunate for a redhead," said Jenny.

"Auburn," Cora corrected.

"If there's leftover yarn, we can do up a muff." Jenny weighed a skein in her hand.

Cora scrutinized the illustration of the cape above the pattern. "I don't trust myself with the instructions. The edge is so intricate."

"Very well. I'll knit it up for you. If you do our

winter stockings." Well aware of Cora's disdain for fussy work, Jenny sang, "Fair's fair."

Cora was considering the question of buttons when they heard a rap on the back door. As Cora and Jenny entered the kitchen to answer it, their neighbor, Moira Kelly, tumbled in and closed the door swiftly behind her. She waved the newspaper gripped in her fat, pink hand.

"I don't think yous get the *Trumpet,* so I brung it," she said, somewhat breathlessly. "I know you'll want to read today's paper."

"Thank you, Moira." Jenny directed their guest into the sitting room with a wave of her hand. "Sit a minute, and we'll get you a cup of tea."

Cora tried to glimpse the headline as she crossed to the stove to pour a mug of tea, but as Moira wiped her feet, she tucked the paper under a plump arm, and it was hidden from Cora's passing eyes.

As Cora followed the two older women through the passage with the steaming drink, Moira said, "I shoulda mentioned already. It's good news, not bad, and now I've gone and worried yous." She plopped into the rocking chair, held the *Trumpet* up for inspection, and quoted proudly, "Phila...Philano...Oh whatever. Man Donates Generously to Orphanage. That's only the headline, mind." Moira's grin broadened. "It's about Doc Patton's little wanderers. They'll be having toffee pudding tonight, I expect."

Jenny pursed her lips and frowned. Though Moira didn't notice Jenny's expression, Cora did. She exchanged the mug for the newspaper with Moira, and asked brightly, "Shall I read the article aloud?"

"You might as well. I don't know where I've left my spectacles," sniffed Jenny who knew full well they rested on a pile of patterns.

"Very well." Cora settled onto the loveseat, cleared her throat, and read:

Philanthropist Donates Generously to Orphanage
By William J. Smith

Mr. Robert Helston of Maryville heroically ventured to the neighboring town of Brucedale yesterday on a mission to save the "Protestant Home for Little Wanderers" from destitution. Mr. Helston presented a check to the grateful head mistress, Miss Ivy MacDonnell, for the generous sum of $20,000. Said Miss MacDonnell, "The orphans look forward to their merriest Christmas ever thanks to Mr. Helston's kind assistance."

Mr. Helston bashfully avoided comment, but did allow that, as a Christian gentleman, he would never countenance any deprivation harming innocent children and he had to act when he heard of the plight of the Little Wanderers who have been sustained on salt pork, turnip, and oatmeal of late. Mr. Helston also stated that he was inspired to donate to the orphanage in the memory of the esteemed Dr. John Patton, late of Maryville, who funded the orphanage to the meager extent he was able.

"Thank you, Mr. Helston," exclaimed five-year-old Georgie Quinn. "I hope we can have toffee pudding for our supper." Mr. Helston chuckled, fondly ruffled the flaxen hair of the spritely lad, and declared that he hoped for a similar meal when he returned to Maryville and his daily toil.

As Cora folded the paper over, Moira clapped her pudgy hands together. "I know just what I'll make for Mr. Kelly's dessert tonight. Toffee pudding! Mind he's usually home late from the tavern and sups there. Isn't it the most delightful story though! Doc Patton would be so glad."

"Indeed he would, Moira," Cora passed the newspaper back to their guest.

Moira raised her hand in protest. "Pray keep it, Cora. Mr. Kelly receives a copy at the tavern, and you can have this one as a memento, seeing as the article mentions your father."

"Thank you, Moira," said Cora.

"More tea?" Jenny broke in.

"No, no," Moira quickly responded to Jenny's visible impatience. "I'd best get a stew on the stove and tend to my darning. I can tell by all the acorns in the garden, we're in for a nasty winter. Mr. Kelly will need warm socks with no holes. Well, except where his feet go in at the top," she laughed merrily.

"Thank you for coming," Jenny said.

Cora remembered the raisin scones in the breadbox and wondered at Aunt Jenny's failure to offer them. Moira would surely linger for a treat and a second mug of tea if pressed. Cora shrugged the thought away as they saw Moira to the door.

When they'd returned to their seats at the sewing table, Jenny said, "At risk of seeming uncharitable and cynical, I shall only say this once. Robert Helston is trying to buy you, Cora. His actions are transparent. He's playing on your ideals to steal your heart by donating to a children's charity that your father held dearly in his own heart. I also know for a fact that meals are far more varied at the orphanage than is stated in the article. When this man calls, you have no duty to oblige his whims."

"Once? And no more on this subject? That's your promise?" asked Cora in a voice of molten steel.

"Yes. My speech is quite finished, and I shan't return to the matter," replied Jenny with understated ferocity.

"Shall I put the newspaper in the kindling bin?"

"Yes, I believe you should."

"May I cast off the black crepe and don cheerful colors again?"

"Dress as you wish, my dear Cora." Jenny rose and collected Moira's empty mug. "You don't need my permission. Your destiny lies in your own hands."

With a discouraged sigh, Cora sifted half-heartedly through the button tin. She was disappointed in Aunt Jenny. Obviously, Robert cared for the orphans as much as Father had and could provide them with far more comfort. To assume the motive for Robert's donation was to selfishly lure her was profoundly unchristian. Why did Aunt Jenny have to ruin her chance of happiness by being so sour?

Chapter 9

Three days later, Cora answered the front door to receive the delivery of a dozen red roses with a card attached.

"Oh, someone loves you," Jenny said with an air of mystery. "I wonder who it could be. I suppose the Maryville spy ring has noticed your change of wardrobe and a certain gentleman wishes to court you."

Blushing, Cora took the flowers into the kitchen and placed the bouquet in a pitcher of water to keep the blooms fresh until she prepared a vase. Jenny hovered in the doorway, forcing Cora to turn her back to her to read the note with a modicum of privacy. She withdrew a small, white card from its envelope. The writer's penmanship was masculine, even, and confident.

Dearest Cora,

May this floral token mitigate the dull gray of November and brighten your room. I hope you will not be offended by my boldness in asking if I may entice you to join me on a carriage ride this Saturday afternoon. Pray reply in the afternoon post, if able. I'm on tenterhooks hoping you'll accept.

Your humble servant,

Robert

Cora suppressed the urge to jump up and down and dance around the kitchen whooping with joy. Until she received this missive, she couldn't be absolutely sure of

Robert's feelings, but now she had confirmation of his romantic interest. The roses and note changed everything. The only cloud hanging over her happiness was Aunt Jenny's dark view of Robert. Cora turned, smiling in spite of herself.

Jenny leaned against the doorframe, arms crossed, her mouth set in a thin, straight line.

"Well?" she asked.

"Well?" Cora repeated. "Well, Robert wishes to take me on a carriage ride on Saturday afternoon." She braced herself against Jenny's disapproval and denial of permission.

Instead, Jenny's expression softened. "What do you plan to wear on this momentous occasion?"

"You mean I can go?"

"It's up to you."

"Then I shall. I've reduced the size of the bustle on Betsy's green frock and I've only to remove the fancy bows on the sleeves to make it tasteful. It's a deep enough shade for the time of year." Cora bit her lip as she considered what she would wear for warmth. Her black boots would do, but her woolen cloak was a nondescript gray and fraying at the hem and would look forlorn in contrast to the dress.

Jenny seemed to read her mind. "I've made quick progress on your cape. If I apply myself to the task, I can finish it by Saturday."

"Oh!" Cora squealed. "I don't know how to thank you, Aunt Jenny."

"Your happiness is thanks enough," Jenny said, matter-of-factly.

"I'd better write back. Robert asked for a reply in the afternoon post. I believe he's worried I'll decline."

Jenny shrugged and stepped aside so Cora could hasten to the sitting room.

Cora sat at the desk, took up a quill pen, and thought. And thought more. What would she write? She had to strike a balance between warmth and reserve, to cloak a signal of passion under cool-headed dispassion. Display her affection without being a push-over. She'd ask Aunt Jenny for advice, but what would a spinster know of such matters?

Cora cradled her chin in her hand and gazed pensively through the windowpane. Unlike the Helstons, the Pattons' resources were limited, and Cora couldn't afford to waste paper on numerous drafts. In the garden, a crow flew down from the spruce tree and perched on the roof of the chicken coop, his beady eyes scanning for kernels of corn that the chickens had missed. Silhouetted in the weak, November sunshine, the crow bided his time until the rooster scratched and pecked his way to the farthest corner of the enclosure.

"Patience," murmured Cora. "That is your lesson for me, isn't it, Mr. Crow? A gentleman's demands mustn't be dignified with immediate satisfaction lest the object of his desire lose value in his eyes."

Cora dipped her pen in the inkpot and wrote in her best hand across a leaf of fine paper,

Dear Robert,

Thank you for the beautiful bouquet of roses. The flowers are fragrant and brighten the sitting room considerably. You are so thoughtful.

I accept your invitation of a carriage ride on Saturday.

Yours sincerely,

Cora

She folded the letter into thirds, tucked it into an envelope, and placed it in the drawer. Robert would receive his reply in Friday's post and not a moment sooner.

****

Workday over, Jim and Tom dropped by the office of the millworks to pick up their weekly pay packets. Mr. Brockett, pillar of Maryville civilization, was sequestered in his office, but his daughter, Adeline, bounced out of her chair when Jim and Tom crossed the threshold and approached the clerk's desk.

"Daddy's clerk is ill, so I'm filling in," she grinned. Adeline looked every inch a businesswoman in her navy frock and work sleeves. Her rich, chestnut hair was piled atop her head, and she'd tucked a pencil behind her ear.

"For some reason, I don't miss the lad," Tom said under his breath.

Adeline pretended she hadn't heard him as she pushed his envelope across the desk.

"Thank you, Miss Brockett." Tom smiled as he pocketed his pay, then turned to Jim. "You still going to the bank instead of directly to the tavern like a normal man?"

"Yes," replied Jim.

"Then I'll meet you at the S 'n T in an hour." Tom swaggered off.

"Here's yours, Jim, and something even better." Adeline handed Jim two envelopes, one the usual work-a-day beige and the other pink with a scalloped flap. "It's an invitation."

"Thank you, Adeline." Jim tucked both envelopes into his shirt pocket.

"Won't you read it?" she pleaded with eager brown

eyes.

"As you wish." Jim withdrew the invitation, opened it, and read, "You are cordially invited to a party at the home of Mr. and Mrs. Brockett on Saturday evening, the 14th of November to welcome Miss Diana Jones home from her year abroad in Europe…"

"Oh, do say you'll come, Jim," cajoled Adeline. "A party is always merrier when you're there."

"You realize when you flatter me, I'm yours."

"Yes, I do. So you'll come?"

"I'd be delighted."

Adeline bobbed up and down with her hands clasped before her. "Wonderful!" she exclaimed. "November is less dreary already."

With a quick smile, Jim thanked her once more and hastened to the Commercial Bank before it closed. The mortgage payment on the farm was soon due, and he'd put a little of his wage aside for tuition. His savings account was his best defense against the nimble fingers of James senior, the unluckiest gambler in Maryville.

Chapter 10

So what if Robert arrived late? Surely it was due to the demands of business rather than callous arrogance as Aunt Jenny alleged. Concealed behind the window curtain, Cora watched Robert loop a rein around the fence post and mount the porch stairs. From his black top hat and tailored frock coat to his polished boots, he looked positively gallant, and she wouldn't ruin a splendid afternoon on petty interrogation. She pushed by Aunt Jenny before the older woman could answer the door dressed in her riotously patterned, sleeved quilt and say something mortifying. Cora got to the door on the first knock and her first date with Mr. Robert Helston commenced.

The sun cast its rays at a low angle, tinting the countryside in warm sepia and golden tones as Robert tucked the carriage blanket around her. Despite the November chill, it was a fine afternoon for an outing.

"I thought we could drive around the millpond and over to the lake range," said Robert. "However, you look so beautiful, it's rather selfish to keep you to myself. I could drive through Maryville to show you off."

Cora felt a heat rise in her cheeks. Blushing over compliments was the curse of the ginger-haired, yet she did feel beautiful. She'd arranged her hair in a crown of loose loops, and her royal blue cape and green frock fit her just so. However, she only wished to dazzle Robert's eyes on this fine afternoon.

"I believe I'd prefer a countryside drive," said Cora.

"I as well," said Robert. "Let's go to the lake range."

They departed from Jenny's prim, whitewashed cottage with square pillared porch and regimented gardens, and drove through the neighborhood of simple brick and clapboard dwellings on Maryville's western fringe. Scrawny chickens scratched for half-frozen bugs among the cabbages and chard in unruly kitchen gardens. A mangy mutt pulled a bone from a steaming compost heap while a snotty-nosed boy in a tattered jacket looked on. Robert tapped his whip on his horse's back, and the horse quickened his pace.

Cora noted a stiffness in Robert's bearing and a subtle twitch in his nose that revealed an unease, a covert disgust, with the poverty on the western edge of town. Never mind. Best to forgive him this, for Robert's lofty sense of propriety had served him well. Born into Anglican privilege, he'd magnified his family's wealth. Surely these mild signs of snobbery could be overlooked.

"What's the name of your horse?" asked Cora, admiring the trim, black gelding.

"Prince."

Robert slid closer, eased his arm over hers and she let herself shelter at his side. "You'll be warmer now," he said softly, taking the rein in his right hand.

They drove past the millpond, placid and glassy with a ruff of silky cattail and milk weed around its edge, then gained the road to the lake. They were blessedly alone. As they approached an avenue of spruce, Robert produced a flask from a leather case under the seat.

"I hope you'll join me for a glass of brandy, against the chill."

Cora agreed she would, agreed they could share a single glass, and she would hold it while Robert handled the reins. Presently, they stopped at a copse of willow with a view across the water, a mirror for the dusky hills on the opposite shore. Prince drank at the lake's edge while Cora and Robert slouched under the carriage blanket, the brandy loosening their tongues and obliterating all sense of time. By the second glass, Cora felt as if they'd known each other all their lives, such was the easiness of their laughter and the depth of their revelation.

As they finished their third glass, Prince pawed the ground, impatient for his stall and a reward of oats. Robert looked at his pocket watch. Quarter past five. After two hours of blissful conviviality, the sun was setting on a perfect afternoon. Aunt Jenny would be frantic if they didn't return before dark, yet Cora scarcely cared. Only couldn't this afternoon go on forever?

They started back at a brisk trot, Prince eager for his barn, racing against the sinking sun.

When Robert slipped his free hand under the blanket and rested it on Cora's thigh, a strange, magnetic energy pulled her toward him. His intimacy, his lingering touch was all she craved during the short journey back to town. Robert didn't move his hand, he didn't caress, he didn't speak. He merely linked himself to her with the warmth of his hand in the fold of her skirt and signaled that they, Robert and Cora, were on a different journey, destined for a different place, than the workaday world of Maryville.

****

In the rarified atmosphere of the Brocketts' drawing room, Jim poured punch with a silver ladle into crystal glasses for Adeline Brockett, Helen Jones, Betsy Meyer, and the guest of honor, Miss Diana Jones, recently returned from Europe by way of New York City. Nearby, four young men played whist leaving Jim the odd man out, much to his relief. Cards were a dull amusement compared to Diana's breathless tales of Italy, Switzerland, and France and the other girls' envious yet curious commentary.

Presently, the conversation drifted from the exotic delicacies of continental cuisine to the outlandish fashions of Paris, and Jim's attention wandered. What if Cora were to appear and—

Adeline tugged Jim's sleeve and pulled him away from the others as Betsy watched after them.

Not to be overheard, Adeline hissed, "Cora's not coming, so stop looking toward the door."

"Am I that obvious?" Jim asked, sheepish that Adeline had read him.

"Yes. Always. You are utterly incapable of hiding your feelings. It's one of your many endearing qualities."

"Is she busy?"

"I truly don't know. We didn't invite her. Mother thought it unseemly for Cora to attend a party when she should be in mourning."

"I see." Though the exclusion stung him, Jim held his tongue. Adeline and he both knew that Cora's absence had more to do with her status and her lack of membership in the Anglican Church than arcane rules of bereavement. Although Jim shared Cora's middling rung on the social ladder, he was welcome in Adeline's circle because he added a dash of color to the party.

"Don't be like that, Jim."

"Like what?"

"Sulky. You're a mopey old Basset hound. It doesn't become you."

"I'm sorry." He affected a winsome expression.

Mollified, Adeline smiled. "You should be. You have a bottomless cup of punch and four beautiful ladies buzzing around you with literally no competition for their attention." She looked pointedly at his empty glass and nodded toward the crystal bowl. "What else could you possibly desire?"

Cora's presence. "Nothing at all," he replied contritely as they refilled their glasses.

"You're not the only one whose love is unrequited," said Adeline. "Cheers." They clinked glasses, and after a sip of the sweet refreshment, she continued. "Mother was hoping Robert Helston would attend."

"Now that's a scandal," said Jim, regaining his usual good humor. "How's your father taking it?"

"Silly, daft, adorable Jim. She and Mrs. Jones want to match Diana with Mr. Helston."

"But he's so old," exclaimed Jim.

"Diana is twenty-four and he's only thirty. He just seems old because he's more mature than you lot." Adeline glared theatrically at the card players who were arguing over the tally.

"Well, I have no objection to the match," said Jim.

"No, you wouldn't, would you, given Cora's obvious interest in Mr. Helston," Adeline smirked.

"Adeline, tell me seriously: what does an intelligent girl like Cora, or Diana, see in a man like Robert Helston?"

Adeline wrinkled her nose. "Well, he's not my cup of tea. I prefer a strongly built man with wavy black hair and dreamy, dark eyes." She straightened Jim's lapel and peered up at him flirtatiously. "However, some women are attracted to wealth and power, and he has both in spades. And objectively speaking, he's as handsome as you."

"Damned with faint praise."

"Remember what I said about sulking."

"Yes, Mother."

Adeline swatted Jim's shoulder. "Do you want to discuss ecclesiastical architecture with Diana or play a duet on the piano with me?"

"Um…"

"Quite right. Please listen carefully for once. The left hand is only three notes in a dead-easy waltz rhythm. Even you can manage that."

Chapter 11

"You're sure you're not working too hard? Martin is only six weeks old, and here you are, managing the store on your own." Concern etched Cora's forehead.

Hilda Beck laughed. "I've not had an easier baby than Martin, but for my sore bosom. The older ones are in school, the store is quiet in the afternoon, and Hans is here for the morning and afternoon rush with time between for the heavy work. This is my version of heaven, Cora. A clean, well-stocked store, friendly customers for chit chat and, dare I say, a spell of gossip, and a baby sleeping in his cradle, content as can be. If only my left side didn't look and feel like a giant coconut."

"And we have a plan to make that right."

"We do. Thanks for writing everything down, Cora. About the salve and such. My mind leaks like a sieve. Always does till the babes sleep through the night."

"I understand why you like it here, behind the counter, Hilda. Actually, I can smell it." Cora closed her eyes and inhaled deeply through her nose. They were perched on stools next to a row of glass jars filled with spices. The exotic scents of cinnamon, nutmeg, ginger, and cloves surely tempted customers to splurge on supplies and make a head start on their Christmas baking.

"Fragrant, isn't it? And when Martin starts teething, all I have to do is reach for the jar of cloves and prepare some oil for his gums, just like you and Jenny taught me."

Hilda stood and spoke to Jimmy Sinclair's mother as she entered the store and approached the counter. "How may I help you today, Morag?"

"Hilda. Cora." Mrs. Sinclair, a smile warming her wrinkled, care-worn face, nodded to both women. "I'd like another six yards of denim, please," she said to Hilda. "The boys' trousers wear out faster than I can make them these days."

Hilda fetched a pair of shears from a drawer, a bolt of fabric from a cubby, and took both to a broad table, chattering all the while. "All that sewing and cooking aside, you'll be glad to have Jim home. I expect he's a big help, especially over harvest."

"Aye, so true," Mrs. Sinclair agreed. "He never complains, and he works from dawn to dusk, but I know his heart is in Montreal."

"Is he missing his studies or a girl?" Hilda winked.

"Come to think of it, I couldn't say," Mrs. Sinclair laughed. "Cora? You're just Jim's age. What do you reckon?"

Cora had never considered how Jimmy might feel about anything, and she didn't have a ready answer. Hesitantly, she ventured, "I think he'd miss school more, Mrs. Sinclair. He doesn't want for female attention, but he's bright and in school he read more books than all the other boys put together." And, too clever by far, he played more pranks. Cora felt an unexpected glimmer of empathy for her schoolyard enemy as she continued. "I don't think Jimmy misses a girl. I think he probably misses the challenge of McGill."

"Quite so," Hilda agreed as she measured the heavy

cloth. "And because I so love our Jim, I'm measuring generously, on the house. Montreal's loss is Maryville's gain, especially at a party."

"Why that's eight yards, if an inch, Hilda. I do thank you." Mrs. Sinclair's tired smile melded into one of relieved gratitude and tears welled in her eyes. "Mark my words, I'll be sure to tell Jimmy of your kindness." With calloused hands, she received the roll of denim along with a few candy sticks Hilda tucked inside it for Jim, again, 'on the house'. "We'll pay our account by the end of the month," she assured Hilda.

After Mrs. Sinclair departed, Hilda said, "I make it a rule never to discuss finances, especially where customers are concerned, but I don't think Jim will ever go back to law school. Even if the family could scratch together enough money for tuition, his father is incapable of running the farm on his own and Jim really should take over. They pretend he's helping out temporarily, but they'd be up the creek without a paddle if he weren't home."

"Oh," was all Cora could think to say. It was simpler to be jealous of Jimmy Sinclair when he went off to McGill, or to be irritated by his teasing antagonism, than to feel any sympathy for her old foe.

"Oh indeed. We should all spare a prayer for that poor family. Vice, when it takes a man as it has James senior, is terrible to witness," Hilda said solemnly. "The drink makes a man slovenly, sloppy, and violent, and an easy mark for swindlers and gamblers. Hans likes a nip now and then, as most men do, but I watch him like a hawk. Do yourself a favor and never marry a drinker. Don't even give him the time of day. A drunk man can turn a woman's life into a living hell. Morag Sinclair can only pretend everything's okay."

Cora thought of Robert. Sure, he enjoyed a tipple, but he never let alcohol get the better of him. She didn't have to worry that he'd lose control and do anything stupid or shameful.

Hilda seemed to notice the drift of her thoughts. "If you don't mind me remarking, I find you quite changed these days, Cora."

Oh, oh. Cora wouldn't confirm or dismiss Hilda's assertion.

"You have the faraway look of a woman in love."

Cora objected, "I assure you, I—"

"Have been seen around town on the arm of an older, highly eligible bachelor?" Hilda finished, hands on hips as if challenging Cora to deny it.

"Widower," Cora corrected.

"In practical terms, that's exactly the same thing," Hilda declared, chin rising triumphantly.

"And I'm not in love." Cora felt her face redden as she grasped in vain for a way to dismiss the subject. "We're only—"

Hilda interrupted, "So, it *is* true. You deny it but you *are* in love. I knew it. Don't worry, Cora. I can tell he's in love with you too."

"We spend time together," Cora admitted.

"When the tables are turned, and you need an extra pair of hands when the first little Helston arrives, I'll be at your side."

"Is that a promise or a threat?" Cora joked.

"Both. A threatening promise or a promising threat, take your pick."

On cue, Martin grimaced, batted his tiny fists, and began to grizzle.

"Speaking of which," Hilda said as she plucked him from his cradle.

"Left side first, tuck him under your arm, and gently rub the hard spots," reminded Cora. "I'll warm a towel." Saved from interrogation by a six-week-old, she thought happily.

So happily. Cora *was* in love with Robert Helston, and she no longer cared who knew it.

****

The mercury dropped like a stone that afternoon, and as she left Beck's Dry Goods, Cora wished she'd put her mittens or a muff into her satchel that morning. She rubbed her hands together to warm them, then tucked them under her cape and walked briskly up Main toward the empty lot where her childhood home once stood.

The house was gone but for a neat pile of partially charred wood covered by a canvass that the O'Mallory boys had left. Scavengers dared not disturb it out of respect for the late Dr. Patton. The pieces of wood were too small for construction, but they were handy fuel, and the wood pile at Aunt Jenny's cottage was dwindling quickly with the cold weather. Moira Kelly would lend them firewood, and Robert would send a load, but Cora hated to ask, and the man who usually supplied them was down with the flu. A big bagful would tide them over for a couple days, until Oscar Landry was on his feet again and could deliver a cartload.

Cora pulled a burlap sack from her satchel and uncovered the pile. A pang of sorrow overtook her at the sight of it. Smoke-stained planks, formerly white, and pieces of dark green trim lay in orderly fashion, unlike her father's study which always looked as if a tornado had ripped through, until one really did. At the end of each day, Father would sit at his desk, spectacles sliding down his nose, reading medical journals and looking up treatments in heavy tomes and seldom getting around to his ledger. People paid him mostly out of gratitude, less so because bills appeared in their letter boxes.

And each evening, after supper, Cora would bring a pot of tea into the study to discuss the day's cases or an item of interest he'd found in a journal. "Fascinating," he'd say. "That fellow in Scotland, Lister. He seems to be having great success with carbolic acid, hmm? Cuts the post-surgical infection rate right down. Remarkable. Do you think we might apply his techniques in this colonial backwater, hmm? What do you say, girl?"

Father expected a snappy answer even if it was an admission of ignorance and a promise to learn. Under Father's tutelage, learn she did. Aunt Jenny taught her plenty too: the importance of disease prevention, the preparation of herbal medicines, and how to tune into one's inner voice, one's intuition, something that didn't come naturally to Cora. She preferred to use reason, as Father had. He quizzed her on anatomy and physiology and taught her to follow his diagnosis and treatment methods. He'd say, "If you were a boy, you'd be in medical school, hmm? You have the knack of it, girl, of medicine. I suppose I shall have to manage as your professor, hmm?"

Even with Father gone, she was an eager student, though a student with very few books. How she wished Father were still alive, still setting hard quizzes, still demanding she label each facial bone or list the symptoms of diphtheria. Oh, how she missed him. She stooped and began to fill her sack, grateful for the catharsis of physical labor.

Surely Robert wouldn't mind if she continued practicing her vocation after they married. He hadn't asked for her hand yet, but he hinted broadly he would, and she expected a proposal by Christmas. If only Father were still alive to walk her down the aisle.

****

After he dropped off a grinder he'd borrowed from the O'Mallorys, Jim took the short cut through the orchard to the road. Someone, a woman, was stooped at the woodpile at the Patton place. Bound to happen. A cold autumn, penniless immigrants arriving by the day, hell, even his own family would scavenge if they weren't close to self-sufficient on the farm. The wood might as well go to someone who needed fuel as rot in a pile.

As he drew closer, the female figure came into sharper form. A familiar form. Petite yet curvy though her dress was shapeless and plain, a practical cape, wild curls bouncing under bonnet, sensible boots. Cora. Jim paused under a gnarled tree, obscured in the shadows of the orchard. If Robert Helston were courting Cora, surely she shouldn't want for firewood. Unless she was gathering wood for someone else. But she was too busy for that, and she'd have sent a needy person to gather his own wood. The logical conclusion was that Cora and Jenny Patton needed fuel and Cora was hauling it home herself.

Ever low by Jim's estimation, Robert Helston's standing diminished further. Helston was self-centered, the glowing sun in his own eyes, his very own alpha and omega, and he hadn't seen Cora's situation. Jim stifled his instinct to charge from the orchard and help her. Cora would refuse him, her pride required it, and she'd assume he was lurking. He waited in the orchard till he saw her straighten, heave the sack over her shoulder, pick up her satchel, and tramp away. She forgot to cover the pile, so he covered it with the canvass himself.

Chapter 12

Cora went to the wood box outside the kitchen door to replenish the basket of firewood by the stove. Snow squalls had decorated town and country in whipped cream swirls during the night and now the sky was crystalline blue, the clear air invigorating. After pausing to admire the beauty of the morning, she lifted the lid expecting to reach deep down for the few frozen logs and burnt planks left on the bottom of the box. What a surprise to find it filled with birch logs, evenly split and ready to burn. But who was the kind soul who put them there? Robert? It had to be. Who else would bestow such a thoughtful gift? Back in the kitchen, Cora pushed a few slender logs into the stove, stoked the fire, and filled a pan with water and oatmeal for porridge.

Jenny called from the sitting room, "Mind you conserve that wood. Oscar won't likely be by till late in the day."

"Is that so?" Cora called back.

"Yes, and don't be saucy. He said so when I checked on him yesterday. He was just getting back on his feet, and we aren't his top priority."

With no further word, Cora prepared their breakfast, smiling as she chopped a tart apple into the porridge. Robert's kindness would make a stronger impact on Aunt Jenny if she discovered the firewood herself. They could thank Robert later in the day, Aunt Jenny contritely and Cora affectionately. He'd promised to take her for a sleigh ride when the weather suited, and now the snow was at least a foot deep and squeaky cold. Besides, today was Saturday, usually a light day at the *Trumpet* office.

They were sitting for breakfast when an errand boy arrived with Robert's note. Cora dashed off a reply and pressed it into the boy's hand with a coin and a piece of peppermint candy that Hilda Beck had given her. Aunt Jenny agreed to take over Cora's afternoon patients, although she said she wouldn't thank Robert for the firewood, citing "lack of evidence" that he was the giver.

****

Although over a month away, it felt like Christmas. Robert had fastened bells to Prince's harness, and they jingled with each hoof fall. Although the ice on the pond wasn't thick enough for skating yet, the hill behind the school had attracted a swarm of tobogganers decked out in brightly colored hats, scarves, and mittens. Cora couldn't imagine why people complained about winter, especially on such an afternoon as this.

As they drove behind Brockett's Mill, Cora said, "I thought I'd have to beg at the sawmill for lumber scraps, until you rescued us last night."

"Rescued you?" Robert asked.

"Yes, funny old Robert. Don't be coy with me," Cora teased. "When I opened the wood box this morning, it was filled to the top with birch logs."

Robert frowned slightly as Cora continued. "I don't know how you knew about our predicament. And I don't know how to thank you."

"For the firewood?" Robert brightened. "Yes, well, I can think of something." He wrapped his arm around Cora and pulled her close. "You can keep me warm."

"That's all you want?" Cora laughed.

"No. I'd like to kiss you."

He directed Prince down a quiet lane and halted the cutter in a thick grove of cedars. Apart from gregarious chickadees darting through the air and chipmunks circling the tree trunks, they were entirely alone. Cora looked up into Robert's handsome face. A handsome, troubled face. A lock of brown hair fell over his forehead as he doffed his top hat. His blue eyes challenged her, commanded her, to give him more of herself than she ever had before.

Silent for a moment, he spoke in a low, confessional tone. "Cora. I'm entranced by your beauty, and by your character and your intelligence and your vulnerability. I want you to be comfortable. To be happy and safe. Always. Do you understand that?"

He cupped her cheek in his ungloved hand. Her skin burned under his fingers.

Cora nodded. She was vulnerable to his masculinity, to his authority and experience. She supposed she felt safe…did she feel safe? Robert and she were turning down a strange, perilous corridor of obsession and passion in the seclusion of the cedars. Her heart pounded, her lips parted, and she breathed more deeply as she fought to regain a semblance of rationality, but it was futile. Robert's eyes revealed what words could not: he would kiss her. He would kiss her as a man in love.

Robert had kissed her once before, a chaste peck on her cheek that nevertheless provoked an ache for his touch deep within her, long after they said good night. Now, as he bent his face to hers and drew her chin up to his chin, Cora knew this kiss would be different. His lips parted and sought hers. She closed her eyes to everything, only feeling, only seeking him in return.

At first his kiss was soft and gentle and then it was not. His lips moved hard upon hers as he forced his tongue into her mouth. The sensation, at once fascinating and off-putting, reminded Cora of a garden slug sliding between the leaves of a cabbage. She'd have to convince herself to like it. Robert's hands slid around her waist, and he pulled her to him. Too much. It was too much. The urgent intimacy, the strange feelings. She turned her head to break away.

Robert held her and whispered in her ear. He was hers. She should be his. As cedar boughs swayed over the cutter in a light, cold wind, he clung to her as if parting were impossible.

"One day soon, when you are ready, do you care if you are seen coming into my home?" he asked.

"Unchaperoned?"

"Yes."

"No, I don't care," she replied, covering her nervous ambivalence with false sophistication.

Robert flicked the rein over Prince's back. Arms entwined, they headed back to town. Though warm under the carriage blanket, Cora shivered in a shadow of doubt. She regretted that careless "no".

****

Jim smashed the ice in the trough with the handle of his pitchfork, frigid water splashing him as he broke through. He should've been studying for end-of-semester exams, not toiling on this godforsaken farm and bailing out the old man who pissed away money in the backroom of the Golden Pheasant. Day by day, Jim was stumbling down a dreary trail to nowhere. He had to correct course, find a path back to law school.

He leaned against the rails of the corral. The animals were thirsty. Buttercup snorted with dragon-like puffs from her big, round nostrils as she nudged through a trio of cattle crowding at the trough. Jim rubbed his temple in a vain attempt to relieve the dull throb in his head. A barnyard of nausea-inducing stench, bright white snow, clattering latches, and clanging gates was no place to nurse a hangover.

Thank God, he'd woken in his own bed. Ragged fragments of memory arose in his bleary consciousness and with them a sickening dread in his gut. The evening began with Tom at the S 'n T, then a bet that Adeline wouldn't let Tom over the threshold of the massive front door of the Brockett mansion. Tom lost. Giggling girls…two girls…he between them with an arm around each, on the sofa…blind man's bluff…Mr. Brockett's wine cellar…a lewd game of charades…Mr. Brockett's liquor cabinet…a childish, drunken game of hide and seek…Adeline in the pantry…Adeline pulling his head down and kissing him in the dark…her hand on the fly of his trousers, on his cock…her hand on his bare, hard cock…damn—

"I've brought you a special drink. To fortify you for chores."

Gran. Jim straightened, rigid with shame.

"You've made a late start, and this will keep you till supper."

He turned to face the music in the form of his short, fat grandmother who missed nothing and governed herself with a disarmingly cheerful directness.

"It's a miracle you made it home last night. You could've stumbled into a ditch or frozen to a fence. I suppose the Lord doesn't like the smell of liquor, for

He's in the habit of sparing the drunken."

"I'm sorry, Gran."

"Never mind sorry. You're the one who's suffering, not me. And now you pay your penance." She presented Jim with a large flask. "Drink this."

"Thanks." Jim's tongue shriveled on contact with the malodorous, orange concoction and he barely kept from spitting it out. "I'll drink it later."

"No, no you won't. I made this special and brought it to you when I should be churning the cream. Least you can do is humor my efforts to help you. Drink."

Jim choked down a third of the vile liquid, then wiped his upper lip with the back of his hand. "What's in it?" His mouth contorted with disgust.

"Eggs, tomato juice, buttermilk, dill seed, ginger powder, a few other ingredients. Go on, Jimmy. All of it."

Somehow, he managed to find the bottom of the flask, and he hoped his reward would be solitude. It wasn't.

As Gran received the empty flask, she said, "While the nourishment settles, have you time for a quick word?"

Jim gritted his teeth and nodded gingerly.

"There's no harm in a wee bit of fun, is there Jimmy? At my age, I'm not in the social whirl, yet I do miss it. Why don't you tell me about last night? Cheer me with a story or two."

"There's not much to tell."

"Come now. Surely you weren't alone."

"No. I met Tom O'Mallory at the Shamrock and Thistle, and then we went to the Brocketts' for a small get-together."

"With Isaac Brockett! Isn't he liberal-minded, entertaining the likes of you—the son of an Orangeman and the son of a Fenian, twoscore his junior and not a nickel between you?"

"We stay out of politics." Jim tamped the snow with his boot. Surely Gran would find the weather cold, and she'd shuffle off. Nope. Now she was quoting Burns.

"'The rank is but the guinea's stamp.' Here in the new world, it's true, bless us. What did you talk about then?"

"Nothing much."

"Nothing much?"

Mind sluggish as cold molasses, it finally dawned on Jim that Gran knew more than she was letting on. She was cross-examining him with a competence exceeding that of the crown prosecutor. He stared at a clump of manure in the snow and admitted that Mr. Brockett hadn't been home.

"Not home. Well, who was there?"

"The Jones sisters, Miss Betsy Meyer, Miss Adeline and her cousin."

"You and Tom were foxes in the henhouse."

"It wasn't like that, Gran."

"Like what?"

"Tom and I weren't foxes. We didn't mean any harm."

"No, I suppose not. My Jimmy's a good lad." Gran's soft voice was edged with sarcasm. She reached over the rail and squeezed his cheek, then regarded him narrowly. "However, some folks in Maryville, old-fashioned prudes with queer notions, might disagree. Why, even Mr. Brockett might disagree. Imagine that."

"I can imagine it. I'm sorry."

"No need for sorry. Just mind how you go. And when your head is right, give it a shake, aim your eyes toward your future, and walk so your feet don't stick in the mire. Well, we'd best get back to work."

Gran turned and tramped off until Jim called after her.

"Gran?"

"Aye, Jimmy?"

"How did you find out about—"

"Jenny Patton told me she heard all about you and Tom from one of the Brocketts' servants. At church this morning. Jenny thought your antics were hilarious. Imagine that."

Chapter 13

Jim tucked the mail into his jacket pocket and left the post office for the fresh air of a December afternoon. Mama and Gran would be pleased to have news of family far away. As he descended the stone steps, he spotted Betsy Meyer emerging from the milliner's shop across the street. A quick step back behind the pillar, and she wouldn't see him.

Too late. She was waving with the vigor of a railway flagman. It would be rude to pretend he hadn't seen her. There was nothing for it but to wave back and think of excuses to avoid a long conversation. Comment on the weather, ask after her family, and—

Splat. Jim watched as Betsy, shod in high-heeled boots, skidded on a frozen puddle, and landed flat on her back, limbs splayed, hat lying in the snow like a lost, tropical bird. He crossed the street and was at her service in an instant, hand extended to help her up.

"Are you all right, Betsy?"

She didn't lift her hand, didn't say a word.

"Betsy?"

Quite suddenly, she propped herself on her elbow. "Jim? I'm…I'm…my ankle."

In the slush, Betsy's right leg lay in normal alignment, but her left foot was strangely twisted. A sick shiver ran up Jim's core. Betsy had broken her ankle. Onlookers gathered, informed newcomers about what had happened, and made suggestions. One voice rang above the din, exhorting everyone to step back and give Miss Meyer some space. Cora. It was Cora. Thank God. She'd know what to do.

Cora smiled reassuringly at him as she knelt at Betsy's side. Then, directing her kindness to her patient, Cora asked, "What happened, Betsy?"

"Cora," sighed Betsy. She fell back off her elbow and let her head rest on a rolled-up blanket that some thoughtful soul had placed there. "I was crossing the street to speak to Jim, and I slid on the ice."

"Did you hit your head?" asked Cora.

"No. But I've hurt my leg. My left ankle." Betsy started to sob. "It hurts ever so much."

Still crouched, Cora pivoted and looked at Betsy's lower legs. Cora's expression was placidly inscrutable as she assessed the injury. Jim retrieved Betsy's generously plumed hat and set it by her shoulder. Even if he didn't know what to do, he could make himself useful in small ways.

"Can you lift your right leg?" asked Cora.

Betsy raised her daintily booted right foot and her skirt fell away revealing a lace fringed petticoat and silk stocking.

"Well done, Betsy," soothed Cora. "Now try the left."

Betsy clutched Jim's hand. "Must I?" she wailed.

"No. That's okay." Cora looked up at the crowd. "Has anyone a newspaper?"

"A newspaper?" Betsy echoed. "Whyever—"

Surely it was obvious. "To hold your leg in place while we get you indoors," guessed Jim.

Again, Cora smiled at him, and he felt an

inexplicable lightness. It wasn't charitable, but he couldn't help noticing the contrast between the two young women, Betsy, supine and ineffectual in silks and furs, blond hair coiffed in ringlets and ribbons, and Cora, calm and capable in practical woolen clothing, her wild hair temporarily tamed in a bun under her bonnet.

Someone handed Cora a newspaper, and she said, "Betsy. This may hurt for a moment, but I promise you, you'll feel better after I stabilize your leg. Then we'll take you to your father's office and send for Aunt Jenny."

"What?" Betsy cried. "Your Aunt Jenny? But she's a bonesetter. Surely it's only a sprain. And Daddy doesn't need to know."

"It looks like your ankle's broken," Cora said gently. "Now hold Jim's hand, nice and tight." Cora nodded to Hilda Beck who knelt next to her. "On the count of three, I'm going to lift your leg and Hilda will slip the newspaper around it to give it support."

Jim watched Cora intently, but she paused, frowned at him, and nodded toward Betsy. Right. He had his duty too. Betsy clung to his hand and stared up at him, eyes wide with fear. He smiled back, trying to emulate Cora's reassuring manner.

"Ready?" Cora searched their faces.

"Yes," Jim and Hilda said in unison. Betsy closed her eyes tightly.

"All right. One, two, three." And the deed was done. Cora tied the newspaper splint with strips of gauze from her satchel while Betsy whimpered and gripped his hand.

"Do you think you could carry Betsy to the Commercial Bank?" asked Cora.

Could he? If Cora had asked him to carry Betsy

across a frayed rope bridge over boiling brimstone, he would in an instant. "Yes, of course," he replied.

As he bent to ease his arms under Betsy's legs and back, he felt Cora's gaze upon him, as if she were appraising, and appreciating, his strength. And perhaps his imagination had kidnapped his common sense.

Lifting Betsy was a simple matter. Cradled in his arms, she nestled her head against his shoulder, and murmured of distressed damsels and brave heroes. Her cloying perfume tickled his nose, and he fought the unheroic urge to sneeze. Up the street they went, Cora holding Betsy's leg steady at his side with an entourage of the curious accompanying them.

****

Cora had to admit, it was fortunate that Jimmy Sinclair—no, Jim. Jim Sinclair—was there to carry Betsy into the sanctuary of her father's office, and she told him so.

"It was nothing, Cora," he said. "Any man would've done the same."

But they wouldn't have. He didn't heave Betsy up like a sack of potatoes. He deftly lifted her from the ground without jarring her leg and carried her as if she were as light as a newborn lamb, and that was no mean feat. Now he stood in Mr. Meyer's stuffy office, shifting back and forth in mud-stained boots as if waiting to be dismissed from detention.

"We should be okay now," she said.

There it was. The smile that melted female hearts. "If you're sure I'm not needed…"

"No!" Betsy seized Jim's hand. "I need you here, to comfort me."

Betsy would need comfort, but for the good of them

all, it couldn't be Jim. Young men were of a type and Jim was its epitome. He would sympathize with a patient while pretending to be strong for her, totter with wooziness, and faint, especially in a stuffy room with Mr. Meyer pacing and puffing about and Aunt Jenny's unflinching treatment of the ankle. Bone-setting was a brutal business.

"Perhaps your father could hold your hand?" Cora suggested to Betsy.

"Yes. Yes, it must be me," Mr. Meyer agreed, gruffness disguising his obvious worry.

He took Jim's place at Betsy's side and Jim bolted from the office with relief written all over his rugged face. In spite of herself, Cora smiled after him. With a shake of her head, she searched through her satchel, found a vial of laudanum, pulled out its cork, and poured the liquid into Betsy's mouth. Tape measure round her neck, Jenny was already loosening Betsy's boot laces. Cora closed the office door that Jim had left ajar in his hasty exit.

****

It was meant to be taken as good news, though to Cora it was anything but.

As one of the clerks carried Betsy to the Meyers' sleigh, Mr. Meyer said, "Thank you. Thank you from the bottom of my heart for taking care of our precious Betsy." He shook Aunt Jenny's and her hands as if he were priming a pump. "You both work so hard. Day and night, I'm told. You'll be happy to know that Mayor Jones and Brockett, Tucker, Helston, and I have struck up a committee to find a new doctor. I expect many Maryville citizens will prefer your services, especially those in the lower classes...and the ladies with...well, you know what I mean. A new doctor should reduce your burden considerably."

"Thank you, Mr. Meyer," Jenny said stiffly. She flashed a silencing frown at Cora. "Hadn't you better see Miss Meyer safely home, Cora?"

Cora stammered, "But, but…"

"Go on," Jenny urged. "I'll see you at home."

Dismissed. Cora had no choice but to climb into the sleigh with Mr. Meyer's clerk and a semi-conscious yet whimpering Betsy. Cora's mind spun with the implications of what Mr. Meyer had said. She and Aunt Jenny barely got by on what they earned as it was. A new doctor would absorb their better-heeled patients who paid by cash or check and leave them to barter their services for necessities with Maryville's laborers and heavily mortgaged farmers. As a banker, Mr. Meyer surely understood that. How could he think he was delivering good news?

Betsy yelped as the sleigh lurched over a rut, and Cora put her arm round her friend so she'd jostle less.

The very idea of a committee! Formed without Aunt Jenny's and her knowledge let alone their input. If Aunt Jenny and she were competent enough to care for the people of Maryville, surely they should be consulted on the recruitment of a new doctor. They kept Mr. Tucker from skidding into an ever-beckoning grave. Mr. Brockett's wife sought Aunt Jenny's advice on ailments from dandruff to itchy toes. And Robert…Robert hadn't whispered a single word about a committee. Meanwhile, he was complicit in pulling the carpet from under their feet.

Cora wanted to jump from the sleigh, find him, and confront him that moment, but Betsy had to be settled into bed with instructions given to Mrs. Meyer. The clerk directed the horse up the Meyers' broad lane. Duty first.

****

Night was falling as Cora left the Meyers' mansion. Still livid, she walked over to Robert's house and banged the knocker. A minute later, Polly opened the heavy door.

"Good evening, Miss Patton," she exclaimed. "What a pleasant surprise."

Judging by the lift of her brows, Polly was surprised indeed, though not necessarily pleasantly.

"Good evening, Polly," said Cora. "Is Mr. Helston home?"

"Not as such. No."

"Do you know when he'll return?"

Polly did not, and she looked relieved when Cora didn't press her to speculate on Robert's whereabouts or when he might darken the doorway.

Cora resolved to try his office and she marched briskly from whence the sleigh had carried her an hour and a half before. Besides custom at the taverns, business had stopped for the day and there were few people on Main Street. The *Trumpet* office windows were dark, and no one answered when she pounded on the door.

"Likely at a secret meeting to discuss my future," Cora hissed as she turned to walk home.

Chapter 14

Jenny greeted the prospect of a new doctor with uncharacteristic docility. "I don't like it any better than you do, Cora, but we shouldn't be surprised. Besides, what can we do?" she asked rhetorically.

Plenty, thought Cora. They had to react to the cracking ice beneath their feet. If they didn't, their future would be decided by a small group of wealthy men who had to be reminded to eat their vegetables. The situation was unkind and unjust.

They went to bed early, though Cora was too angry to sleep. All night, she tossed and turned and thought of what she'd say to Robert. As the clock chimed six, she dressed. She'd check on Moira Kelly and her colicky gallbladder, then wait at the *Trumpet* offices for him.

****

Cora arrived as Willy Smith was unlocking the front door.

"Miss Patton. Good morning." He doffed his hat and bowed slightly.

"Good morning, Willy. I'm here to pay Mr. Helston a visit," she said crisply.

Willy pushed the door open and bid her enter the office with a wave of his hand. The main room felt cavernous in the silent morning gloom. Masculine, work-a-day smells of newsprint, ink, and tobacco permeated the air. For a fleeting instant, Cora felt as if she were trespassing into Robert's private world. However, the *Trumpet* building was a place of business and she had come on business.

Willy hung his hat on the coat rack and unbuttoned his coat. "Mr. Helston may be late this morning. May I be of service to you?"

"Late? What time do you expect him?"

"Ten. He may arrive sooner. Usually he arrives promptly at eight, but he went to Toronto last night."

"Toronto." How little she knew of Robert's affairs. He hadn't mentioned that he planned to go to the city, yet she hadn't asked either. "Does he often go there?" She spoke in a conversational tone, as if asking Willy's opinion of the weather or the price of onions.

"Once, sometimes twice a week." Willy's eyes shifted toward the door. "On business."

"Yes, of course," said Cora. On business. How odd that Willy would clarify what should be obvious. What else would Robert do in Toronto? Cora let the matter go.

Again, Willy looked to the door, then back to her. "Um…Would you care to wait for Mr. Helston? His private office is quite comfortable."

Cora hesitated. She had patients to visit. On the other hand, her future had transformed into a looming question mark with yesterday's news. She would wait.

Willy led her to a smartly appointed room with velveteen curtains, bookshelves, a heavy walnut desk and sturdy, well-proportioned chairs. She sank into an upholstered chair and draped her arms onto the arm rests. Best hide her nervousness, her anger, and confront Robert calmly and rationally. As the minutes ticked by, she rehearsed what she'd say.

Finally, Robert entered the room. "Cora! What a

pleasant surprise!" he enthused, though Willy had undoubtedly warned him she was present.

Cora forgot the speech she'd rehearsed, jumped to her feet, and challenged him immediately. "Is it true that you're on a committee to recruit a doctor?"

Robert affected an expression of wounded innocence as he set his briefcase on his desk. "Mayor Jones requested my presence."

"So it *is* true. Robert! How could you?"

"Hold on," he objected, blue eyes twinkling. "I only went to one meeting, as a reporter. I felt I should, but if you think I shouldn't be aware of developments in this town and the *Trumpet* shouldn't report the news, well…" he finished with a shrug.

"Why didn't you tell me? I had to hear about the matter from Mr. Meyer."

Robert stepped toward her, voice gentle as if taming a wild animal. "I would have told you, Cora, but I wanted more information first. So far, the committee is a small group of fat, old men who smoke cigars, drink whisky, and gossip like church ladies, and they've only met once. I was so bored of their boozing and blather, I left the meeting early."

"Do you have any idea what a new doctor means to Aunt Jenny and me?"

"Yes. Do you think I'd let you starve?"

"It's more than the money, Robert. Healing is our vocation."

"And I wouldn't dream of depriving you of it."

Cora said nothing. He sounded so reasonable, but she wouldn't be placated with mushy platitudes. She slumped into the chair, crossed her arms, and turned away. Robert knelt before her.

She wouldn't meet his eyes. Not yet. "Where were you last night?"

"Toronto. On business."

"What sort of business?"

"Railway business. We need investors for a north-south line. I'm frequently called to the city for meetings as is anyone who launches such ventures."

When Cora didn't respond, Robert said, "Polly told me you came to visit last night. I'm sorry I missed you."

Cora's anger crumbled into contrition. How could she remain cross when he was being so patient and sensible? "I'm sorry I spoke crossly," she said, voice low.

"Apology accepted." Robert took her hands in his. "Really. Everything's okay, Cora."

She turned to him and met his earnest gaze. "Only promise me you'll tell me everything from now on—about the committee, about your businesses, about anything important."

"I promise," Robert vowed. "I promise I shall tell you everything you should know."

Cora caught the niggling obfuscation, his "you should know" that qualified his "everything". Yet didn't everyone, even those who were deeply in love, keep certain matters to themselves? She kept harmless secrets. Surely, she must grant him her trust. She shouldn't compare Robert to other men, especially men she didn't care for, like Jim Sinclair. Jim's face was an open book, his emotional state obvious in the set of his eyes and mouth. It would be easy to tell if Jim were lying. Not so Mr. Robert Helston. He was a mystery.

Robert seemed to sense her desire to put the quarrel behind them, for he stroked Cora's cheek and looked into her eyes, lulling her into silent intimacy. And then, he bent toward her and kissed her. As his lips caressed her own, Cora self-consciously slid her hands onto his chest and pushed him away. They were in his office, and anyone might enter the room unbidden. Robert backed off and followed her gaze to the unlocked door. He rose, turned the lock, and knelt before her once more. Then he kissed her again, kissed her aggressively, and forced her back in the chair with the weight of his body until she was beneath him.

How confused she felt. She was intoxicated by the scent of his cologne, intrigued by the unmistakable fullness of his manhood straining against his trousers, against her thigh beneath her skirt, but everything was happening too quickly. He could have her against her will if he chose, for she was trapped beneath him. The door was locked. He might overpower her, take advantage. If she cried out, Willy would probably cover his ears. Cora pushed hard against Robert's chest.

He stopped and sat back on his heels. "This is not the time, and not the place," he murmured. "You deserve to be made love to in a bed of satin with rose petals scattered all about."

She laughed with relief and then he held her, suckled her earlobe, and whispered, "When you are ready, my darling."

****

Over a supper of beef barley soup and biscuits, Aunt Jenny would speak of nothing but her plans for Christmas at the orphanage.

"Do pay attention, Cora," she cajoled. "Miss MacDonnell says in her letter that there are forty-three orphans, twenty girls and twenty-three boys. Thanks to

Mr. Helston's donation, she has procured a toy, a small bag of candy, mittens or socks depending on need, and an orange for each of them as well as books for their library. The cook says they have enough hands in the kitchen for the goose dinner. It's handling the mayhem of gift-giving for forty-three excited children and all the sore tummies unaccustomed to sweets that she needs help with."

"Forty-three children…" Cora said blankly.

"Yes. Forty-three. I said it twice and I'm glad the number is sticking in your head because it appears little else is."

"I'm sorry, Aunt Jenny. I guess I'm a little preoccupied."

"Indeed. And not over that ridiculous committee as you would have said so if that were the trouble."

Cora buttered a piece of biscuit and set it on her plate.

"Where's your appetite? If you don't eat, you'll lose your curves, and then what will Mr. Helston think of you?" Jenny teased.

"I don't care what Robert thinks of me," Cora lied. "I'm not thinking of him at all."

"Well then. Since you seem to have finished your supper, and you're evidently keeping a level head, now is as good a time as any to raise a delicate subject."

Jenny stuffed a hunk of biscuit in her mouth and chewed, leaving the nature of the 'delicate subject' hanging mysteriously between them. Cora was reminded of Jenny's birds and bees lesson when she was eleven. Oh dear.

At last Jenny swallowed, took a gulp of tea, and said, "Have you ever heard the saying, 'Why buy the cow when you can get the milk for free'?"

"Yes."

"And do you understand what it means?"

"Of course." Less said, quicker over.

"Then please explain it to me."

"Pardon?"

"You heard me. When I hear that saying, I look about me and wonder what it means. I'm just a spinster, a half century old, and I've led a sheltered life in this colonial backwater." Jenny seemed to relish Cora's bashfulness. She tapped her spoon on the table like a miniature gavel. "Go on, Cora. Please explain it to me."

"Well…" Cora squirmed in her chair.

"Well?" Jenny affected the expression of a curious schoolgirl.

"It means that a lady shouldn't give away her charms freely. She shouldn't lie with a man until she is his wife. Otherwise, he might take advantage of her and never marry her."

"Good enough," Jenny nodded.

"Is that all?" Cora asked hopefully.

"No." Jenny performed the biscuit-in-mouth trick again to discomfiting effect. Cora looked wistfully toward the door, wishing for escape.

After an uncomfortable interval, Jenny swallowed and continued. "You understand the cow and milk lesson. I was merely reviewing the theory. However, I sense that either you think it doesn't apply to you, or you aren't sophisticated enough to adapt the lesson to your situation."

"Robert would never use me and cast me aside," Cora objected. "He loves me and he's unconventional. And I'm smart enough to—"

"Spare me," Jenny interrupted. "You're twenty-two and entering the battlefield of the sexes for the first time. Mr. Helston is a worldly older man, not a gentleman, who has probably had more lovers than leaves on our plum tree. Wait a minute…it's winter. There aren't any leaves. You know what I mean."

"He was married. Once. Happily." Cora ignored Jenny's eye roll and asked, "Are you suggesting I end our courtship?"

"No, no." Jenny shook her head and waved her hand. "That would be a pointless suggestion. Wise, yes, but you wouldn't think of it."

"That's because Robert *is* a gentleman. And he loves me."

"If you say so."

"I do."

"Well then, moving on, you should be aware that there are many ways for a woman to satisfy her desire without losing her virginity. Stay where you are a moment."

Jenny stood and took the lantern into the sitting room. Cora heard her unlock a drawer and rummage through paper. She returned to the kitchen with a thin, yellowed pamphlet and placed it beside Cora's uneaten soup.

Cora's eyes widened as she read its title. *The Ladies' Guide to Romance with Tips to Prevent Procreation.*

"Even I have my limits, Cora. You'll spare me much embarrassment if you read the guide and follow its instruction rather than forcing me to give you the details."

"Isn't this pamphlet illegal?"

"Illegal, yes. Immoral, no. I only give it to women

when the benefit outweighs the risk in doing so, and I should have given it to you weeks ago. Or years ago."

What a revelation. The very idea that Robert and she could enjoy each other without skating on the knife edge of disgrace. "Thank you, Aunt Jenny," Cora said gratefully.

"You're welcome. In my defense, I thought I was protecting you by keeping this pamphlet hidden from you. Even your father didn't know of its existence. If the wrong person knows you have it, say, one of the men on the committee, we could both land in jail."

Cora turned the pamphlet over to hide its title. "In case Moira pops in. She was feeling better this morning," Cora explained.

"Yes, by all means, hide the front, though don't worry about Moira. Have you ever noticed that she and Mr. Kelly have a small family compared to other couples?" Jenny winked. "Your supper is getting cold."

After such a long day, Cora found she was hungry, and she popped the piece of buttered biscuit into her mouth.

"Now where were we," said Jenny. "Right. I think we should take the last train to Brucedale on Christmas Eve. That's a week from today. Miss MacDonnell says she'll make up beds for us, and then you can return after supper on Christmas Day, and I'll stay at the orphanage another night or two. Moira will feed the chickens and our patients can spare us that long. For once, we're not expecting to deliver any Christmas babies."

Chapter 15

Year-end business took Robert away from Maryville in the days leading up to Christmas. He showered Cora with letters and telegrams, and the flames of their romance burned as ever through their separation. Each day they spent apart intensified Cora's longing for her beau. Although occupied with her work, she thought of Robert and dreamed up various scenarios of reunification in vivid detail. The secret pamphlet, pulled from under her mattress and read by lamplight each evening, was oil on the torrid fire of curiosity that burned within her.

It was selfish to begrudge the orphans anything that would make their lives better, yet she felt an unreasonable resentment that her Christmas should be spent at the Protestant Home for Little Wanderers and not with Robert. Thank goodness Aunt Jenny refrained from commenting on her wistful sighs and faraway glances, and from reminding her that it was their first Christmas without Father. Dreaming of Robert was Cora's comfort, and the orphanage was Jenny's.

At breakfast on the 24th of December, Jenny reviewed their holiday plans.

"I've decided to take the 12:35 train so I can make it to Brucedale by early afternoon instead of travelling with you in the evening. That way, I can take the children tobogganing while Miss MacDonnell prepares for

Christmas. Best tucker the youngsters out so they'll sleep. They'll have their supper, then off to chapel for prayers and to bed. You should come as soon as you're finished in Maryville. The last train's at 8:35 p.m. and mind you're not late, Cora, because the train won't run again till noon on Christmas Day."

"Eight thirty-five at the latest," Cora repeated. "And hopefully I'll catch an earlier train."

"Yes. We'll have a late supper with Miss MacDonnell and her staff after the children have gone to bed. It's Christmas Eve after all. Have you packed your things in my carpet bag?"

"Yes, Aunt Jenny."

"Good. No sense you coming home to fetch anything if you should find you're running late. And you'll have your satchel with you if we need it at the orphanage. It goes without saying that children get sick at Christmas. But there. I said it anyway and it's true."

Cora murmured her agreement and Jenny continued. "The last train back tomorrow is at nine p.m. and the fare is free on Christmas Day. Oh, and here's the orphanage schedule, modified for Christmas, of course. Miss MacDonnell sent it in her letter." Jenny pushed a creased paper across the table.

"Should I keep this?" Cora asked.

"Just review it so you're ready. I need it in my pocket so I can refer to it. I aim to be a help, not a hindrance to Miss MacDonnell…Ivy. She signed her letter as 'Ivy' so I suppose we should call her that now." Jenny's eyes shone with child-like excitement. "Oh, Cora, this will be such fun! Celebrating Christmas with the children. And you!"

"I'm glad you haven't forgotten me," Cora teased.

Jenny laughed and clapped her hands twice, "Now off you go. You've quite a list of people to see and the sooner you finish, the earlier you can join us at the orphanage."

Upon this advice, the hall clock struck eight. Cora drained her teacup and bundled up for the cold.

****

Hastening to Brucedale became impossible when Cora's workday plans went awry due to emergencies. The previous night, Kelly, the barman, had been punched in the nose by a stray fist intended for a customer who ducked, and his nostrils ran like faucets of blood and required packing. The Cameron twins came down with croup. And Charles Tucker, having embarked on a bender on the 21st of December, arrived at the horrible destination of confusion, dehydration, and a belly swollen with fluid that morning. Cora tried to make time on her list by skipping Betsy's visit only to have the Meyers' maid track her down and beg she attend to Betsy's "dangerous" rash, a constellation of pimples scattered over the vain girl's forehead. Well past eight that evening, on tired legs, Cora ran from the home of her last patient to the station, but she was too late. As she hurried to the wicket, the train whistled and pulled away.

Already donning his hat, Jenkins, the station master said, "You can come to mine for supper, Miss Patton. Wife's a Frenchie and a great cook to boot, and we always have tourtiere after Mass on Christmas Eve. I know you're Presbyterian, but Father Finney won't mind you coming to St. Patrick's with us."

Though touched by Jenkins' kindness, Cora declined his invitation. She wished him a Merry Christmas as they left the station and trudged off in opposite directions. The night air was still and fragrant with the smoke of hearth fires. Here and there, Cora heard laughter and carol singing. The full moon lit sparkles in the snow. All of Maryville was celebrating in fine festive form.

Meanwhile, the Pattons' Christmas was ruined. Aunt Jenny would be disappointed, angry, and worried in turns when Cora failed to arrive at the orphanage. On their first Christmas Eve without Father, she should've been at Aunt Jenny's side. However, she wouldn't be, and that was that.

"Merry Christmas, Cora."

She recognized the booming, eternally cheerful baritone of Jim Sinclair and the dull clop of Buttercup's hooves approaching from behind. "Merry Christmas, Jim," she said as she turned. She could be civil. It cost her nothing.

Jim and Buttercup drew up alongside her. "You don't look merry," he said.

"Oh, don't I?" said Cora.

"No. You look like Ebenezer Scrooge after the visitation of the ghost of Christmas present, only you're much younger and prettier than Scrooge."

"Gee, thanks."

"Admittedly, Scrooge set a low bar for beauty, but you exceed him by far, I assure you."

Despite her dark mood, Cora unsuccessfully stifled a smile, and that was all the encouragement Jim needed to dismount his horse and lead her by the rein to walk with Cora.

"Are you going to the Christmas service tomorrow?" he asked.

"No," replied Cora. "Are you?"

"No. Mama and Dad think it's un-Presbyterian to fuss over Christmas and I'd rather not sit in a stuffy church while Reverend Cameron tranquilizes the congregation."

Cora yawned unwittingly. The minister bored her too. "Reverend Cameron is very nice," she said.

"Nice," Jim mocked. "I suppose there are worse epithets."

"He means well," said Cora.

"He could bore the tits off a cow. I'll walk you home?"

Cora didn't object. As they walked in silence, she began to lag.

"Would you like to ride on Buttercup?" Jim asked.

Cora was tired enough to find Jim's proposal tempting, but she declined with a head shake and a firm "No thank you." The mare was large, without a saddle, and infamously prone to bolting and other misbehavior.

Jim defended his horse as if she were a cherished only child. "Go on. She's gentle, Cora. She has a noble spirit. Since I stopped insisting she take a saddle, she's calmed down. She's perfectly obedient as long as she's only ridden bareback."

Cora shook her head.

"Well at least let me carry your satchel," said Jim.

Cora nodded and handed it to Jim, and he rewarded her with that lopsided grin that set girls' hearts racing. Feather-brained girls like Betsy Meyer. He could carry Cora's satchel, but that smile would never work on her. Jim Sinclair was a troublemaker who took pride in sowing chaos.

As they neared the cottage, Jim remarked, "It looks like no one's home. Your place is dark."

"So it is. I can see too," Cora said in a haughty tone.

"You're going to someone else's house for Christmas," Jim guessed.

"No. Robert was away until late this afternoon, I had my work, and Aunt Jenny went to Brucedale to help at the orphanage," she said defensively.

"You're alone then. Alone at Christmas."

Cora realized how pathetic that seemed, and though she owed no explanation, she blurted, "I'm supposed to be in Brucedale at the orphanage too. Only I missed the last train."

"Gee, that's too bad. I'm sorry you're all by yourself, Cora."

Cora wouldn't be disadvantaged by sympathy. "It's fine," she muttered. "Your parents are right. Today's just another date on the calendar." She held out her hand for her satchel and Jim returned it to her. "Thank you," she said as she turned away.

Cora started up the snow-filled lane to the kitchen door. In contrast to the Kelly home next door, the cottage was bitterly desolate. A light snow had covered its roof because its rooms were cold with the lack of a stove fire, and each window was as dark as her mood.

"Won't Miss Patton worry when you don't arrive?" Jim called after her.

"Yes. But nothing can be done about it now," Cora replied irritably.

"We could take you to the orphanage."

"What?" She turned on her heel and looked at Jim.

"I think you meant to say, 'Pardon'. Buttercup and I. We can take you. Brucedale is eight miles from here, and we can cover that distance before midnight." Jim gazed fondly at his horse and patted her shoulder, and

Buttercup snorted and tossed her head as if she understood every word her master uttered.

Cora said, "It's late. I couldn't."

"You can. We can, Cora. I don't want to go to any silly parties. I definitely don't want to go home. All the taverns are closed. I have nowhere to go but Brucedale."

"But you'll have to walk the whole way."

"I'll ride home."

"You'll be exhausted."

"Buttercup is a superbly conditioned horse. The snow is packed on the road, the moon is bright, and I'll have an excuse to sleep the day away tomorrow. It's fine."

Cora hesitated long enough for Jim to settle the matter. "We'll wait while you get ready."

"I'm ready," she shrugged.

Before Cora could change her mind, Jim knelt in the snow and clasped his hands to make a step for her and boost her onto Buttercup's back.

****

As he tugged the bridle and clicked his tongue to command Buttercup to walk, Jim, again, wondered how girls like Cora ended up with men like Helston. Such matches were a mystery for the ages. She would spend Christmas at an orphanage while he rested in a soft armchair by a fire, fattening himself on plum pudding and eggnog. However, Jim had to concede that Cora's beau had much to recommend him by any measure. Helston was handsome and would age into a commanding dignity if he didn't let his girth expand overmuch. He dressed well, though his taste was effete, and he had nice things. He was wealthy and powerful. Yet, there was a sneaky oiliness about him that set Jim's teeth on edge. Perhaps part of Jim's dislike for Helston sprang from envy...perhaps one percent. The other ninety-nine percent was borne of suspicion. The very idea of Helston leering and pawing and eventually bedding Cora made Jim sick.

Now, he had roughly two and a half hours with Cora, alone, in the moonlight, on Christmas Eve. He wasn't tongue-tied with any other girl. Why then Cora? Oh, right. Because he loved her. For a mile he led Buttercup in silence while Cora struggled to keep her seat, even with him carrying her satchel.

"You could sit astride, Cora. Our secret," he suggested.

"I'm okay," said Cora.

"No, you're not. Swing your leg over. It's much easier to ride that way. I promise I won't stare at your leg." He couldn't resist teasing.

"Promise?"

"Of course."

Cora did as she was bid.

"Better?" he asked.

"Much better," she sighed with relief. "The world isn't fair to women."

"I suppose it isn't," agreed Jim. "But being a man is no Sunday school picnic either. By the way, I can see your leg."

"Why you brazen, rude—"

"Impertinent bounder," he finished. "Yup. I've heard it all. Most girls can't get enough of my nonsense."

"I'm not 'most girls' and you promised not to look."

"I'm sorry. Game?"

"Sure," Cora said slowly, as if she thought the idea might be a trap.

"What's your favorite Christmas carol?" asked Jim.

"Good King Wenceslas," answered Cora. "Yours?"

"Same."

"No way. You're just saying that."

"On my honor, it is true, fair lady. Favorite Christmas food?"

"Mincemeat tarts."

"Same again," Jim exclaimed. "That's uncanny."

"It's also not true, is it?" said Cora. "So I'll ask you this time, and you have to answer first. Favorite color?"

"Green. As green as your beautiful eyes, and the pond in August, and the willows in spring. You?"

"Turquoise. Not the same at all," said Cora.

"Completely different," he agreed. "Favorite writer?"

"Umm, Dickens I suppose."

"There you go. Me too. I've read every Dickens novel except the long ones."

They passed the time and miles in pleasant banter and in laughter. The road ran through a cluster of shacks and roughly built commercial buildings with a sign welcoming them to the Village of Burnside. They were almost halfway to Brucedale.

Halfway and that was all. Cora shivered and drew her cape closely about her. The cloudless night grew colder. The north wind blowing across the bleak fields would steal her warmth. The joking was over.

Jim said, "You're getting cold."

"I'm okay." Cora shivered again. "You keep warm by walking, so you don't feel the cold as much. We're already halfway."

"Only halfway. We have to pick up the pace, Cora, and get you to shelter. Now, don't say 'no' right away.

Just listen. We'll get to Brucedale more quickly if we ride double. You're small, so I'll sit behind you and shield your back from the wind. Buttercup would be happier if she could trot…or canter. She feels the cold too."

Cora knew he was right. She didn't object. He gave her back her bag and, taking care to avoid unseating her, he swung himself up behind her, adjusted the reins, and nudged the mare into a smooth run with a tap of his heel and a click of his tongue. Awkward and ill-timed at first, the trio eased into the rhythm of the ride. Cora leaned back into Jim's chest as he protectively embraced her body in his arms and anchored her legs with his. He had ridden with girls before but tonight was different. Cora was submitting to his strength and warmth because she needed him, not because she wanted him.

"Better?" Jim asked over the thumping of hooves.

"Yes, thank you. Only we mustn't tell anyone about this, especially Robert."

"Oh, I agree. We mustn't tell Robert," Jim mocked. "He'd far rather court a virtuously frozen girl than a healthy, daring girl. Any gentleman of his station would."

"You make him out to be a priggish snob," Cora said crossly. "What do you know of him anyway?"

"Nothing," replied Jim. "Only that we mustn't tell him."

"Can we stop talking about him now?"

"As you wish. And for the record, you mentioned him, not me."

They rode through the night, neither speaking though neither angry despite their quarrelsome words. Jim couldn't hide how he felt. They shared a sacred intimacy in riding a horse together. Cora's bottom was snug between his legs, for she didn't wear a bustle. Her back sank into his torso and chest, and she rested her head against his collar bone. He inhaled the lightly floral scent of her hair mingled with the earthy equine smell of horse. He felt himself harden, yet he wasn't ashamed. He could tell by her pliancy that she knew what was happening, and she was enjoying it too. She didn't recoil when his cock pressed against her. He had to muster every ounce of his self-control not to kiss her as they submitted to the sensuality of their ride.

As they neared Brucedale, he drew up on the reins and held Cora close. She melded into his embrace as Buttercup slowed to a walk. He kissed Cora's temple. She tilted her head to expose her neck and he savored the saltiness of her soft skin from the tender place under her ear to the hollow of her collar bone, and when she shuddered, and whispered "no" he withdrew.

Cora quickly wrapped her cape about her again. He'd breached the boundary of appropriate behavior with a girl whom he loved but who belonged to another. Jim dismounted and resumed walking to quell his turmoil, his shame. When at last he mustered the courage to look up at her in apology, he saw tears in her eyes.

He hadn't meant harm. "I'm sorry, Cora. Forgive me," Jim pleaded. "I took advantage."

"No, Jim. You have nothing to forgive. I let it happen. I'm the one who's sorry."

****

Cora listened to the snores and snuffles of a half dozen sleeping women, among them Aunt Jenny, two cots over. Down the hall, Jim slept in the men's dormitory. Jim was near and Robert was far, far away.

116

How strange it was to think upon.

Celebrating Christmas Eve at the orphanage with Aunt Jenny, Ivy, and her staff was worth every mile of the journey and tomorrow she'd get to meet the children. Now she had to sleep. Cora rolled onto her side and gazed through the window. Hanging from the eave, an icicle shimmered. How fortunate that she and Jim had the full moon to light the way to Brucedale.

What a journey it was. She hadn't laughed like that since Father's death. It wasn't that her life was joyless. Only that Robert sanitized his anecdotes for female ears, Aunt Jenny's wit was barbed with discomfiting truth, and Cora's few friends spoke carefully in her presence lest they provoke a fit of grief. Bereavement had drained her life of conviviality and humor. How odd that she should rediscover laughter with Jim Sinclair on a desolate road on a cold winter night. After they'd discussed books and music, their banter drifted to an outrageous game of 'truth or lie'. Smiling to herself in the darkness among the sleeping, she recalled their game as if it were a play on a lantern-lit stage.

From high on Buttercup's back, Cora started the challenge with an inquisitor's glare. "Is it true, Mr. James Sinclair, that you dressed a statue of James McGill, the founder of your college, in a tiara and ballgown?"

"No, it isn't true, your honor." Jim's eyes glinted in the moonlight. "The allegation is false."

"You dare deny it?"

"Yes, I deny it because the inaccuracy of your honor's allegation diminishes the towering achievement of the crime. It was Admiral Horatio Nelson whom we dressed."

"What?" Cora dropped the pretense of stern

judgement. "But doesn't Nelson stand on a tall pillar?"

"Indeed he does. The great man stands proudly upon a column sixty feet in height. Among the mob, I drew the short straw and had to ascend to his lofty perch by means of rope and whisky. If you'll permit me to boast, Cora, the Admiral looked mighty fetching when I was through."

"What did he wear?"

"A ragged, red frock that a harlot sold us for the price of a week's honest work in her peculiar trade and a crown fashioned from a length of chain and some nails. The wealthiest man among us paid the harlot. She was thrilled to see her frock on old Horatio and thanked us profusely for thusly cheering her. Unfortunately, the authorities weren't as amused."

"So there's some truth to the rumor that you were expelled for the prank?"

"Not at all, Cora. I ran with no ordinary mob. They're the sons of the ruling mob. The incident was dismissed as boys being boys and after a reprimand, all was forgiven. I came home because I ran out of money. If I'd studied harder, they might've extended my scholarship so it's my own fault."

"I'm so sorry."

"Why?"

"Because it must be terribly disappointing to have your dream of becoming a lawyer dashed like that."

"Not dashed. Only delayed. I aim to return to McGill as soon as I've saved enough money."

With Jim's declaration, the game had ended, and they'd fallen into their own thoughts. As they passed a faded sign announcing they'd reached Burnside, a sharp, north wind stabbed Cora's back with icy daggers. Try as she might, she couldn't stay warm, and she couldn't reasonably object to Jim's suggestion that he join her on Buttercup's back.

And then, in an instant, they were riding double, the heat of Jim's body warming her. At first, she was desperately clumsy riding partnered. Clumsy until she yielded to Jim's unspoken command. The more she relaxed and attuned to Jim's cues, the more gracefully they rode.

She'd tried to convince herself that Robert wouldn't mind. However, Jim's strong arms were about her, his firm thighs braced hers, his chest rose and fell against her back, and his body rocked her to the mare's rhythm. Even the scent of him, a mix of smoke, sweat, and raw, masculine sex, enveloped her. His breath, warm against her temple, carried the faintest sweetness of liquor.

He'd be a fearsome match against any foe and Cora felt safe against the night but not safe with herself. As she sensed Jim's arousal, a heat rose within her, and they were pulled into a mystical dance. As they approached Brucedale, Jim slowed them to a walk, but the spell didn't break. His hot breath upon her, he nuzzled her ear, softly kissed her neck and collar bone, grazed her skin with his stubble. Her skin sizzled under the touch of his lips. She had to stop him. It was madness.

So quietly Jim could've pretended he didn't hear, she'd whispered, "no," and he'd pulled away immediately. She straightened and fixed her cape and he dismounted. They'd crossed a line. She'd tasted forbidden fruit and spat it out in the nick of time, before she betrayed Robert. Before she ruined her future.

Then the cold of night descended once more. When Jim begged her forgiveness, the night froze into a solid, black wall of regret. She'd tried to breach the wall with an apology, but she'd failed. For the rest of the journey, Jim didn't speak beyond polite necessity, and after he'd stabled Buttercup and joined the party on Aunt Jenny's orders, he behaved as if nothing had happened.

But it had. Cora hugged herself under the thick woolen blanket and imagined Jim's arms about her once more.

Chapter 16

Cora, Jenny, and Ivy watched from across the yard as Jim held Buttercup's bridle, and Jacob the groundskeeper lifted children onto her back. Buttercup could carry four small riders at a time and didn't flinch when they wiggled, kicked, or pulled her mane. Other children waited their turn in an unruly queue, jumping, shouting, and playing tug-of-war with brand new skipping ropes and even a scarf which Ivy promptly put a stop to with a whistle and a loud reprimand. All the adults were nursing mild hangovers from the celebratory sherry that Ivy served when Jim and Cora arrived. While food and drink had been plentiful, sleep had been short for everyone, with several children waking early to check if Father Christmas had visited. He had, and with this discovery, mayhem ensued.

"We're lucky Jim stayed the night. Just look at the fun the children are having," Ivy remarked.

"More hands on deck. And he's a natural with children. Cora, wherever did you find that wonderful man?" Jenny drawled like a socialite.

Cora blushed. "I didn't find him. He found me."

"Either way, could we keep him? Ivy and I have fallen in love." Jenny pretended to swoon with Ivy catching her, and both women broke into a gale of giggles.

Jenny spoke again, in her normal voice, much to

Cora's relief. "I was with Jim's mother when he was born. Let me see…that'll be twenty-three years ago in January. As I recall, he presented himself to the world with nary a whimper. His eyes popped open, and he took everything in, curious and smart as can be from day one. Now Cora, on the other hand, was born in April, and she screamed like a banshee."

How mortifying. According to Aunt Jenny, Jim was Christ's second coming though too modest to realize it, his childhood sins absolved and forgotten, while she had been the devil incarnate. Cora felt a tug on her skirt and looked down to find a girl of about four cradling a doll in her arms.

"Please, Miss Patton. Dolly's blanket is loose. Could you help me wrap her?"

Cora replied with a friendly smile and nod, relieved to escape from the conversation, and she knelt before the brown-eyed, pig-tailed girl. "It's very cold. You're wise to keep Dolly snuggled in a warm blanket."

With a grateful smile, the girl handed the doll to Cora.

As Cora swaddled the toy, she said, "Dolly is a good name for your baby. What's your name?"

"Faith."

"Faith. That's a good, strong name too. My name's Cora. You may call me that if you like." She returned the doll to its little mother who once again cradled it lovingly.

"Thank you, Miss Cora." The girl curtsied and skipped away.

Aunt Jenny was right. She'd been a spirited, ill-mannered child, at least compared to Faith. Standing away from Jenny and Ivy, Cora surveyed the yard again.

The older children played tag and younger children crawled in the snow. Against the odds, forty-three parentless youngsters were growing up healthy and literate under Ivy's loving care. The Protestant Home for Little Wanderers was an unmitigated success in its mission. Father would've been so proud.

A bell rang. It was dinnertime. Some children ran to line up at the doors; other children, absorbed in their games, dawdled, and complained that dinner came too soon. Jim and Jacob helped three riders dismount to join the line.

After assisting in the service of the mid-day Christmas meal, Cora would return to Maryville by train. If she'd arrived last night by the means she'd intended, she would be much the same woman. However, Jim had stirred something undefinable, something deep within her soul. Their encounter had pushed her off-balance, and she welcomed time alone on the train to think, to regain her footing, before Aunt Jenny sidled in for a heart to heart and before she saw Robert again.

Ivy opened the door and the children filed into the yellow brick building. Jenny picked up a tiny youngster who hadn't obeyed the bell and carried him indoors. Jim led Buttercup across the yard to where Cora stood.

"You could stay for dinner."

Jim shook his head. "Dinner's for the children, not for a stray dog like me."

"But there's more than enough. The children would love it if you joined them."

"Cora, I can't. I've been gone too long from the farm as it is. I'll give Buttercup a drink and a bag of oats and we'll be on our way."

"Well then. Merry Christmas."

123

"Merry Christmas." Jim extended his hand and smiled, dark eyes unreadable, a two-day beard thick on his square jaw. "Friends?"

So that was what they would be. "Yes. Friends." Cora shook his warm, rough hand, and made herself smile in return.

Her tears came later, when she stared from the window of the train carriage and caught glimpses of the road that ran parallel to the tracks from Brucedale to Maryville.

Chapter 17

On Boxing Day, Robert hosted a mid-day dinner with his mother and aunt in his dining room. Though intimidated by the grandeur of Robert's house and the sumptuous formality of the occasion, Cora resolved to relate to the Helston ladies as if they were her own adored yet highly respected family members. The stakes were high. Although Robert didn't require his mother's permission to remarry, her nod would make a proposal almost certain.

Cora felt like a circus bear, dancing for the approbation of Robert's mother, Mrs. Josephine Helston, and Josephine's sister-in-law, Miss Eugenia Helston, who sat opposite at a table laden with a roast turkey and all manner of Yuletide delicacies. So far, Cora was passing the Helston ladies' tests with flying colors. She'd dressed modestly, chose the correct piece of cutlery for each dish, laughed demurely at Miss Eugenia's limp jokes, took only enough wine to be sociable, and spoke pleasantly of the food and season. Judging by Mrs. Helston's gracious friendliness, permission to marry would be granted.

At three o'clock, Polly entered the room with a crystal decanter of sherry and offered to refill their goblets. Josephine and Eugenia wouldn't take more, not with their sensitive stomachs and the dyspepsia which inevitably followed the slightest dietary indiscretion.

Cora commended Mrs. and Miss Helston's restraint and the meal was over. Finally.

Could they see Cora home? No, no. Robert would drive her. Wasn't this irregular? Polly and Martha, the cook, were present as chaperones, and Robert, a man of thirty, was well aware of the importance of reputation and honor. Would Cora come to dine at their home on a mutually suitable Sunday in January? She'd be delighted! At last, Robert helped the ladies into their cloaks, assisted them into their sleigh, and they drove off with their hired man at the reins.

Cora and Robert were alone.

He led her to a loveseat in the drawing room, closed the door, and poured them both a celebratory drink.

"I mustn't stay long," Cora warned as she accepted the glass. "I have quite a lot to do before Aunt Jenny returns."

"Christmas comes but once a year. Let's not be boring," scolded Robert as he sat beside her and raised his glass. "To us."

"To us." Cora sipped the sweet, honey-colored wine and set her glass at a distance on the table.

Robert did likewise, and Cora realized he had misinterpreted her action as a signal for a session of intimacy rather than a wish to avoid inebriation.

"Your mother and aunt are very kind," she remarked.

"Yes, to you they're kind because they like you. They can be downright horrid too." Robert gripped Cora's hands in his. "But let's not talk of them. This is our Christmas. My God, how I've missed you, Cora."

"Thank you for your letters while you were away."

"My letters? Jesus, Cora. What's wrong?"

"I don't know." Which approached the truth. She was sharing a loveseat with a confident, urbane, powerful man. He was about to shower her with praise and gifts. She saw the pastel boxes on the rosewood table. He would kiss her ardently. He loved her yet she'd nearly betrayed him only two days ago and imagined betraying him every time she remembered Jim. "I suppose I'm tired," she lied.

"Come. Rest in my arms." Robert drew Cora close by his side and gently guided her head to the crook of his shoulder. "We mustn't quarrel, but you must tell me if something is bothering you."

She gazed up at him with doe-like eyes to mend the rift and he answered her silent appeal by drawing her chin up and kissing her. As Robert's mouth commanded hers, she thought of Jim again. Imagining Jim while in the arms of Robert solved her problem—temporarily.

Robert ended the kiss and pressed his forehead against hers. "Better?"

"Yes. Better."

"Good." Robert released her from his arms and retrieved the boxes from the table, pink and mint green wrapped up in bows.

"May I give you my present first?" asked Cora. "I'm afraid it isn't much, and it will suffer by comparison if I open my gifts before you."

"Okay." Robert smiled indulgently.

Cora presented a box wrapped in paper that she'd decorated with an ink print.

"The paper itself is a gift," he remarked. He untied the string and the paper fell away to reveal an expertly crafted checkerboard box with a brass latch and hinges. Inside the box were thirty-two ornately carved chess pieces. "It's exquisite, Cora. I'll treasure this gift forever." His words were imbued with genuine admiration for his new possession. "Thank you."

"My grandfather made it from elm and walnut. Fortunately, since Aunt Jenny was my chess teacher and kept it on her shelf in the sitting room, it wasn't lost in the fire."

"The craftsmanship is remarkable. Do you play well?"

"No. I'm hopeless."

"Then we're an even match." Robert latched the box, set it on the table, and kissed Cora again, though this time he didn't linger.

Brightening, he said, "Now it's your turn." Cora was struck by Robert's childlike demeanor. As if by magic, Christmas transformed mature adults, including her beau, into sentimental, giddy children.

"Should I begin with the largest or the smallest box?"

"That's up to you." Robert winked.

Cora reached for the middle-sized box, pulled the ribbon, and removed the lid only to find another box within it. A hatbox. Lifting its lid, she found a fashionable hat of turquoise silk with a profusion of navy and yellow feathers fixed to its brim. She lifted it from the box. The hat was beautiful, but wherever would she wear it?

"Go ahead, Cora. Try it on," said Robert. "And if it doesn't fit or you don't like it, we can find another one."

"I love it," Cora said, as much to convince herself as to reassure Robert. She placed the hat on her head and Robert grinned appreciatively.

"It almost does justice to your beauty. I described

you to the milliner and he designed and made it especially for you."

"Thank you," said Cora. "I shan't take it off just yet."

"Okay, next box," urged Robert, his expression animated with glee.

Cora took up the small box and removed its lid. "It's a pearl pendant." Her brows rose in surprise. "In the shape of a butterfly."

"And the chain is gold. Do you like it?"

"Yes." Cora dangled the necklace in her fingers, certain she had never handled anything so precious.

"Then you must wear it as well, Cora."

Without a word, she unfastened the clasp, gave the necklace to Robert, turned, and presented her neck so he could place it on her. Necklace fastened, he removed her hat and kissed her neck, unknowingly reminding her of Jim's kiss.

"One more box," Robert whispered into her ear.

The large box contained a dress. A gorgeous dress fit for a whirl in the city. The bodice was sleekly fitted and the skirt full in layered turquoise silk with navy and yellow frilled borders to match her new hat. The three-quarter length sleeves and deep square neckline were trimmed in harmony with the skirt. The dress would've cost a small fortune. "Thank you," said Cora, holding the garment before her.

"You must try it on," said Robert.

"I must not," protested Cora. "I want it to fit perfectly when I wear it for you, and it must be altered first. Oh, Robert, I do love my gifts."

"I'm glad."

"But wherever shall I wear them?"

"You'll wear your outfit when you accompany me to the city. My darling, you have the beauty, intelligence, manners, and charm to hold your own in any company and now you have a fashionable ensemble worthy of Paris to match your finest qualities."

As she carefully replaced her gifts in their boxes, he asked, "Are you still tired?"

Cora shook her head, and they resumed their embrace. She spoke through his kisses to ensure he understood her limits, as the pamphlet told her she must. At last, when she was certain that she'd convinced him of her passion, she broke away.

"Stay longer," begged Robert.

"I mustn't," said Cora, recoiling from his neediness. Though they never spoke of Eliza, Cora wondered if his late wife's memory haunted him still, even when he was with her.

"Very well." Rather abruptly, Robert stood.

Their Christmas was over.

Chapter 18

"Should we exchange gifts tonight or wait for Hogmanay?" Jenny asked, pushing aside the mending as Cora entered the sitting room.

"Which would you prefer?" Cora set mugs of herbal tea on the sewing table.

"Tonight. I can't see to sew under lamplight anymore. My eyesight's gotten terribly fuzzy in low light. Why don't you cut us a bit of fruit cake and we'll have our own little party? We've earned it."

After Cora retrieved her gift for Jenny and cut two generous slices of cake, she returned to find a heavy, rectangular parcel on the sewing table.

"I hid it in the basket of yarn." An impish grin spread over Jenny's face. "I knew you'd be too busy to knit while I was in Brucedale, and you wouldn't find it."

Cora picked the gift up and felt the weight and shape of a large book beneath the paper wrapping. A child of three could guess what her gift was. She put the parcel back on the table. "Why don't you go first, Aunt Jenny?"

"No, you go."

"Very well." Cora slipped her finger along a fold and the paper covering fell away. "*Gray's Anatomy,*" she exclaimed, wide eyed as she flipped the cover open. "And it's the latest edition! It's brand new! Thank you, Aunt Jenny."

Without looking up, Cora turned the pages to

examine the book's many drawings and descriptions. "Why, this is better than the texts Father had. I've no end of learning here."

"There's plenty to occupy you," said Jenny.

"Oh, this is the best present I've ever received, Aunt Jenny. But it must've been expensive."

"Never you mind about that. You'll learn Dr. Gray's lessons for the benefit of humanity, and it's cheaper than medical school."

"Women can't go to medical school."

"Yet." Jenny lifted her chin defiantly. "It's only a matter of time till the world wakes up to the fact that a woman is a man's equal in the treatment of the ill and injured."

"And reading," said Cora. She looked at a drawing of a nose. Each fold, prominence, and hollow had a name. She flipped to the illustration of the kidney and marveled at its detail. Within her new tome, every nook and cranny of the human body had been accurately rendered and systematically labelled. At last, she lifted her eyes to Jenny. "I fear your present can't possibly compare against this." Cora closed the book and hugged it to her chest.

"I'll judge that for myself." Jenny picked up her gift. "If the gift disappoints, at least the paper is pretty," she joked.

"I carved potato slices into shapes and used them as ink stamps."

"I'll keep this paper. It's too nice to spoil or burn," declared Jenny as she turned the gift this way and that. "I can't guess what this is."

"Then open it," Cora laughed.

Jenny removed and folded the paper to reveal a box

the size of a small tea pot. She lifted the lid. "A mortar and pestle!"

"So it is," said Cora. "To replace the one you cracked. It's white marble so you can clearly see what you're grinding."

"It's a good size too, and beautiful. Thank you, Cora. It's just what I need."

"You're welcome."

"Do you know what I think?" Jenny tested the pestle in her bowl.

"No. I'm not a mind reader," Cora said, relieved that Jenny liked her gift.

"We gave each other gifts to help with our work. I think we mean to continue in our vocation, regardless of whether or not you marry, or a new doctor sets up practice, or I go blind." Jenny rubbed her eyes theatrically.

"Is that so?" said Cora.

"Yes. And what's more, I believe your father would've approved whole-heartedly. He wouldn't have wanted your talents to go to waste."

"Oh, Aunt Jenny. Whatever talent I possess I owe to him and you," Cora said wistfully.

"He'd also want us to celebrate the season," said Jenny. "Did you know, this fruitcake was a recipe of your mother's."

"I believe you've mentioned it." Cora set her new book on the table and cut a bite-sized morsel from her slice with the edge of her fork.

Jenny poked her own slice with the tines of her fork. "Do you think we might have overbaked this a touch?"

"It may have stayed in the oven a bit too long," Cora agreed as she chewed. The cake's texture was gummy, the edge bitter and rock-hard from excessive heat.

"We can serve it to Mr. Helston if he visits on New Year's Day."

"Aunt Jenny!" scolded Cora. "We'll do no such thing."

Chapter 19

Above all other holidays, New Year celebrations captured the souls of the St. Andrew's Presbyterian congregation. Old-timers pined for Scotland and Northern Ireland, families dined on haggis, and everyone had shiny coins in pocket or purse. Men and boys marauded Maryville, drinking and making merry at each home they visited, while women and girls, dressed in their finery, welcomed them in from the cold. Everyone wondered who would be the "first footer", tradition holding that a dark-haired man crossing the threshold of one's home before any other visitor in the new year portended good fortune.

"I love Christmas, but it's Hogmanay that pulls the heartstrings," Jenny waxed nostalgically. "Your father, being sandy-haired, wasn't in demand socially but he loved new year too. I believe it was on the first of January in 1851 that he proposed to your mother."

Cora had heard the story often enough to be bored by it. "Who do you think will have the first baby of 1875?"

"The MacTavish girl. She's still carrying high, but her time's near. Either she or Mary O'Mallory. Won't Kate be tickled to have a grandchild."

Cora murmured her agreement and gazed toward the doorway.

"He'll come when he's good and ready," said Jenny.

"It's only just past midnight. I'm not expecting him anytime soon," Cora fibbed.

Jenny cast Cora a look of disbelief, stood, and stretched. "I've sat enough," she said. "I think I'll stoke the fire and mull the cider." When Cora moved to help her, she waved her off. "Not in that dress, Cora. Your only chore tonight is to wait for visitors and look pretty."

Again, Cora's eyes shifted toward the door. If only she could set to a task to occupy her mind. However, she was dressed in her new frock. Only two days prior, Jenny had knelt at its hem, mumbling through the pins she held between her lips that only mistresses received gifts of clothing from men and that Cora shouldn't expect a proposal anytime soon. Despite her disapproval of Robert's gift, Jenny altered the dress and now Cora wore it. Uncomfortably. Cora might be fashionable, but she felt confined under the garment's weight, ridiculous in colors reminding her of a parrot, and disloyal to Robert for feeling so.

She could read *Gray's* while she waited. She leafed through its pages but couldn't concentrate. Robert would visit first, of course. Any time now and how pleased he would be to see her dressed like a duchess. Yet what if another dark-haired man should visit?

Guiltily, Cora twisted her new pearl pendant in her fingers and imagined opening the door to Jim Sinclair. Though not dressed as smartly as Robert, he'd fill out a plain wool jacket dashingly with his wide shoulders and muscular build. His dark, deep-set eyes twinkling, he'd twirl her off her feet in his strong arms, wish her a hearty happy new year, and kiss her on the cheek with that appealing mouth, stubble tickling her face, and if they were alone, he'd surely kiss her mouth.

Except she was dressed in weird garments that precluded being spun in a man's arms, and Jim would stay away because Robert was her beau.

She heard a knock, sharp and clear, and Jenny, unhampered by frippery, got to the door before Cora had risen from her chair. Oh, dash it. Wouldn't it be wonderful if it were Jim?

From the end of the hallway, she watched as Jenny pushed the door open. Robert exclaimed, "Happy New Year," doffed his top hat and, with a quick bow, presented a box of candy and a sack of oranges.

"Thank you." Jenny seized the gifts and hesitated in the doorway long enough to be rude.

"You're our first foot, Robert." Cora grasped Jenny's elbow and pulled her away. "That's if you'll come in."

As Jenny retreated, Robert stepped over the threshold and into the hallway.

"How honored I am to be first across your threshold, my darling," Robert declared.

Ashamed of her disloyalty, Cora turned her face away as he bent to kiss her cheek.

"You are radiant, especially tonight," he added.

From the kitchen doorway, Jenny proffered a plate and glass and nodded toward the sitting room. "Would you care for some cake and mulled cider, Mr. Helston?"

"How kind of you, Miss Patton," said Robert. "I'd be delighted."

Cora glared at Jenny as she led Robert through the narrow hall to the sitting room. She gestured to the tiny sofa, granting him the comfort of a soft seat and her company by his side.

"So this is the headquarters of the Patton ladies,"

Robert ventured. "And it's a pleasing room indeed."

Unceremoniously, Jenny handed Robert the celebratory victuals, stationed herself in the rocking chair, and crossed her arms and legs to indicate that she would remain in the room for the duration of Robert's visit.

Cora glanced at his plate, looked to Jenny, then looked at the plate once more. "I'm afraid the cake came out too dark, Robert. Pray allow me to find you something else to eat. We…we have shortbread and tarts," she stammered.

"It looks delicious." Robert set his glass on an adjacent low table and took up his fork. "I'm sure I'll enjoy every bite of it."

"I hope you do," said Jenny. "It's an old family recipe."

"You deserve to have a slice too, Aunt Jenny," suggested Cora, angry heat rising in her cheeks. "You've been busy all evening while I've been idle."

Jenny waved off Cora's suggestion while Robert chewed and swallowed a forkful of cake. He took a swig of cider to ease the passage of the sticky, bitter mass down his throat.

The strangling silence of the over-crowded room, Jenny's relentless surveillance, Robert's struggle with the awful cake, and the unaccustomed tightness of her corset—all these oppressive elements bore upon Cora, and she could barely breathe let alone converse. As Robert mashed a sticky, black raisin under his fork, Cora slumped at his side.

"I could do with some fresh air," she gasped.

"I as well." Robert set his plate aside, rose, and offered his hand to Cora. "My darling? Would you accompany me on a stroll in the moonlight?"

****

As the trio were enduring their Hogmanay party inside the Patton cottage, Jim walked up the road. He'd visit Cora before dropping in at Betsy's house and then he'd head to the tail end of the New Year's party at the Jones' home. Since Christmas, thoughts of Cora tormented his every waking moment. However painful, he had to find out whether his love for her was hopelessly unrequited, whether there was even a sliver of possibility of mutual love. If Cora rejected him, Jenny Patton's welcome would save him from total humiliation.

A quarter moon had risen in the east, casting enough light to make a lantern unnecessary. He hurried. Although Hogmanay celebrations were not the Meyers' custom, Jim had promised Mr. Meyer he'd visit Betsy before the stroke of one. Jim felt sorry for Betsy. Still convalescing from her accident, she was captive in the gilded cage of the Meyers' parlor, away from the parties and friends who sustained her. His secret agreement with Mr. Meyer only made Jim pity her more.

Yet pity wasn't love.

As he neared the Pattons' front garden, Jim saw man-sized footprints in the snow. They marked a trail from the road, up the walkway, and onto the porch in one direction only: in. Helston. But he had to be sure.

Jim went to the east side of the cottage, peered into the sitting room window, and then he turned and walked away.

****

Cora had always rejected the notion of fate. Whatever happened, whether good or ill, one responded according to one's will. Even such a tragic, random event as a life-extinguishing tornado and fire presented choices to the survivors. Would one collapse into pathetic, helpless misery and rely on the charity of others, or pick up the pieces of one's life and set to work? Would one be a giver or a taker? Do good or evil?

Tonight, however, Cora's life ran on the tracks of fate, for she cast her lot with Robert.

Ironically, it was Jenny, immovable in her rocking chair, who set the chain of causation into motion. If Jenny wouldn't budge, Robert would. The nocturnal stroll was presented as an invitation, but it was a rescue. Jenny seemed oblivious to the fact that her own bloody-minded stubbornness pushed Cora into Robert's orbit.

And so they went, Cora's arm linked in Robert's, over the threshold and into the future.

Anything might have derailed them. Another visitor, a medical emergency, Jim Sinclair come to bring good luck to an old spinster who was fond of him. Yet no circumstance, no fatherly voice in her head, no chance event, nothing, nothing at all, intervened.

Cora and Robert walked to the stone bridge and stood upon it, frigid, black water tumbling over the rocks beneath their feet. On that crisp January night, Robert asked the question that turned the wheel of destiny. He took Cora into his arms and said, "Will you marry me?"

"Yes, Robert. I will," she replied.

Chapter 20

Betsy rested on the chaise lounge with her left foot propped on a satin pillow and a magazine on her lap. Three Kings Day hadn't even passed, and she was already complaining that 1875 was the most boring year ever. The Christmas tree was dropping needles, the decorations were dusty, and everyone had forgotten that she was an invalid. Betsy even accused Cora of lacking sympathy for her plight.

"You might try the crutches your father bought you," Cora suggested.

"I have and they didn't suit me. I'm ever so clumsy with them," sighed Betsy. "Ow!" she cried as Cora lifted her left foot.

"I'm sorry." Cora unwound Betsy's bandage as gently as she could.

"It's okay, Cora," said Betsy. "Let's talk of new years and parties and all the gossip, and I'm certain I won't feel as much pain."

Cora nodded as she rolled up the soiled bandage and put it in a basket for the Meyers' laundress.

"Who was your first footer?" Betsy asked.

"Mr. Helston," Cora replied.

"I knew it! He's ever so handsome and dark, though awfully old, if you don't mind me saying it."

"He's only thirty, remember."

"Thirty. And already gray at his temples, though I

suppose some girls like older, more worldly gentlemen," Betsy baited. "They say he plans to marry this year."

"Oh?"

"And I've heard your name paired with his."

"Is that so?"

"Yes. And you're blushing and taking too much interest in the bandages, so now I know it's true. Oh, Cora, that's ever so romantic. Being swept off your feet and lifted from poverty by a dashing, wealthy, lonely gentleman who finds solace in your love."

"I neither confirm nor deny the rumor, and I'll thank you to speak of it no more," said Cora. "Besides, I'm not poor."

"By not denying the rumor, you reveal that it's true. I think you make a perfect couple. I've read that opposites make the best matches. You're short and he's tall. You're fair, and I can't help but notice, so don't be vexed when I say it, you're also freckled. He's dark and even-toned. He lives by his wits, and you live by your labor."

"Enough already," Cora interrupted. "I use my wits too."

"When will you marry?"

Cora fended off the question with a shake of her head as she examined Betsy's ankle. "You still have some bruising, but the bones are well-aligned. And the swelling is gone."

"Will I ever dance again?" Betsy feigned the expression of a tragic heroine with a limp hand turned over her forehead.

"You know you will," Cora laughed. "Maybe even by St. Valentine's Day."

"Good. Because there is someone I shall accept as a

dance partner and beau. You'll never guess who our first footer was."

"I didn't know German families celebrated Hogmanay." Cora pressed her fingers onto the top of Betsy's foot and felt a strong, healthy pulse.

"We don't. But Mummy said we could this year as I was ever so lonesome with my ankle and all. Can't you guess? Oh, please do."

"Um, Rumpelstiltskin?" Cora joked as she shifted her fingers to the soft flesh behind Betsy's ankle bone.

"No, silly. Ouch, that hurts. If you can't guess, I'll have to give you a clue."

"Okay." Cora gently lowered Betsy's foot to the pillow.

"Remember what I said about opposites? You know, blonde and dark, rich and poor, weak and strong…"

"Uh huh."

"Aren't you going to guess?"

"No. You tell me," Cora said absently as she loosened the string on a fresh bandage.

"Jim Sinclair."

"What?" Cora felt as if her heart had fallen into her belly, cold and still as a river rock. A terrible chill overcame her, and she froze in place.

"Yes. Jim. So you're surprised. You shouldn't be, Cora. Ever since he came to my rescue and carried me into Daddy's office on that horrid day, we've had a special connection. I feel it here, in my heart."

"Can you wiggle your toes?" Cora asked, fighting to control a maelstrom of emotion.

Betsy could, vigorously. "Aren't you going to ask me about his visit?"

"No," Cora quickly replied. "I can see by your smile

that you had a wonderful time together."

"We did. He was ever so jolly and amusing though I wonder if he wasn't a little drunk. Now, tell me, Cora. Have you delivered a new year's baby yet?"

"Not yet." Thank God Betsy had changed the subject. Cora began wrapping the clean bandage around Betsy's foot beginning just above her toes. "Aunt Jenny is attending a woman now, and I should be on my way to help her."

"Who is it?"

"I mustn't spoil the surprise. Announcing the birth is a blessed privilege for the new parents."

"New parents. So, it's their first child."

"You don't miss a single beat." Cora forced a smile and placed her index finger over her lips. "Not a word to anyone, Betsy, assuming that brilliant mind of yours will work out who they are."

"Mum's the word," promised Betsy. "It's ever so exciting though. You'll probably be with child yourself before the year is out."

Cora ignored the comment and fastened the bandage at Betsy's lower leg. "How does that feel?"

"Comfortable."

"Good. Even though it's tender, your ankle's healing well," reported Cora.

Again, she urged Betsy to rise from the chaise lounge and use her crutches and after receiving Betsy's noncommittal assent, Cora rushed away.

****

Pleasantly tired from clearing brush at the back of the farm, Jim leaned on the bar at the Shamrock and Thistle and sipped his ale. He deserved a quiet pint, before the tavern buzzed with the voices of men, boasting, teasing, taletelling, and filling the space with amusing nonsense. To his credit, Kelly kept the place friendly by brooking no provocative language among his patrons, the fistfight just before Christmas notwithstanding. Although Kelly was Catholic, Orangemen, and Protestants in general, were welcome in his establishment if they paid their tab, minded their manners, and left the conflicts of Ireland on the other side of the Atlantic. Jim happily complied with Kelly's unwritten rules.

"I reckon we won't see Tom today." Kelly drained the last of the whisky from one bottle into another bottle to top it up.

"Oh? Don't tell me he's up and joined the temperance society," said Jim. "A new year brings out the worst in people, doesn't it? All that resolving and vowing and moralizing."

"No, no. Nothing so terrible as that. When I went home this afternoon, Moira told me that Mary O'Mallory is squeezing out her baby today. Today or tomorrow. The first usually takes its sweet time."

"So Tom's to become an uncle finally. But the women won't want him underfoot."

"No. That's so. Jenny Patton and Kate will run him off before he makes himself a nuisance, but he has to keep his brother company. Nervous as a nun in a whorehouse, that one is. Jeez, there's so many O'Mallorys, I've up and forgotten his name."

"Timothy."

"Right. That's it." Kelly pushed a cork into the bottle and set to arranging his empties in a crate.

"How old were you when your first was born?" asked Jim.

"Twenty-two. Same age as you are now. Guess that makes you a laggard." Kelly winked.

He'd be twenty-three in a week. Jim took a sip of ale. Kelly meant no offence, but the comment cut close to the bone.

"I didn't mean nothing by that, Jim. Lord knows you've encountered a few obstacles along the way."

"And I won't add another in the form of self-pity." Jim smiled. "I can afford a pint of your best when I want one. That's a blessing, isn't it?" He raised his tankard in a mock toast.

Kelly leaned across the bar and said in a serious tone, "A man can't choose his father—"

Oh no, thought Jim. Kelly's about to impart sympathetic advice. This is getting embarrassing.

"But he can choose a rich girl to marry," Kelly laughed and winked again.

"Not many of those about," said Jim.

"So you're going to make me come out and ask it directly, are you?"

"Ask what?"

"Ask about you and Betsy Meyer. You were seen at the Meyers' place just after midnight on the first of January. I have it on reliable sources that Betsy speaks of no one else but you."

Jim didn't dare mention the disgraceful facts underlying his visit to the Meyer family. That the Commercial Bank held the mortgage on the Sinclair farm. That a father had been cowed by his spoiled daughter. That across the ledger, Meyer delivered a strong suggestion in confidence to Jim as end-of-year accounts were settled.

Filling the silence, Kelly said, "She's a pretty gal."

"So she is, Kelly. No denying it. But I was all over town on Hogmanay, so don't think too hard on my varied love life or you'll regret your wedded state."

"Moira's all the woman I can handle," said Kelly. "And she reminds me daily in case I forget it."

Kelly looked past Jim's shoulder. "Well look who's here. Father and uncle?" Kelly asked as Tom O'Mallory pulled his brother Timothy into the tavern.

"Not yet," said Tom. "Jenny Patton told me I should take Tim away for one last drink before his life changes forever."

"That sounds ominous," said Jim.

"It's an understatement," said Kelly. "No one can prepare you for the upheaval that a tiny, squalling bundle brings you."

Tom said, "She told us the baby won't come till tonight, but she'd have someone fetch us if she's wrong."

"Tim, my man. A whisky with an ale chaser for you, on the house." Kelly reached for a shot glass.

Tim nodded, by all appearances too nervous to speak, and on his behalf, Tom said, "Why thank you, Kelly. That's mighty generous."

"You'll pay for yours, Tom."

Tom feigned offence, then laughed. "'Twas worth a try."

"Looks like Mary and you will win the New Year's baby basket at Beck's," Jim said to Tim.

Tim shook his head and bestowed the weakest of smiles on Kelly who pushed a full shot glass of whisky across the counter.

Tom said, "You haven't heard. It's a two-way race for first baby now. Alice MacTavish is having hers too. Ian junior fetched Cora away from our place, oh, about an hour ago. Jeez, word travels slowly in Maryville."

"Those poor ladies are run off their feet," said Kelly.

"Maybe not for much longer," said Tom. "Father Finney told me, and no one tell anyone else because it might be a tale, that a new doctor's moving to town, probably in February. Setting up in the Brockett building on Water Street. Apparently old Brockett's giving him a break on rent."

"There's some will beat it to the new doctor, and others will stick with the Pattons," said Kelly. "I reckon Moira and me will be in the latter class."

The men all murmured their agreement with that sentiment, and Jim said, "Those who have the money will go to the doctor and those with restricted means will not. Cora and Jenny are the equal of any doctor, but they'll suffer a loss of income once he sets up his practice."

"I wouldn't worry about them money-wise." Kelly looked at Tim's rapidly emptying glass and started pulling tankards of ale from the cask. "Robert Helston will keep them in comfort."

"Keep?" asked Jim. "What's that supposed to mean?" Kelly's casual remark felt like a punch in the gut and an attack on Cora's honor.

"Take it how you like," Kelly shrugged. "All's I'm saying is Helston has taken a mighty close interest in our Cora."

"I think he aims to take her honestly," said Tom. "I'd wager my life savings that wedding bells will ring before the ice breaks up."

"Who told you that?" Jim asked, muscles tensing for battle with an invisible, unnamable enemy.

"No one," said Tom. "It's plain to see for any who

take a passing interest in the affairs of their fellow man."

"I grant you both that they may be courting, but only yesterday Jenny Patton told me Cora puts her work first," said Jim. "Always. Jenny said that even if she were engaged, Cora wouldn't be rushed into marriage."

"Jenny Patton oughta inform Helston of that," joked Kelly as he pushed a fresh tankard across the bar to Jim.

Jim shook his head and pushed the unrequested drink back.

"Oh, come on Jim," protested Kelly. "This ain't exactly breaking news. Helston and Cora are together constantly." He gave the tankard to Tom instead.

Tom nodded his thanks. "Only a matter of days till Helston puts an announcement in the *Trumpet*."

Sensing trouble, Kelly said, "Lighten up, Jim. As you yourself admitted, you were all over town on New Year's Eve. Many a man envies you your way with the ladies and that probably includes Helston."

Jim shrugged, backing down from further argument. If he had an adversary, it was Helston, not these jocular men. As Jim fished a couple of coins from his pocket to pay his tab, Tim said, "I feel like I'm going to be sick."

Jim laid a hand on his shoulder and steered him toward the door. "Come on, Tim," he said. "I think we both need fresh air."

Chapter 21

Bathed in dawn's glow, Alice dozed with her hours-old daughter at her breast. There'd been a worrisome gush of blood after the birth, but the heavy bleeding resolved with fundal massage and nursing, and the new mother and her baby, yet unnamed, looked healthy and tranquil, cocooned under a fresh quilt in the daybed near the kitchen stove.

"You'll stay for breakfast, Cora?" asked Alice's elder sister Grace who'd come from Burnside for the month. "We've bacon from Dad's Tamworths and Alice baked cornbread yesterday, just before she went into labor."

"Thank you, Grace. I'd stay but Aunt Jenny will be watching for me. I really should be going." Cora picked up her satchel.

"I'll drive you, Cora," said Ian junior. "It'll take but a few minutes to hitch the cutter."

Cora shook her head. "No, no. Thank you, though. I prefer to walk. I'll sleep better when I get home that way. You stay with Alice and the baby and mind you fetch me if either one shows any sign of being sick. Remember: fever, pain—"

"Chills, paleness, drowsiness, trouble breathing, vomiting, anything that doesn't seem right, even if I can't pin it," finished Ian junior, the pride of new fatherhood animating his face.

"Correct," Cora smiled at Ian and Grace. "Mother and babe are in capable hands with the two of you."

Cora had done all that she could for the new family, and now it was time for her to stop hovering and let them get to know the youngest MacTavish in privacy, without anyone peering over their shoulders.

Outside, pink, purple, and orange ribbons of cloud lit the eastern sky and deep blue shadows played upon the snow. Awaking to a fine winter morning, people and birds alike greeted the day and began their routines. A wagon driver offered Cora a lift, but she waved him off and thanked him for his kindness. Walking helped her to shed the demands and stresses of midwifery and clear her head.

Though bone-tired, Cora loved her work. She couldn't imagine casting it aside to join the ranks of Maryville's matrons, organizing church picnics and charity bazaars, chattering over cream teas, and enforcing their oppressive moral code through punishing gossip and ostracism of those who broke their rules. Yet hadn't Robert suggested she do just that? Frequently, he spoke of marriage as an idyll in which she'd never have to lift a finger aside from hanging off his arm as they maneuvered through society. When she hinted she'd continue to work with Aunt Jenny, he scoffed, albeit subtly, and said he'd see to Cora's every desire.

Perhaps he was trying to protect her like a pearl in an oyster shell. In the year following Eliza's death, Robert sank into such a deep melancholy that his friends and acquaintances, including Father, worried that one day he would be found lifeless and cold in the *Trumpet* offices and be buried beside his beloved wife. He'd recovered with scars and Cora wondered if his smothering affection might be a strategy to ward off a repetition of his unhappy past.

Cora didn't doubt his love, but she yearned to be more than a wifely adornment and lover. She yearned to entwine and bond spiritually, as an intellectual equal, as she had with Jim Sinclair during the journey to Brucedale.

There. She'd thought the unthinkable. Again. What was wrong with her?

Feather-brained girls lost their minds for Jim Sinclair. Accustomed to getting whatever she wanted, Betsy Meyer chased him relentlessly. At church, dowagers and debutantes dropped gloves, flirted coquettishly, and admired Jim with stolen glances and slack-jawed stares. Even Aunt Jenny, on the cusp of cronehood and cynical in matters of romance, adored him. Since Christmas Eve, Jim had given Cora no hint that he thought of her differently than any other girl. Still, she couldn't forget how she felt when she was with him. When they rode together, Jim enveloped her in his strength and easy simplicity, and she feared she would never experience such a connection with Robert.

For the sake of a happy marriage, she had to banish Jim from her mind. Robert Helston was a good man, and he deserved the loyalty and devotion of a good wife. Today, after a long nap, Cora would start planning the wedding.

As she walked up the lane to the cottage, the kitchen door swung open.

"What time did Alice's arrive?" called Jenny, evidently too curious to greet her niece before nailing down the facts.

"A little after three," replied Cora. "And Mary's?"

"Half past two. Girl or boy?"

"A girl. A fair size with a few whisps of red hair. No name yet. And Mary's?" Cora stamped the snow from her boots.

"A boy. 'Patrick' for his grandpa. And he's a big boy too, for an O'Mallory."

"The O'Mallory family wins the basket from Beck's. Congratulations, Aunt Jenny."

"Why are you congratulating me? I didn't win a prize."

"If you say so," Cora grinned. "Why aren't you in bed already?"

"I wanted to gloat. Even though I didn't win a prize."

Both women laughed and then yawned, and a half hour later they slept in the contentment of those who are confident they've earned their rest honestly.

****

"As you've insisted we marry in your church, I've spoken to Reverend Cameron, and he's agreed to read the banns beginning this Sunday," said Robert.

"So soon?" asked Cora. "That would mean an early February wedding."

"Yes, before Lent. If we delay, we won't be able to marry till after Easter."

They fell into silence as they walked arm in arm along Silver Creek near the stone bridge where they'd pledged their love and intention to marry only the previous week. Now the creek was frozen and swift cold water carried bubbles and bits of debris under the clear ice. Why couldn't they wait till spring? She kicked a hunk of snow onto the ice with the side of her boot. Robert seemed to stiffen with disapproval over her childish action.

"I imagined the church decorated in spring flowers," Cora said.

"Hardly anything blooms till May, and that's months away. Then May being unlucky, we'd delay to June," Robert countered. "Anyway, we can buy flowers in the city. Roses, carnations, or whatever you please, my darling."

My darling. Once endearing, now the words sounded patronizing and domestic.

"How about lilies?" she asked with an edge of sarcasm.

"Lilies too, though we're planning a wedding, not a funeral."

"I was joking."

"Were you?" He slowed his pace and frowned at her.

"Yes," she insisted, meeting his eyes.

After another spell of silence, Cora spoke again. "I'm sorry, Robert. I guess I imagined a spring wedding with bunting and bouquets and sunshine to bless us."

"My darling, the sun shines in February. And I hate to remind you, as the past belongs firmly in the past, but this is my second marriage. A fancy wedding would be unseemly."

"You're right, of course. Our wedding might be a painful reminder to Eliza's family of their loss, though I'm sure they think of her every day regardless."

"Thank you for understanding that, Cora. We can have a modest wedding and an extravagant honeymoon." He squeezed her hand affectionately.

Cora wouldn't object and hurt this good man whose only motive for a February wedding was to spare others pain. And to bed her properly. "Yes. All right. February," she shrugged.

"Ash Wednesday is on the tenth of February," said Robert.

"Then we must set a date in the first week of the month," said Cora.

"Monday for health, Tuesday for wealth, and Wednesday the best day of all," Robert recited.

"If Wednesday is the best day according to an ancient nursery rhyme, then I suppose I'm in favor," Cora agreed with covert reluctance. She had the dizzying sensation of riding on a run-away train.

"Wednesday, the third," Robert exclaimed as he lifted Cora off her feet in a bear hug. "My darling, we shall be the happiest married couple in the world." After he set her down, he asked, "Have you ever been to Niagara Falls?"

"I have not," replied Cora. "But isn't it rather far? How will Aunt Jenny manage?"

"Oh, let's not worry about that just now," Robert interrupted. "Such matters have a way of working themselves out. Now imagine if this creek and the dam just upriver were a million times bigger, and instead of draining Brockett's millpond, they're draining Lake Erie, with water and ice thundering over the ledge and raising great clouds of mist."

"You're describing Niagara Falls," laughed Cora.

"I am, my darling. I shall take you there and we will dine on caviar and champagne and make love all day long."

****

The organist was only playing the prelude and already Jim was hopelessly bored. He'd offered to take

Gran to church and now he suffered the consequences. As he slouched in a futile attempt to find a comfortable position, latecomers hurried to their pews, Reverend Cameron shuffled reams of notes, and Gran bookmarked her Bible. A couple hours in the scheme of his life were no great sacrifice, and church was the highlight of Gran's week.

Jim looked toward the Patton pew. Face impassive, Cora sat as still as a stone statue of a goddess. Next to her, Jenny read the Bible or possibly an earthlier book, pausing now and again to push her glasses up her long nose. Cora whispered something to Jenny, and they looked toward the opposite side of the church. Jim followed their gaze. There Robert Helston squeezed into a pew between his Aunt Eugenia and his mother and waved to Cora. Strange. Strange and foreboding. The Helston family was Anglican, not Presbyterian. Cora smiled and nodded back to Helston, then turned toward the pulpit, her face statue-like once more.

Reverend Cameron cleared his throat and called the congregation to worship. And then, after several announcements with a lengthy prayer tailored for each, Reverend Cameron bestowed a smugly benevolent smile upon Cora and Helston and issued the words that shattered Jim's heart:

"I've published the banns of marriage between Mr. Robert Thomas Helston of Maryville and Miss Cora Jane Patton, daughter of the late Dr. John Alexander Patton, also of Maryville. God willing, the groom and his bride will be joined in holy matrimony in this church on Wednesday, the third of February at two o'clock in the afternoon. This is the first announcement of banns. If any of you know of just cause or impediment for why the wedding should be prevented, I implore you to declare it."

Reverend Cameron again smiled at the prospective bride and groom. "Robert and Cora, the congregation shares your joy." After intoning another prayer, he cleared his throat and bid the congregation rise for the first hymn.

"How lovely," Gran whispered, taking Jim's arm as she stood. "I do love a winter wedding. Cheers everyone up. Mind I always thought Cora would be perfect for you, she being so smart and capable and all."

Jim patted Gran's knobby hand and said nothing. He couldn't look at Cora or her fiancé. He stared blankly at the choir, stifling his emotions, forcing himself to attend to the melody and mumble the lyrics of the hymn. Time after time he'd ignored reality. He thought they'd plan a spring wedding with enough temporal distance from the present for Cora to discover that Helston was unworthy as her groom. Now the woman he loved was to be wed to a snake within the month and become another of the snake's possessions. Why didn't anyone else see that? Why couldn't she see it?

Jim could do nothing to stop the wedding. He couldn't register an objection; he hadn't grounds. Obviously, he couldn't murder Robert Helston, although the thought crossed his mind. And he couldn't talk Cora out of marriage to a man she seemed to respect and adore. Jim was a college drop-out who managed his father's heavily mortgaged farm and nothing more. Against Helston, Jim stood on quicksand.

The rest of the service passed in blurry torment and two hours later the congregation spilled from the church onto the snow-covered lawn. Men shook Helston's hand

and thumped his shoulder in hearty congratulations. Women gathered around Cora and hugged her in turn, Gran among them.

"I hoped she'd marry you."

Jim turned. It was Jenny Patton.

"Me too." Upon the confession, a tidal wave of sadness washed over him.

"I don't suppose there's anything to be done," said Jenny.

"No, I suppose there isn't," said Jim.

"Pity." Jenny regarded him with sympathy, shook her head, and trudged away.

Chapter 22

Before she entered the sick room, Cora spoke with Mrs. Tucker who informed her that Mr. Tucker was in a rare lucid state though already calling for spirits at daybreak.

"If he doesn't get the drink, he flies into a rage and says the ugliest things. Yesterday, after he screamed blue murder and called me Satan's witchy spawn, his eyes rolled back, and he went into fits. When he came to his senses, I spooned an ounce of brandy into his mouth and that calmed him, though he soon wanted more."

"You did the right thing, Mrs. Tucker," said Cora. "The drink will take him. It's likely only a matter of days, but he'll suffer less if he receives what he craves."

"But didn't you tell him to lay off it?" Mrs. Tucker took Cora's cape and hung it on a hook by the door.

"Yes, I did. And if he had, it might have bought him some time, given his liver a chance to heal. But now his organs are so weak, he's past the point of no return and it's better if he has the comfort of his vice."

"The drink."

"Precisely. I'll look in on him, Mrs. Tucker, but by what you're telling me, I think it mightn't be too soon to fetch your vicar."

"Very well." Mrs. Tucker's eyes glistened with tears. "You warned me the final days would come."

Cora took Mrs. Tucker's hand and spoke softly.

"You've kept Mr. Tucker alive longer than most wives would've managed."

"Because I love him, Cora," she sobbed. "When he's sober, or at least only a little drunk, he's the kindest, most thoughtful husband a wife could want. Charles' good days more than make up for the bad days. And on those days, well…" Mrs. Tucker scowled. "Those days he's the very devil."

Cora frowned in empathy. "Drink is a curse and the ruin of many a man. Mr. Tucker has always been very kind to Aunt Jenny and me. Father valued his friendship very highly and respected his advice."

"So many people have told me the same, and it's bittersweet to hear it."

After she collected herself, Mrs. Tucker said, "Could you take him a glass? I feel as if I'm poisoning him whenever I bring it to him. As if I'm kicking him closer to the edge of a cliff."

"Yes, I can do that," Cora nodded. "You mentioned he's lucid, so I'll broach the subject of his future. Better he has a drink in hand than—"

From the floor above, a startling, shrill cry lifted the fine hair on Cora's neck. "Sweetums! Where's my bottle?"

"Coming, Charles," Mrs. Tucker called back. "Cora's here and she'll bring it up."

"Tell her to hurry, will you? I don't have all day."

With a pained look up the stairs, Mrs. Tucker muttered, "You do have all day, you bloody old buzzard." Seeing Cora's raised eyebrows, she said, "He is an old buzzard. A lovable old buzzard and he shall have whatever he wants, bless the old devil. On Cora's orders."

****

For the reward of a glass of brandy, Charles Tucker mustered the strength to transfer from his bed to his armchair with Cora's support and now she sat near him, on a footstool.

"Cheers." He accepted his glass with a tremulous hand, took a swig and looked Cora in the eye. "Does Beatrice know how sick I am?"

"Yes," Cora replied.

"I see. Yes. Quite right. As she should," he murmured, then drank again in sips.

Cora noted his jaundiced skin and yellow, raccoon-circled eyes. The old man's belly was tautly bloated, his breath labored and fetid, and his extremities swollen with fluid. If he opened his robe, she expected she'd see an ominous bruising around his umbilicus.

She asked, "How do you feel, Mr. Tucker?"

"Lousy. Lousy! I'm nauseous, jittery, weak, and muddled. It's the dipsomania, you see."

"Yes, I see. Are you in pain?"

"Not as such. My skin crawls with tiny bugs. They torment me. I want to jump out of my skin. It's the bugs, you see. Brandy chases them away and then it wears off and they start again. Crawling."

"How unpleasant."

Tucker nodded.

"Are you eating?" asked Cora.

Tucker shook his head, face contorted with disgust at the mention of nutrition.

"And the commode?"

"My urine is a queer color of brown and my movements are black and sticky." Tucker took another drink, then asked, "Does it matter?"

"I shouldn't think so, Mr. Tucker." Given the gravity of the man's illness, Cora judged that frankness would be a better servant than platitudes if he hoped to die with his affairs in order and a semblance of peace in his soul. "Things like that don't matter anymore." Gently yet directly, she looked him in the eye. "You're dying."

"Dying," sputtered Tucker. "Surely you have medicine for me. You always have medicine."

Cora shook her head and abided in silence while Tucker stared blankly at his glass with rheumy eyes. He took down the last of the fiery liquid. "I believe I'll have another."

"I'll pour you one," said Cora.

After he had drunk again, she said, "Mr. Tucker. I don't know how long you'll live. Besides the Lord above, no one can predict the length of anyone's life. However…"

"However, you're telling me that my time will be brief. Truncated. Short."

"Yes, I'm sorry to say I am. We can keep you comfortable, no nagging, and you can have whatever you like—"

Tucker sat straight in his chair. "I'll not hear of it. No, indeed. I'll not."

Cora was speechless. What did he see when he peered into the looking glass? When he tried to stuff his feet into shoes or fasten his belt? Scoured by booze and self-neglect, Tucker's life was bleeding away and only God could save him.

Tucker believed differently. "We'll have a new doctor in Maryville soon. College educated, trained by the best. He'll know what to do."

"A second opinion," said Cora.

162

"A medical opinion," corrected Tucker. "I'll pay Mr. Helston for all you've done and send for the new fellow. You needn't return if there's nothing you can do for me."

"You may pay me, if you're so inclined," said Cora.

"Helston will be your husband soon." Tucker refused to meet her eye.

"Very well, Mr. Tucker." Cora hid her hurt behind steely professionalism. "I'll go now. And I'll pray your outcome is as you wish it. Do you want to return to bed, or remain in the chair?"

He stared at his glass and mumbled, "The chair suits me at present. Thank you."

Dismissed, Cora took her leave of Mr. Tucker, relayed his requests to Mrs. Tucker, and left their residence before she said anything she might regret.

****

Outdoors, Cora breathed deeply and slowly to try to rid herself of her irrational shame. She couldn't dismiss Mr. Tucker's words as the addled raving of a drunk. He was lucid and honest when he spoke. She was most insulted that he questioned her judgement. She and Aunt Jenny had poured over texts and written to Father's colleagues in other towns for advice on treating his myriad illnesses. No competent doctor would fault their care, but she couldn't argue with a dying man in denial of his mortality. In such a case as Mr. Tucker's, her acceptance of his need to grasp for a wispy straw was the compassionate route forward. He hoped for a cure, and she'd done all she could. It was cold comfort to Cora that the new doctor would have the same chance of successfully treating Charles Tucker as she and Aunt Jenny had.

"New doctor." Those words cut like a knife in the gut. Naturally the citizens of a burgeoning town such as Maryville would want a doctor and eventually a hospital. Deep down, she'd understood that all along. But why hadn't Robert mentioned that a new doctor was already on his way? He knew. He had to know. He published the newspaper and furthermore, he moved in the same lofty circle as Charles Tucker. Cora decided to go to Robert's office, wait for him, and confront him, after she checked in on the MacTavish family.

****

Once again, Willy would warn Robert that she was waiting to ambush him in his office. Cora didn't care. She also didn't care that she wore a plain dress Robert disliked, that she hadn't bothered with her appearance, and that she had no idea what she'd say to him. Too angry to be still, she paced back and forth over the thick Persian rug.

After a half hour, Robert entered the room and she stopped in her tracks, turned, and threw her outrage at him like a bucket of slops over a pigsty wall.

"How could you, Robert?"

Slowly, as if to show that at least he had control of his senses, Robert closed the door behind him and smiled. "My darling. How could I what?"

"You know what I'm talking about."

He shrugged, blue eyes conveying an expression of surprised innocence.

"I visited a patient this morning who told me that a new doctor is expected in Maryville any day now."

Robert gestured to a chair. "You heard correctly, Cora, but I can't break the news until details of the physician's arrival are finalized."

Cora stepped forward aggressively. "I thought we'd agreed. You would tell me everything. We wouldn't keep secrets from each other."

"We did agree. Trust is our foundation. That and love."

"If that's true, then I should have been told. Instead, I feel as if I stepped on a garden hoe that you knew was there, buried under leaves all along. Do you have any idea how humiliating it is to be told that you're no longer needed? That a stranger to this town will arrive any day and kick you from your place?"

Robert shook his head. "No, I don't—"

"Of course you don't," Cora hissed. "You're a man. You're university educated. No one has ever questioned your competence. Or considered you inferior."

"Cora."

"Robert," she mocked.

"Cora, I've never considered you inferior. The fact is that Maryville needs a doctor and doctors are men."

Robert took her elbow, but Cora jerked her arm away.

He took a heavy breath, spread his arms, and opened his hands expansively. "My darling. Let's begin again. Tell me exactly what is troubling you."

She stamped her foot. "I already told you."

"All right. Then perhaps you should read this." Robert circled round his desk, unlocked a drawer, removed a leaf of paper, and handed it to Cora. "This is a draft of an article for the front page of the paper. Third paragraph down. Aloud, if you please."

Cora nodded, scanned to the third paragraph, and read Robert's angular handwriting:

"Although the date of the arrival of Maryville's new

physician is unconfirmed, the Trumpet *editorial department states emphatically and unequivocally that Maryville has been well served by Miss Jennifer Patton and her niece, Miss Cora Patton, who courageously stepped into the breach upon the tragic passing of Dr. John Patton. The pair have toiled tirelessly for their patients, from infants newly born to frail elders breathing their last, and they understand the medical needs of Maryville better than any, especially a newcomer. That is why the Editorial Department is calling for Miss Jennifer Patton and Miss Cora Patton to assist in forming a new and important committee to plan for the construction of a hospital. It is the opinion of many, including Maryville's leading citizens, that the Pattons' expert medical advice and their knowledge of this fair and growing town should be put to expedient use now and in the future."*

Cora placed the paper on the desk and, eyes narrowed, regarded Robert with suspicion. The article seemed too pat, as if its author wrote it to appease. She wasn't ready to let go of her anger just yet.

"We can discuss the idea of a committee another time. I beg to know, when is the new doctor coming, Robert? Surely you can tell me that."

"He's expected in a week or two. As soon as I receive his telegram, I'll revise the article with the details and publish it after I tell you everything I know."

"What's his name?"

"Dr. August Blackmore."

"How long have you known that?"

"Since the tenth of January." Shoulders slumped, Robert sat on the edge of the desk and looked forlornly at her. "I wanted to tell you, but you've been too busy to

166

meet me."

"I suppose I have been busy," Cora conceded.

"You must not let your work come between us, my darling. Ever again," Robert said solemnly.

"You've been busy too."

"Yes, that's true. I'm sorry." As if exhausted by bearing the weight of the world, he sighed and spoke in a low, confessional voice. "How I hate it when we quarrel."

As she considered his burdens, likely greater than her own, Cora's anger dissolved. "Truce?"

"Everlasting peace. Do you have some time to spare for the lovelorn?" Robert grasped her hand and pulled her close.

"Only a few minutes." Cora replied.

Hands firm on her back, Robert was already kissing her neck. His lips grazed her jaw, then her cheek, his breath hot on her skin.

"I'm sorry too," she whispered in his ear.

"Ssh. It's okay." He stopped her from further apology by covering her mouth with his. As their kiss deepened, he drew her against him and caressed her, his hands circling ever lower. He ventured below the small of her back and Cora tried to break away. He ceased his exploration yet tightened his hold.

"Robert. You mustn't." She wriggled in his arms. "I have to…I have to get back to work."

"You're right, my darling. Forgive me." Robert released her and smiled. "You have such power over me."

It was a lie. They both knew who had more power and it wasn't Cora.

Chapter 23

Jim and Tom sat on overturned crates and drank coffee from pewter mugs, away from the racket of the sawmill. Both men had picked up steady jobs for the winter, Jim for tuition and to cover the mortgage on the Sinclair farm and Tom to save money for land of his own. Their employer, Mr. Brockett, hired seasonally and paid his men well if they worked hard and were never tardy, an arrangement that suited Jim.

As usual, Tom was a bubbling fountain of gossip, though everything he relayed was in the previous day's *Trumpet* and if Jim were inclined, he could have read the news himself.

"His name's Dr. August Blackmore," said Tom. "They reckon he'll arrive next week and be ready to see patients by the end of January. Trained at Oxford and left England for a life of service and adventure on the frontier. A God-fearing Christian, lepidopterist, and amateur playwright who hopes to elevate Maryville with theatrical plays and dramatic readings."

"Where do I buy tickets?" Jim asked.

"Maybe Dr. Blackmore will be a blast of fresh air, though he could be one of those insufferable Englishmen who is hellbent on civilizing the colonies."

"Maryville isn't exactly the frontier," said Jim. "I hope he's not disappointed when he can't put on shows for cowboys and natives."

"You know what a posh Englishman fresh off the boat is like," snickered Tom. "He'll strut around and complain that Beck's doesn't stock a decent claret and send home letters bragging that he wrestled a grizzly bear and discovered a secret valley, as if he were Daniel Boone."

Jim drank his coffee, and Tom continued, "Whatever he's like, he'll be here on time to release Cora from her work so she can marry. The wedding's on the first Wednesday of February."

"I'm aware," said Jim.

"And the newlyweds will honeymoon in Niagara."

"The timing is perfect." Jim mounded a ridge of snow with his boot, then flicked it away with his toe. "Perfect timing for a perfect couple."

"You're being sarcastic, bitter, and cynical," accused Tom. "It doesn't suit you."

"No?"

"No. God damn it, Jim. You're such a pathetic patsy boy lately. Mooning around, feeling sorry for yourself."

"Break's almost over." Jim finished his coffee and tossed the dregs into the snow. He wouldn't be baited.

Tom stood and playfully kicked Jim's boot, then made to punch him. "If you're sweet on Cora, you should fight for her. You'll regret it forever if you don't try to stop her from making the biggest mistake of her life."

Jim looked up at his friend and read his face. Tom wasn't taunting. He was advising.

"Tom, I have to be realistic. I dropped out of college and I haven't got two red cents to rub together. Against Helston, what chance could I possibly have?"

"Jesus, Joseph, and Mary! What have you got to lose? Helston's an arsehole, and you know it. Quit the self-pity and do something. For your sake and Cora's."

"Like what?"

"You're not as stupid as you look, Jim. You'll think of something." Tom kicked Jim's boot again, this time harder. "Time to work, lazy bones."

****

The sun was sinking at the horizon as Jim rode Buttercup back to the barn and gave her a vigorous combing and rubdown. After work, he'd turned her out of the barn and did his chores, but she pestered and whinnied and nudged until he finally relented with, "Okay my girl. A quick run and then your supper." And run they did, over the wind-packed snow on the west side of the fence lines, Buttercup saddleless, Jim reining just enough to remind her he was master.

As they galloped, he thought of Christmas Eve with Cora, her easy laughter, the scent of her skin after a long day's work, the warmth of her body as she eased against him, each taking pleasure in the embrace. Without saying so, she'd paid him the compliment of feeling safe with him and she yielded. How he longed to laugh with her and meld with her again.

Tom told him he'd think of something…find some way to reach her. A letter?

****

Jim found his supper on the kitchen table, something that was happening with increasing frequency. Mama's headaches stole hours from her days and sent her to bed early most evenings, though she refused to seek the Pattons' aid. Gran was away at Aunt Sophie's. No doubt Dad was squandering the weekly allowance Jim had given him that morning. Like most incorrigible gamblers with coins in their pockets, his father's poker nights began in grandiose delusion, and Jim preferred to be out of the house when the old man departed with a swagger to the card table in the back room of the Golden Pheasant.

Jim took his supper to his room, lit a candle, and ate at his desk. He cut his food and chewed each forkful methodically. Tonight was chicken and dumplings though it could have been anything on his plate, even a bar of soap, for all he tasted. He had a task. He had to find the right words. He had to reach Cora.

After he pushed his empty plate aside, he pulled a box from under his bed, and found ink, a pen, and paper, all leftover from law school. After agonizing deliberation, he decided to begin by contemplating his goal, Cora's happiness, and leave space for his sentences to form. The candle had burned halfway down before Jim was prepared to commit ink to paper and this is what he wrote:

Dear Cora,

I only wish for your happiness. I fear you will take displeasure in the contents of this letter, and you may choose to avoid my company forever, but I take this risk willingly. Please know that I shall always place your wellbeing above my own.

I fear your fiancé is unworthy of your love. You are far and away the better half of the match. You are clever while he is cunning. You are honest while he is sly. You serve the unfortunate and he is served by them. You give your heart and he takes it. Cora, there are few men on this earth who are your equal in character and Robert Helston is not one of them.

You and I grew up together. Despite what you might think of me, I have loved you from the start. Till my dying day, I shall hold in my heart the memory of our time together on Christmas Eve, and I shall love you always.

If you ever need anything, Cora, please do not hesitate to call upon me. And by all means, marry whomever you wish, only please consider if Robert Helston is good enough for you.

Jim

He folded the letter and put it in his vest pocket. He'd carry it with him for two or three days, give time for his sentiment to solidify into conviction or soften into misgiving. Jim would either send the letter or burn it. Now it was time to sleep on his words, as any wise lawyer would. As he blew out the candle, Jim did not know that his letter would drift to the bottom of Brockett's millpond and the paper would disintegrate without anyone ever reading the words it contained.

Chapter 24

Betsy Meyer was now under the care of Dr. Blackmore. On her last visit, Cora left the doctor her notes about his new patient and today she visited Betsy as a friend. Cora was at peace with passing the baton of Betsy's care to Dr. Blackmore given Mr. Meyer's standing in Maryville and his participation in the recruitment committee. Indeed, Cora's transition from being Betsy's medic to being her friend was inevitable and not unwelcome.

On a late January day, at a small, skirted table in a sunny bay window, the pair celebrated Cora's engagement and upcoming wedding, now only a week away.

As Betsy poured the tea, Cora asked, "What is Dr. Blackmore like?"

"Haven't you met him?" Betsy asked in return.

"No, I'm afraid I haven't. Robert met him at the station and conveyed him to his new apartments on Water Street and by his report, Dr. Blackmore was warm and polite and spoke in glowing terms of our little town, but I've been too busy to meet him, with a wedding to plan and all."

"He's ever so wonderful," Betsy giggled. "He's blond, and he wears his hair parted to the side just so. He has the dreamiest pale blue eyes, a very handsome mustache, and he's trim and neat."

"And his character?" Cora dropped a lump of sugar into her tea and stirred.

"Also dreamy. Cora, he paid ever so much attention to me. He visited for nearly an hour, and he listened to all of my problems. Although it was just a 'getting to know you' visit, he made a very careful examination of my ankle."

"He sounds thorough."

"Oh, he is." Betsy pouted. "He told me I mustn't dance yet, but he'd work with me to build strength in my ankle."

"Sensible." Cora sipped her tea and basked in the warmth of the sunny window.

Betsy leaned toward Cora as if to emphasize the confidential nature of their conversation. "When I met Dr. Blackmore, 'August', for that's what he told me to call him, I forgot all about Jim Sinclair. It's so strange. Last week I was head over heels in love with Jim and I felt that we were finally developing a deep connection, but this week, I'm not so sure."

"Oh? What changed?"

"Well for one thing, August is a highly educated gentleman. He speaks with a proper, upper-class English accent, and he's seen ever so much of the world including France. When I compare him to Jim, with his homely clothes and country ways, I'm afraid Jim doesn't come off as well." She crinkled her brow. "As I get to know August, I'm cooling on Jim. I do hope Jim isn't dreadfully disappointed."

"You're gracious to consider Jim's feelings, Betsy. I wouldn't worry too much about Jim. He's resilient. His broken heart will mend if you decide that Dr. Blackmore should be your beau."

"Do you think so, Cora?"

"Yes, I do."

"I suppose Jim's heart is mending already with the fuss that Adeline, Helen, and Diana make of him. Adeline will win him in the end. They make a perfect match. Mrs. Brockett will convince Mr. Brockett to overlook James senior's antics and accept Jim as a potential son-in-law eventually."

With a stab of jealousy in Cora's gut, a scowl passed over her face though Betsy was too absorbed in enumerating the charms of her latest infatuation to notice.

"Anyhow, it's just as well for I think Mummy and Daddy prefer August too. He's twenty-eight, the perfect age for a man to marry, and we're both blond so we'd have the most adorable, fair-haired children."

"I look forward to meeting Dr. August Blackmore," Cora declared, recovering her social graces.

Betsy nudged a plate of dainty cookies toward Cora. "You'll like him, Cora, and since you're marrying Mr. Helston, I don't have to worry about you stealing him away."

"Betsy!" Cora laughed. "I would never let a man come between my friends and me. Besides, you're by far the prettier of the two of us with your blond ringlets, ivory skin, and narrow waist. Isn't it I who should worry?"

"No. You command respect and that's attractive to men. You're a lioness and I'm a cute little kitten."

Cora was surprised by Betsy's remark, and she protested the characterization.

Betsy poured more tea, then rang a bell to summon the maid to refresh the pot. After the maid left, she asked,

"What does it feel like to be kissed by a man?"

"Pardon?"

"You know. Really and truly and properly kissed. Not a peck on the cheek, but a full kiss on the mouth."

Cora stammered slightly. "It's, um, interesting. It's a way to know someone without using words."

"Mr. Helston kisses you," said Betsy.

"He does." Cora's cheeks flushed and she knew her face was scarlet.

"Is he good at it?"

"Betsy. Such questions. Yes, I suppose he is, though I've no one to compare him to, and I'll not say anything else on this subject."

Betsy giggled. "I knew it anyway. Now you must tell me all about your wedding plans."

Relieved to speak on the less intimate aspects of love and marriage, Cora described her plans for a modest wedding, from Robert's red rose boutonniere to their departure on the evening train with all the luggage Robert insisted they'd need during their honeymoon. The two friends chatted away the afternoon in happy companionship and, as she left the Meyers' residence, Cora was almost convinced she was glad to marry Robert Helston and not in the least interested in news of Jim Sinclair. Almost convinced, which is to say, completely and utterly vexed by the matter.

****

Each year for a few days in January, the weather warmed, the sun shone brightly, and children abandoned their skates and toboggans for the fun of making snowmen and forts with melting snow that clumped obligingly.

Within a spell of warm, sunny weather, this day was

glorious. Jim couldn't help but look wistfully from the crude window over the millpond, see the dazzling snow, and wish he had the afternoon off to go hunting. The snow lay in drifts over thick ice, though at the edges and up the center of the pond where water flowed toward the millrace, the ice was thin. With the warmer temperature, ice fishing was out of the question. Deer hunting, on the other hand—

A dog ran across the ice. A big, black, energetic dog darting here and there, zigging and zagging on the millpond, unaware of the danger. With four legs to distribute his weight and speed in his favor, he'd probably be okay. A boy stood on the edge of the pond waving his arms frantically. Likely shouting too, though Jim couldn't hear that over the noise of the mill. If the creature would only listen to his young master. Jim couldn't abide a poorly trained animal. Dogs were happier when they knew their place. A dog who ran about aimlessly and made mischief spelled trouble.

The mill was running smoothly. Maybe he should go down and help. As he watched, the boy ventured onto the ice. He had no choice now. He had to go and stop him. The foreman would understand. Jim dashed down the stairs, fairly jumping from landing to landing, and hurried to the pond.

"Stop," Jim yelled to the boy. "Stop. The ice isn't safe."

"I have to get Dart," the boy called back.

The dog likely caught a scent or saw a squirrel, for he bounded across the pond, the boy after him. Jim was close enough now to recognize the boy. Peter Beck.

"Pete! Stop!"

"I won't! I have to get Dart."

Pete strode off, calling for his dog, and Jim heard an ominous crack.

"Turn back!" Jim shouted.

Too late. Pete broke through where the current was fastest. He bobbed up and clung to the ice, but the water pulled him. If he let go, he'd be carried under the ice.

"Can you pull yourself up, onto your belly?" Jim shouted.

Though struggling and kicking mightily, Pete couldn't fight the current. Soon he'd weaken with effort and cold and go under. There was no time to fetch rope. No time to think. On hands and knees to spread out his weight, listening to the ice all the while, Jim crawled to Pete.

"Keep holding on!"

On the thinnest ice, Jim went down on his front, legs and arms spread, and he reached for Pete.

His fingertips touched Pete's mitten. Almost there. "Kick hard!"

Pete kicked and Jim grabbed his hand. Alas, the current twisted the boy and he slipped away. All Jim had of the boy was a mitten. A mitten to give to Mrs. Beck. He had to think fast. Act and think.

Due to fluctuations in level, there was an ice-free area down the pond where the water collected before spilling into the millrace. If he followed Pete's path under the ice, he could grab him and come up there. Jim took as deep a breath as ever he could and pulled himself over the edge of the ice, headfirst, into the frigid water.

He kicked with the current, eyes wide open in the dark water, watching for any sign of Pete. He was only a second or two behind the boy. The water's course wouldn't vary. If he could keep his breath and swim along in the channel, he could grab him. Jim's chest burned and his throat seized. Come on, where was he? An indistinct form, a boot…Pete. He had him!

Jim grabbed the back of the boy's jacket and pulled him under his arm. Dangerously short of air, choking in darkness, fighting to hold his breath, Jim kicked with the current. Seconds later the water swirled into an area clear of ice. Not a moment too soon. Jim grabbed the edge of the ice with his free hand and held on. Their chests heaved and they gasped and filled their lungs with air. As he held Pete up, Jim went under and inhaled murky water. A man threw them a rope and Jim gasped for air and mustered his dwindling strength to tie it round Pete so he could be pulled to safety.

The men pulled Pete across the ice like a harpooned seal.

Jim's consciousness narrowed, dimmed. So cold. So hard to breathe. Men's voices. Rope thrown to him. The man missed and tried again. Grip, grip hard, and kick and hold on. Ungodly cold, shivering, numb. Lying wet on the snow. A horse blanket and…nothing.

****

Reveling in the sunshine, Cora walked with a skip in her step to the music of birdsong all the way home. Home for one more week. She doubted that Jim would ever have proposed to Betsy Meyer but hearing that Betsy had turned her sights on Dr. Blackmore made Cora inexplicably happy. Surely Betsy's report of a match between Adeline and Jim could only be rumor. Mr. Brockett would forbid a courtship between Adeline and any young man who hadn't established himself financially.

How petty Cora was being. She should wish for

179

Jim's happiness. She tried to push him out of her mind and think of Niagara Falls and Robert and their wedding night. She would marry a rich and powerful man, a man who was most attentive to her needs and loved her very much, and she would love him in return. Jim would be her friend—they'd shaken on it on Christmas Day—and that would be that.

Pre-wedding jitters were normal and expected. Many a girl thought of the boy she could have married if life had taken a different turn. Everything was as it should be, wasn't it? Cora walked up the slushy lane and entered the cottage.

Odd. Aunt Jenny's carpet bag sat on the kitchen table.

Cora called out, "I'm home," and hung her cape on the coat rack.

Jenny walked into the kitchen, brushing her long silver hair all the while. "I'm glad," she said. "How's Betsy?"

"Thrilled to bits over the new doctor. She says she's in love."

"Good. Now Jim Sinclair can stop hiding."

"Aunt Jenny!" Cora shook her head. "Why is your bag on the table? And why are you arranging your hair in the middle of the afternoon?"

Jenny set down her brush and opened the top of her bag to extract a letter. "This is why." She handed the letter to Cora.

Cora read rapidly. The letter was from Miss Ivy MacDonnell's assistant. Ivy was unwell. Very unwell. Paralysis in her limbs, slurred speech. They didn't know what was wrong. A doctor in Brucedale diagnosed apoplexy and prescribed bedrest, but couldn't Miss

Patton come at once to see her dear friend and offer her opinion?"

"You must go," Cora agreed.

"The trouble is, I don't know how long I'll be needed. Your wedding is next week, but Ivy sounds terribly sick. I'll go, see Ivy, and send you a letter as soon as I have more information."

Cora nodded. "What train will you take?"

"The first one that comes. I'll go to the station as soon as I'm ready and wait there."

Cora saw her aunt's worry in the set of her mouth and her frenetic hair brushing. An old Patton habit. Suppress alarm with action. Push worry aside with work. Cora held out her arms to her aunt, and Jenny accepted her hug.

"Thank you, Cora. That's just what I needed," she whispered as she broke away.

Then, Jenny took a big breath, smoothed her skirt, and finished preparing for her journey to the orphanage.

****

As soon as Jenny left, Cora donned an apron, flung open the windows, and set to dusting and sweeping. For too long, they'd neglected their housekeeping. With the spring-like thaw and worry pressing once more, cleaning the cottage was Cora's ideal occupation until she heard a frantic knocking.

She opened the kitchen door. "Tom?" Cora's mind leapt to Mary, Tim, and baby Patrick.

Tom panted from exertion, and Cora bid him enter and sit, but he remained standing.

"It's Jim. They're getting a horse to fetch you. I ran ahead."

"Jim? Tom, please—"

"Jim went through the ice at the millpond, rescuing the Beck boy. Jim got him all right, but he's in a bad way."

"You mean Jim."

"Yes. Pete Beck is fine. Just cold and scared. It's Jim who's bad. He's not coming round."

Cora glanced at her open windows and at her satchel. At least she hadn't stoked the fire. She heard the beat of hooves in slush. "Quick, close the windows while I get my boots on."

Tom nodded and seconds later, Cora grabbed her satchel, and they rushed out the door.

Chapter 25

Mrs. Sinclair held the back door open and ushered Cora into the farmhouse kitchen with Tim and Tom close behind.

"Thank the Lord, you're here." Mrs. Sinclair's words tumbled forth in panic. "We've got Jimmy's wet clothes off and covered him in quilts. He's in the daybed by the stove. I sent the other boys away so you can do your work."

Cora nodded to her, crossed the kitchen, and knelt by the bed. Jim looked like death. His lips were blue, his skin was pale, and his hair was matted with muck. Cora assumed the same mucky substance had entered his lungs in some measure, and besides hypothermia, would present the chief obstacle to Jim's recovery.

"Jim. It's Cora. Can you hear me?" She peered closely at him, looking for any sign that he heard her and understood, but he only frowned briefly. It was something.

Cora slid her hand under the blankets to palpate his pulse. His wrist, heavy and thick from hard work, felt corpse-like, clammy, and limp, and his pulse was weak and thready. He needed warmth. Without warmth, Jim wouldn't stand a chance against any infection fomenting in his lungs.

Cora looked up at Mrs. Sinclair who hovered next to the bed, terrified for her son. "Do you have any more quilts?" Cora asked.

"Aye. Including one almost finished, on the frame."

"Fetch them please, Mrs. Sinclair, and we'll set Tom and Tim to warming them at the stove."

Mrs. Sinclair rushed away before Cora could ask if the kettle was full, so she told Tom to fill it. "He'll want a warm drink when he comes around," she said. If he would come around.

Cora found her stethoscope and listened to Jim's breathing. Through the earpiece, she heard what she dreaded most. Every breath Jim took was shallow, wet, and ragged and expended his precious energy. She sat back on her heels and thought. They had to warm him, and they had to reposition him to drain his lungs, and it was difficult to do both at once. She had to prioritize. She'd helped her father treat a similar case, the Finney girl who'd fallen down a well and made a full recovery. Cora mumbled Father's slogan to herself. "Breathing first, above all else."

Mrs. Sinclair returned with blankets and quilts and she and the O'Mallorys' covered Jim with a fumbling inefficiency universal to frightened loved ones. Cora glanced at the trio and considered her options. The brothers were strong, and Mrs. Sinclair was less distraught when she was assigned a task. In a few minutes, Tom and Tim had shifted Jim onto his front over pillows and Mrs. Sinclair had placed a basin of steaming water at the head of the bed. While the boys supported Jim, Cora percussed his back, praying her blows and the steam would loosen up the muck in his chest.

"Oh no," Tim exclaimed, sensing a change in his friend. "He's going to be—"

"Sick," yelped Tom as Jim's body heaved violently and he vomited all manner of filth into the basin. And then Jim coughed, and Cora thought it the most wonderful sound she had ever heard.

"That's it, love. Cough some more," she coached, and cough he did.

Cora was peripherally aware of Tom and Tim looking curiously at each other and Mrs. Sinclair sighing with relief.

Cora sponged and dried Jim's face, and the brothers eased him onto his side. Mrs. Sinclair and Cora tucked the warm blankets all around him. And then everyone stood and watched their patient.

If only Father were at the bedside with them. Or Aunt Jenny. Cora had a plan, but Jim's condition was grave, and she might have missed a detail, a new treatment, that would make a difference to him.

"His color's a little better," Mrs. Sinclair said hopefully.

Cora touched her shoulder and nodded. "Yes, Mrs. Sinclair, but he's very ill and he hasn't turned the corner yet. I'd like for the boys to fetch Dr. Blackmore."

"But Cora...we can't afford him," Mrs. Sinclair protested.

"Mr. Helston can. And will," said Cora. "Jim should have the best care possible."

Tom and Tim were already donning their hats and coats. "Water Street. We won't be long," said Tom as they hurried away.

After they left, Cora asked, "What about Mr. Sinclair? Shouldn't we fetch him too?"

Mrs. Sinclair shook her head sadly. "I don't think so, lass. He'll be in his cups at the poker table. Best leave him where he'll do less harm. Give Jim a wee bit o' peace."

Cora felt sick. She hadn't understood the extent of Jim's burden. "Mind if I stay and watch over him tonight, Mrs. Sinclair?"

"Mind? I'd like that very much. Stay, lass. Stay with him. Mind we're in your debt and we'll find a way to pay—"

"No need," said Cora. This was no time to think of anything other than Jim's recovery. They had to work together. Jim deserved all they could do for him and she could only pray it was enough. Cora returned to the bedside and sat with Jim and Mrs. Sinclair until Dr. Blackmore arrived.

****

An hour later he did. There was a sharp tap on the kitchen door, and carrying a walking stick and a black medical bag, Dr. Blackmore entered the kitchen with the O'Mallory boys close on his heels.

A pink flush had risen in Jim's cheeks and his breathing was regular, though it was still ragged and wet.

Blackmore assessed his new patient with a cursory glance. "Mr. James Sinclair. Well, well. Asleep, is he? I dare say, he requires sleep."

Obviously, thought Cora. Even a donkey knew enough to sleep off illness and injury. She rose from her chair and extended her hand. "Cora Patton."

"Miss Cora Patton. Well, well." Blackmore shook with a smooth hand. "I've made the acquaintance of your fiancé, and if I may be so bold, you are even more beautiful than Mr. Helston's description of you."

"Thank you," she said, averting her eyes from Blackmore and looking toward Jim. Cora felt as judged as a prize heifer at the county fair, and she was impatient to address the pressing matter of her patient's fragile health. "I trust the O'Mallorys told you what happened."

"Yes. Quite. A true hero is our Mr. Sinclair. Foolish to venture onto thin ice, however, and now he pays the piper."

"He saved a boy's life," Tom said. "He didn't have a choice now, did he, doc?"

Blackmore shrugged to suggest that Tom's assertion was an open question, then turned to Cora. "You've examined him."

"Yes. He was very hypothermic, so we wrapped him in hot blankets and he's warming up now. He was breathing at about twenty-eight breaths a minute. I percussed his chest and he coughed and expectorated a good deal and now he's breathing better, as you can see. Unfortunately, he hasn't been sufficiently alert to eat or drink safely."

Blackmore twisted his mustache thoughtfully. "Have you administered morphia?"

"No," said Cora. "That would suppress his cough and make him even more drowsy. We want him awake and coughing."

"Quite. Have you bled him?"

"No. My late father—he trained me—he rarely performed that procedure. He usually counselled his patients against it even if they requested it. There isn't evidence for its efficacy."

"Miss Patton," Blackmore scolded. "Bloodletting has been practiced for centuries and it's a standard treatment for pneumonia, which this patient will surely develop. I must insist…"

From her seat by her son, Mrs. Sinclair spoke up.

"Dr. Patton always said bleeding was quackery, except in rare cases. He said it sapped people's strength and the best it did was to make money for the doctor."

Evidently, Blackmore wasn't accustomed to being challenged. His voice rose. "If I'm to be your son's physician then I must treat him as I know best and that includes bloodletting."

"You're not his physician. Cora only wanted your opinion," said Mrs. Sinclair.

It occurred to Cora that Mrs. Sinclair was stretching the truth, though Cora herself wouldn't permit a knife to so much as scratch Jim's arm.

Blackmore smacked his walking stick on the floor. "Mrs. Sinclair. I am a fellow of the Royal College of Physicians. Do you actually mean to ignore my advice and leave him in the care of this girl?"

Mrs. Sinclair nodded. "The lass will do for my Jimmy."

"Quite. Well. I take my leave of you then. If I may be taken to Mr. Helston's residence. We have much to discuss," Blackmore said to Tim, seeming to prefer to address the timid brother.

Tom met Cora's eye, and he winked at her as he followed Tim and Dr. Blackmore out the door.

After they left, there was little to do but watch Jim and tend to his needs as they arose. Cora noticed Mrs. Sinclair's obvious fatigue and urged her to rest, which Mrs. Sinclair did after setting out bread and cheese for Cora. The only light in the kitchen was a single candle, burning on the table near the daybed. Alone with her patient, Cora settled back in her chair for a night of hopeful observation.

Through long hours, Cora left the cheese and bread

untouched.

Jim's slightest stirring jolted her to attention. On the other hand, if he lay quietly, she feared he was slipping away. If only he'd wake and call her "Spotsy" or "Miss Polka Dot", she could scold him for putting his life on the line. Yet Tom was right. Jim did what came naturally to him, always, and he had to dive into the frigid water to rescue Peter Beck. Any red-blooded Maryville man would have done the same, wouldn't he? Cora pushed the notion from her mind that some men would've stayed on the bank and let the boy drown.

Shortly before midnight, Mr. Sinclair stumbled through the door, bragging that he took the final hand with a full house of aces and queens for his heroic lad Jimmy. Cora suggested he tell his son about his win in the morning, and to her relief, he staggered off to bed, as certain he'd see his son alive in a few hours as the sun would rise.

The kitchen was quiet again and cooling off. For Jim's sake, Cora had to keep the room warm. She opened the stove door for light, went to the bin, and filled her arm with evenly split birch logs, a routine chore and one she undertook several times a day in winter. As she pushed the logs into the stove, she realized they were cut and split in the same expert way as the logs that had been secretly placed in the wood box at the cottage in November. She felt as if she were wiping a frosty window and seeing through it clearly for the first time. Jim had filled the wood box, not Robert, though Robert had claimed the credit. She pushed the implications of this fact from her mind.

Fire fueled and stoked, Cora dropped back in her chair and looked at Jim. Fast asleep, face mercifully untroubled, eyes closed under thick, dark brows, lips parted to ease his labored breath. Tomorrow his mother and she would wash his matted hair, sponge him down, and pull a night shirt over him, if he was strong enough. He had to be strong enough. Cora prayed to God to make him strong enough.

Jim frowned and mumbled indistinctly and beads of sweat broke over his brow. Cora sat up. Too soon to know if these signs marked improvement or decline.

She leaned close to his ear. "Jim. It's Cora. I'm right here beside you."

Jim's frown softened and his face relaxed.

"Nod if you hear me," she whispered, and he nodded once.

"You need to drink. I'm going to give you some broth and medicine."

After she propped him up on a pillow, Cora dribbled a few small spoonsful of salty broth and a spoonful of expectorant into Jim's mouth before he lapsed back into a fitful sleep. With her fingers, she combed his hair from his forehead and whispered again, "You must be strong, love. Promise me you will be strong."

More mumbling, more restlessness, and a cough, and then Jim slept calmly. An hour later, Cora heard a soft rap on the door. It was Kate O'Mallory.

"I was up with Mary and the baby, and once they settled, I had Patrick bring me. I knows where I'm needed," said Kate. "The Catholic women will see he's cared for proper."

And the Lutheran, Methodist, and Anglican women as well as the women of Jim's own Presbyterian church, thought Cora.

"Sleep a spell, Cora. I'll watch over him and wake

you if we need you," said Kate. "Take the rocking chair and I'll take the chair by the bed."

Though Kate was bossy, Cora was content to be bossed. She left a bottle of medicine on the table for Kate to administer if Jim woke and she napped fitfully for an hour. Cora awakened with a wry neck, but she didn't complain.

Everyone in the Sinclair farmhouse survived the night.

Chapter 26

Cora collapsed into her own bed early in the morning after receiving Kate's promise that she'd be summoned immediately if Jim's condition changed. When she awoke at eleven, she set a fire in the stove, heated some water, and washed at the basin before the looking glass. She'd spent the night at the Sinclairs' in the same frock she'd worn to visit Betsy, and when she got home, she'd changed into her nightgown and left the frock draped in all its satin glory over the foot of the bed. Cora hung the fussy garment in the wardrobe and slipped on her gray dress, ready for whatever the day would bring.

That was plenty.

As she dined on a cold lunch of oat biscuits and cheese, the postman pushed the day's mail through the letter slot in the front door. Cora fetched two letters and read them while eating. The first was a note from the elder Mrs. MacTavish to confirm the menu of refreshments that the Presbyterian ladies would provide for the wedding reception, and could Cora please reply at her earliest convenience? Cora tucked the missive back in its envelope and pushed it aside.

The second letter was from the orphanage, hastily written last evening and sent on the first train to Maryville that very morning. Cora stopped chewing as she read Aunt Jenny's staccato scrawl. Ivy was profoundly ill. Worse than Aunt Jenny had expected. Not only were Ivy's limbs flaccid, but the poor woman was incontinent. No one else was sick, Aunt Jenny ruled out food poisoning, and though she didn't think the cause was infectious because Ivy had no fever, Aunt Jenny was isolating her from the staff and children, just in case. Cora wasn't to come to the orphanage as she was surely needed in Maryville, but Aunt Jenny couldn't predict how long she would stay in Brucedale. She might even miss Cora's wedding.

Cora decided to search their medical texts for any information that might help and write a reply. And she'd share the awful news of Jim's near drowning. As she finished her lunch, there was a knock on the front door. Cora's heart leapt with trepidation, and she hastened to answer it. Thank God, it was only Robert and not a panicked member of Jim's circle.

"My darling. I hoped I'd find you home." Robert smiled broadly.

Despite the confusion of the last twenty-four hours, Cora was glad to see him, and she cared not a jot that Aunt Jenny wasn't home to chaperone. He stepped inside, doffed his hat and frockcoat, and swept her into his arms. How good it felt to be held, to be supported, to not have to think for a moment but only exist in the arms of a man who loved her. If she ever told him of her friendship with Jim, Robert wouldn't understand, let alone tolerate it, but he could understand the distress of her duty and her sorrow for an old classmate.

"I wondered if you had need of your fiancé," said Robert.

She led him to the sitting room, and they sat close on the loveseat, Cora relating the terrible news of the prior day, Robert listening and murmuring his sympathy.

After she shared her burden, Robert said quietly, "Dr. Blackmore paid me a visit last night."

So that was it. That was the real reason for Robert's visit. As Cora began to rebut the unfounded accusations Dr. Blackmore had surely made, Robert placed his index finger lightly over her lips.

"Hush, my dear Cora. You've no need to defend yourself." He kissed her forehead, then continued. "I'm only telling you, so you're apprised of Dr. Blackmore's animosity toward you, and you can govern yourself accordingly."

Cora sat back and said archly, "How might that be, Robert?"

"Don't confront him. Go about your work diligently in your aunt's absence. Let me handle him, man to man. And when we marry, take a long break from caring for others, entirely devote yourself to being my wife, and let him either find his sea legs or founder."

"His sea legs? You mean I should let him bleed Maryville dry and seduce his young, female patients?"

"Cora, you can't fight every battle. Whether you like it or not, Maryville has a new doctor. Admittedly not the caliber of your late father, yet he is a proud 'fellow of the Royal College'. Don't roll your eyes. Hear me out, please."

"Go on."

"Charles Tucker will soon imbibe from Heaven's pearly brandy snifter, and justified or not, people will blame the doctor for his death. Blackmore will probably slide his hand up Miss Meyer's leg a little too far for her father's liking. In other words, he'll make mistakes, Cora, and he'll either sink or swim."

Cora stared straight ahead, and Robert continued. "Don't you see how this could play out? You'll marry me on Wednesday and give him plenty of rope to either hang or save himself. If need be, Maryville can start searching for a new doctor sooner rather than later. If Blackmore shows himself to be an incompetent scoundrel, you can step in until the committee recruits another doctor. If he proves his mettle, you can apply your talent to advising on a new hospital."

With misgiving, Cora nodded. Sometimes Robert's Machiavellian intellect frightened her. And yet, it attracted her too. He understood the world in ways she did not. As he drew her close, she realized she was in love with two men, both clever, both tall and darkly handsome, both brazenly proud, masculine, and confident.

The only guarantee in life was death, and in this moment, Robert and she were alive together. The day itself would die with nightfall and never return. Cora was tired of struggling alone. She had to learn to trust this man who would be her husband.

Robert's eyes beheld hers with ice-blue intensity. He whispered, "I love you," and then he kissed her deeply, passionately, as they had kissed so often before.

"May I amuse you in a new way?" His voice was a low, husky growl.

Before she could answer, Cora felt the slip of his hand at the top of her bodice. He meant to fondle her.

"No!" she cried.

He squeezed her softness, hard enough to hurt her.

"Oh!" She winced and tried to twist away, but he held her tightly. "Please stop!"

"Darling. Did I hurt you?" Too slowly, he removed

his hand.

"Yes." Tears stung her eyes. How could he think she would welcome such a violation?

"I thought you'd enjoy that."

He must have known she wouldn't. She wiggled away. He sat next to her, but he didn't touch her.

"My darling. What do you think will happen on our wedding night?" he asked in a low voice.

What indeed? Cora didn't dare answer. If Robert were angry, he could do far worse than grope her.

"I'm sorry." He pulled her against him and hugged her. "I shouldn't have."

"It's okay," Cora said warily. For several minutes they sat together, and she pretended to be comforted. When his body relaxed and she was quite certain his lust had abated, she asked casually, "Robert, who delivers your firewood?"

"Oscar Landry."

"He doesn't usually supply birch."

"No, I suppose not. Though I don't notice things like that. Why do you ask?"

"Aunt Jenny likes to keep birch on hand so it's easier for her to start the stove. She'll need a steady supply when I'm not here."

"That's my darling Cora. Always thinking of others," said Robert.

Cora laughed to cover her sorrow. She loved her fiancé, and she knew he loved her, but for some time she'd doubted his honesty. Now she had proof that he could hurt her and lie to her, and she could lie to him. They could be utterly false while pretending they were true. They would build their life together on a foundation of sand. Rifts were already forming between them.

Perhaps Robert knew and didn't mind, for with marriage he would possess her regardless. The wedding was six days away. How she wished she could seek Father's counsel.

Cora kissed Robert on his cheek and rose from the loveseat. After he left, she wrote to Aunt Jenny to broach the idea of postponing the wedding and posted the letter enroute to the Sinclair farm.

****

By mid-afternoon, the clouds dispersed, and the sun glowed like a torch across the icy fields. Clear skies and a northern breeze portended a return to cold nights. The snow crackled underfoot as Cora walked up the Sinclairs' lane. Fritz, the farm's deaf, one-eyed mutt, greeted her with a tail wag then resumed his afternoon round of the barnyard. Pitchfork in hand, Tom waved from the paddock where Buttercup, a dairy cow, and a couple of Highland steers placidly munched on hay before their return to the barn for the night. As soon as Cora entered the kitchen, Kate donned her coat.

"Your turn, Cora," she said gruffly. "It's you he wants anyway. Broke into a bit of a fever, oh, about two o'clock, and mumbled your name. You'll find him mostly unchanged."

"Has he eaten?" Cora hung her cape and bonnet on a peg.

"A half cup of broth. And the medicine, every four hours like you wrote on the bottle. He coughs but he's not strong enough to sit and cough up the phlegm proper."

"Has he passed water?"

"Yes. Dark and only a little, mind."

"How's Mrs. Sinclair holding up?"

Kate took Cora's elbow, steered her outside where they wouldn't be overheard, and spoke in a low tone. "They're the queerest family I ever did see. I'm Morag's friend so I'll say it plain. She knows how sick her son is, but she moaned and whimpered over her 'headache' until I sent her off to bed. Don't get me started on James senior. If ever a more useless excuse for a man walked God's green earth, I haven't made his acquaintance."

"Oh," said Cora. "Mrs. Sinclair has never mentioned a headache to me."

"No. Why would she? She can suffer as if she were Job and take to her bed when it suits, whenever things get tough. Does a spot of work in the morning, feeds the chickens and such, and by afternoon she's done for the day. If you gave her medicine, she might get better, and that wouldn't do. I don't know where Jim got his character, but it wasn't from his parents."

"Thanks for telling me all this, Kate," said Cora. "Do you think we should send for Jim's grandmother?"

"I don't know. She's only away at her daughter's a couple more days. Let's leave her be unless Jim gets worse." Kate tightened her boot lace, speaking all the while. "There's plenty of food. Everyone loves our Jim and the women of Maryville seem to think their cooking will snatch him back from the brink. Adeline Brockett even sent a case of grapefruit. I can't imagine what it cost. Anyway, you won't starve tonight."

"Am I to stay, then?"

Kate straightened and gave Cora an odd smile. "I don't think anyone else will do."

After a quick good-bye, Cora went to sit with Jim. He slept fitfully with a single quilt for cover. His forehead glistened with perspiration, and he shivered.

Someone, presumably Kate, had washed him and dressed him in a cotton nightshirt. His thick, wavy black hair was clean though damp with sweat, and he'd soon have a beard if his stubble weren't addressed. Cora wouldn't shave him. Let Jim grow a beard. Maybe when he was well again, he'd keep it.

When he was well again. He had to get better. She had so many things to say to him. She'd been cruelly indifferent to his natural decency. She'd made the mistake of condemning him for his wildness. His fearsome recklessness blinded her to his goodness. Jim was a man who lived by his own rules, not those imposed by others, and he lived passionately, freely, honestly, and generously because of it. To voice her apologies when he was so sick would be self-serving and hollow and wouldn't help him. The only thing she could do for Jim now was to follow his example. Abandon rules of decorum and do what mattered.

She leaned closer. "Jim. It's me, Cora."

His dark, deep-set eyes fluttered open and rolled closed again.

"Jim. Can you hear me?"

He nodded, then tried and failed to turn in bed to face her.

"I'll roll you onto your side, okay?"

Another weak nod.

Cora took hold of Jim's far shoulder and found him feverish. "Roll on the count of three and I'll pull too."

The task accomplished, Jim coughed hard, expectorating a wad of phlegm.

"Good work," Cora praised. "I'll bet no one has ever complimented you for that."

Jim smiled, barely perceptibly, only a tiny tension at

the corners of his mouth, but unmistakable.

"Rest. I'll heat some broth."

Though the broth couldn't be too hot on account of that fever. If Aunt Jenny or Father were here, she would ask for advice. Cora had tucked a text on respiratory ailments in her satchel, but she knew what it said without reading it. Fever was nature's way of fighting pneumonia. On the other hand, too high a fever damaged organs and could bring on seizures, even death. Father's brand-new oral thermometer was lost with him, and she'd only her wrist to judge Jim's temperature. Should she let his fever run its course, or lower it with cool compresses and willow bark powder?

Jim was dehydrated. Kate said he'd only voided a small amount, and he was losing fluid through perspiration and phlegm. Cora felt his forehead with her wrist. Definitely febrile. After a momentary deliberation, she made her decision and stood.

Jim had to drink to loosen the phlegm and fight the infection and he would drink more if he felt better. "Time for supper," she muttered as she poured broth into a shallow pan on the stove. Lukewarm would be plenty hot. She'd heat it only enough to make it palatable. She mixed the willow bark powder with a spoonful of jam. No mixing medicine with his supper. That could break trust. As the broth warmed, she went outside and scooped some snow into a bowl to cool some flannel cloths.

At the bedside again, supper tray ready. She had to prop Jim up so he wouldn't choke. By the look of him, he weighed nearly two hundred pounds, all muscle. Should she find his parents? Maybe Tom was still in the barn? Cora looked at Jim and shrugged. They'd manage.

Cora got two big pillows ready. "Time to sit up. You're going to help me. Understand?"

A faint, "yes."

Good enough. "I'll help you too. I'm putting your arms around my shoulders and, on the count of three, you sit."

By the grace of God and bare necessity, they managed. With Cora's help, Jim sat up and she whisked the pillows behind his back. She mopped his face with a cold cloth to wake him more. Medicine first, willow bark and expectorant, and then a cup of broth, taken by spoon.

Finally, Jim drank enough broth to do him good. Cora could have cried with relief. He'd earned a rest and afterward she'd listen to his lungs with her stethoscope and try to loosen up the phlegm wherever it was blocking his breathing.

Chapter 27

Jim existed in a limbo between life and death. He had a vague awareness of day and night. He heard women's voices…Cora, Mama, Kate, Agnes Cameron, Moira Kelly, Gran…a choir of angels who soothed, coaxed, sang, whispered, and prayed. When he moved, he felt broken, as if he'd been trampled by a bull. He fought for air, fought hard, but he was under the ice, suffocating.

Where was Peter Beck? He must find Pete.

From the surface, Cora's voice called to Jim, and he called back. If she heard him, she'd know what to do. She'd understand. "Cora." The syllables gurgled in his throat. "Cora."

"I'm here, love."

Cora. Love. He tried to lift his arm, tried to reach out to her. Too weak, too weak to struggle anymore, drifting back into the mud. All was darkness.

Jim lost time itself.

He felt something cold pressing against his forehead. He burned like a boiler.

Her voice again. "Here love. It's me, Cora. Can you open your eyes?"

He could. Colors. A copper halo, creamy skin, a graceful gray form, open-armed. Cora. His angel Cora.

"Jim. Stay with me. Open your eyes again, love."

He had to tell her. Tell her about the boy. Under the

ice. "Pete."

"Peter Beck? He's fine, Jim. He'll be back at school today. It's Monday, the first of February."

He slept again.

****

After five long days and nights, Jim slept quietly without chill or fever for the first time. Cora watched his chest rise and fall evenly. The tension in his face eased, and though his cheeks were hollow, his color was normal. At last, he was out of the woods.

Cora wished she could stay by his side and watch him awaken to the world, but that morning she had to visit Robert to postpone their wedding. She could predict Robert's reaction—crestfallen yet understanding.

What Robert didn't know and what she would never tell him was that Jim was strong enough to do without her presence now. A force, an invisible bond, pulled Cora to Jim, and though logic dictated she should sever it and simply love her fiancé, she could not. It was selfish and wrong and utterly bewildering, but she loved both men.

More time. Today that was all she would ask of Robert.

****

"Darling!" exclaimed Robert when Cora knocked on the door jamb and peeked into his office. A wide smile on his face, he placed his pen on his blotter, and stood with open arms to welcome her.

"May I interrupt your work, Robert?" She stood in the doorway.

"Of course you may, Cora. Always and ever." Observing her cool attitude, he slumped back in his chair.

The wan cast of Robert's face, his damp shirt with sleeves rolled up, the papers piled upon his desk, and his earnest blue eyes scolded Cora more deeply than words could ever. She should leave. Instead, she took the chair opposite him.

Before she could change her mind, she blurted, "I think we should postpone our wedding."

At once, his features crumpled into an expression of wounded shock. "Postpone?" he echoed. "Why?"

"With everything happening. Aunt Jenny away, a patient in grave condition, the demands of your business affairs." She gestured over his desk. "Wouldn't it be better to wait until spring? June is the luckiest of months and I've heard Niagara is beautiful in late spring."

"Cora, I'm working hard now so we can marry on Wednesday. As we planned, together. Your aunt despises me, so her absence is preferable. The feeble and ill are always among us. You're not superstitious and Niagara is beautiful in any season. Your excuses for a postponement are nonsensical."

He was right. She had no defense against his accusation. "I need more time," Cora said gently.

Robert slouched back and rubbed his day-old beard as if negotiating a tricky deal, though the sadness in his eyes betrayed his pain. "All right. May I ask what has changed?"

"Nothing's changed. I still wish to marry you."

"Come now. If that were true, we'd marry on Wednesday. In fairness, you must tell me, so I'll ask again. What has changed?"

"I assure you it's nothing, Robert. Only my feminine foibles. Only my intuition that it would be better to begin our marriage with unhurried dignity. I feel as if our wedding is a looming deadline instead of a celebration. If fate is kind to us, I will only be a bride once, and I want our wedding to be perfect. The time is too short. I only ask for more of it. More time."

"Very well. You may have it."

"Thank you," said Cora.

Robert didn't rise from his chair to embrace her. He only nodded once. "You'll inform those who must know of our decision to postpone."

"Yes," said Cora. "I will."

As she walked down Main Street, Cora met Mrs. Brockett and Mrs. Jones walking arm in arm, each dressed in somber shades, wearing a black veiled hat, and carrying a basket. Someone had died.

"Good day, Mrs. Brockett, Mrs. Jones." One couldn't simply ask, who was it? Cora bowed slightly. "So sad, isn't it?" she ventured.

"Indeed, it is, my child," said Mrs. Brockett. "But you and Dr. Blackmore did your best for Mr. Tucker, so you mustn't fret. The good man is with our Shepherd in Heaven now, and his suffering mercifully has ended."

"Poor Mrs. Tucker," said Cora.

"They loved each other to the end," agreed Mrs. Jones. "All we can do is offer our comfort in her time of sorrow."

"I mustn't delay you from your condolence call." Cora stopped herself from curtsying in the presence of these esteemed ladies. "Please, could you tell me when I might pay my respects?"

Mrs. Brockett replied, "Any time, Miss Patton. As you are to be married, I'm certain Mrs. Tucker will understand if you are absent from the funeral on Thursday and pay your respects either prior to or after your wedding."

"Mrs. Tucker speaks highly of your care for Mr. Tucker," added Mrs. Jones. "I believe I'm on firm ground when I say that she shall be most pleased to receive you."

"Thank you," Cora said bashfully. "Mr. Helston will wish to delay our wedding when he receives the news of Mr. Tucker's passing. They were firm friends and he'll be stricken with grief."

"In times of trial, one makes sacrifices," said Mrs. Brockett. "By the way, how is young Mr. Sinclair?"

"Improving day by day," said Cora.

"How wonderful. Adeline has been in knots with worry, and she'll be so pleased to hear it. At her request, the vicar led our entire congregation in a special prayer vigil at St. George's on Sunday. God intervenes for those in his broad flock who are deserving."

"So He does, Mrs. Brockett," said Cora.

Mrs. Jones puffed her chest proudly. "Jim certainly cheered up my Helen when she suffered from mumps last December. She's a pretty girl, though vain, and she had cheeks like a chipmunk gathering nuts, but he entertained her as if she were a beautiful princess and he a court jester, and he restored her spirits. Eighteen is such a difficult age for a girl. Jim had the mumps as a small boy and felt quite safe spending time with her while she was housebound."

"That's so like him. Always cheering people up," said Cora. Now she did curtsy—involuntarily. "I mustn't keep you from Mrs. Tucker."

"As ever, duty beckons its Christian women," said Mrs. Brockett. "Good day, Miss Patton."

As Cora parted from the matrons, she felt as if the

world were rocking under her feet. How could she be so stupid? Only minutes ago, she postponed her wedding to a man who would make a wonderful husband because she believed she shared a special bond with Jim. However, half the women in Maryville felt the same way as evidenced by the avalanche of food, calling cards, and letters entering the Sinclair home every day and the hastily organized, well-attended prayer circle petitioning for divine intervention on Jim's behalf. When Jim recovered, Cora would join a queue of women who thought he adored them exclusively and who vied for his favors.

She could turn around this very second, run to Robert, tell him she'd changed her mind, and beg his forgiveness for hurting him. She wouldn't. She'd asked for more time, he'd granted it, and she'd take it.

Before she had met Mrs. Brockett and Mrs. Jones, Cora had planned to stop in at Beck's to check on Hilda and Martin, ask after Peter, and buy some tea, flour, and soda powder. Numb with confusion, fatigue, and regret, she walked directly home instead.

****

On schedule, the mail arrived as Cora awoke. Befogged from sleep, she collected it at the front door and shuffled through it in the hallway. A letter from a cousin in Scotland addressed to Aunt Jenny, an invitation to a meeting of the Maryville chapter of the Temperance Union, and a letter from Brucedale. Cora added the first two letters to the pile of mail waiting for Aunt Jenny on the desk, then opened the third.

Dear Cora,

We'll converse at length when I return to Maryville, probably Thursday (you've been warned!), so I'll keep this letter short.

Ivy is getting better, little by little. Fortunately, the paralysis hasn't affected her breathing. She's coming to her senses, able to sit up for short periods, grasp weakly, move her toes, and I hope to God the worst is behind us. Sometimes you have to almost lose someone before you realize how precious they are. Aren't I the wise old sage?

I'm not a prayerful person as I doubt God intercedes in earthly affairs, but for Ivy and Jim, I'm making an exception. I do hope he's getting better. I'm glad you're considering cancelling your wedding so Jim has you with him.

Oceans of love,
Aunt Jenny

"Postponing, not cancelling," muttered Cora. Perhaps the "wise old sage" would help Cora right her up-side-down world when she returned on Thursday. The future was a giant question mark for all of them and Cora could only hope she wasn't making the biggest mistake of her life.

Chapter 28

Late in the afternoon, Cora returned to the farmhouse to find Jim seated in a chair, being shaved by his doting grandmother.

"Got to look handsome," old Mrs. Sinclair cooed. "What do you think, Cora?"

"Handsome is as handsome does," Cora replied breezily as she took off her cape and readied herself for work.

"Ach, then it's a mighty good thing he does as he looks." Mrs. Sinclair laughed and pinched Jim's cheek. "Too thin though."

Jim looked helplessly at Cora, then grinned dangerously, dark eyes lively with mischief. "Cora will fatten me up."

"Aye. So, she will," agreed Mrs. Sinclair. The old woman, as wide as she was tall, turned to Cora. "I've chicken soup in the heavy pot, and a gruel of oats and cream in the saucepan. Take your pick. Either meal will do for the likes of him." She toweled off Jim's face with a damp cloth. "There. Presentable."

"Thank you, Gran," said Jim.

As if by predetermined arrangement, Mrs. Sinclair took the basin to the door, threw the sudsy water into the snow, and bustled out of the kitchen leaving Cora and Jim alone. Cora was used to caring for a semi-comatose, inert Jim, not a fully conscious, virile Jim dressed in a loose linen shirt and wool trousers, slouching casually in a chair. Though she'd seen all of him when he was sick, today was different. Her eyes wandered over his broad shoulders, his powerful chest and arms, and the curl of hair at the opening of his collar. Even after a week's illness, he looked as if he could pull a locomotive single-handedly.

Cora looked about the room to keep from staring. To make matters worse, the bed was made and the kitchen was spic and span, with no chore undone to occupy her. The Sinclairs should have sent word that they didn't need her. Now she stood in their house with nothing to do, awkward as a mule on skates, before a man she loved but hadn't admitted openly to loving.

"Are you hungry?" she asked.

"No. Gran force-fed me some stew an hour ago."

"Well then, I should—"

"Make us some tea and sit with me, Cora. Please." He nudged a chair toward her with his foot. "Don't be a stranger."

"But you're so much better. You don't need me now."

"I do need you." Jim forced a cough for effect, and then coughed for real, a benign hack of the sort that lingered long after the patient was better otherwise. "I need to talk to you."

Cora nodded, and they spoke of trivial matters as she prepared the tea.

After she took the proffered chair, Jim said, "First of all, thank you. You saved my life."

"The men at the mill saved you," she corrected. "And I'm not the only one who watched over you."

"I'll thank them too when I see them. Gran told me

you've been here every night, bringing medicine and keeping me alive. She said I'd be dead if it weren't for you."

Cora poured the tea into mugs. "You were strong enough to survive an ordeal that would have killed most men. Peter Beck was lucky you were there for him."

Jim fixed his eyes on Cora's with an intensity that flustered her. He said, "I'm missing five days of my life. I want to know what happened."

"What do you remember?"

"Strange things. Sometimes I felt like I was being smothered and I was really scared. Other times, when I heard your voice or felt your touch, I was at peace. I was delirious but everything felt real. It was as if you were pulling me up to a garden in paradise and everything would be okay. You were with me at my lowest. I was unwashed, messy, and helpless and you didn't turn away. I was in a desolate hell, and you were my angel."

"I'm flattered you think so, but I didn't do anything remarkable, Jim. We all supported you through it…your mother and your grandma, Kate, Moira, Agnes, and Tom."

"How close did I come to not making it?"

"Very close. Your lungs were filled with fluid. I was terrified we'd lose you."

"So Gran wasn't overstating the matter then."

"No."

"It's ironic. I almost lost my life and I feel stronger."

"You'll be well again soon."

"Don't misunderstand me, Cora. What I mean is, I've gained courage. The courage to say what I think, to say what I have to say. And do what is right, regardless of consequences."

"After confronting death, any other risk seems small by comparison? That kind of courage?"

"Exactly." Jim's black eyes pierced Cora's defenses, demanding honest courage in return. "Do you ever think of Christmas Eve? The night we rode together to Brucedale? How happy we were in each other's company? How natural and right everything felt?"

"Yes. Every single day," Cora replied softly.

"I do too."

Neither spoke for a moment. Each peered at the other, acknowledging their unspoken bond for the first time since that night. Jim extended his hand, still rough from manual work, and Cora took it. How right it felt to touch him. He wasn't her patient now. He was simply a man.

"After they took off my wet clothes, did anyone mention finding a letter? In my vest pocket?"

"No. Not as I recall. Was it important?"

"Yes. I wrote it to you. I carried it with me for days because I was too afraid to mail it, too afraid to give it to you myself in case you wouldn't speak to me again after you read it."

"Me?"

"You."

"I suppose you must tell me what you wrote."

"I wrote that I love you and I asked you not to marry Robert Helston. And this week you'll be married."

"Jim, the wedding is postponed."

"Postponed? That's fantastic!" First he laughed, and then he questioned her. "It's a technicality, but you said 'postponed', not 'cancelled'. You're still his fiancée?"

"At this point, yes. I was worried to pieces about you, and I didn't want to vanish when you needed care."

"What does 'at this point' mean?"

"Just what you think it does."

"How about 'needed care'? If I hadn't gotten sick, would you marry Helston this week?"

"I don't know." She shrugged. "Probably."

A shadow of disappointment fell over Jim's face. "Fair enough. Now that I'm okay, are you going to run back to Helston?"

"No." Cora pulled her hand away, exasperated. How vexing Jim's questions were. If she answered with a lie, he would see through it, and the truth hurt him. Choosing her words carefully, she said, "I asked for the postponement because I need time, and Robert generously granted it."

"Generously? Cora, Helston is many things and generous isn't one of them. Whatever he gives is an investment with an expectation of profit."

"You know nothing about him," Cora protested. "I think you're jealous."

"Yes, I am. Because I love you."

"Jim, you could marry any girl in Maryville and judging by what I've heard, you've been very thorough in your selection process. Maybe I'm the one who should question you."

"I haven't made promises to anyone."

"But you toy with girls' hearts. How do I know I'm not another bead on a string of girls to whom you've pledged you love?"

"Because you aren't. I'm many terrible things, Cora, but I'm not a liar and I don't trick women by pledging love I don't feel. The other party understands the terms and joins me willingly. You're the only woman I love."

In a flash, envy consumed Cora. She imagined him

with other women. How could she be so naïve? A stolen kiss under mistletoe, a lingering hand on a waist while dancing, the offer of his arm on the stairs—that was tolerable. However, the idea of Jim performing acts on other women that should be reserved for marriage was not. She was losing control of her emotions and giving away her power. As ever, Jim was gaining the advantage even in his weakened state.

Worse, he read her like a book, and he teased her. "I won't fool around anymore if you break your engagement," he said. "It's an exclusive offer."

How she longed for him to hold her, but he was too smart and too proud by half. He thought she was a pushover. Their Christmas Eve ride was in keeping with the pattern of his life. A few clever jokes, a dash of charm, a hang-dog look, and she'd eat from his hand like Betsy Meyer, Adeline Brockett, Helen Jones, and God knew who else. He was dangerous. He had to be tamed.

Cora spoke coldly as she rose. "I'm not negotiating a contract with you, Jim. I have to go."

Her response had the effect of a card table upended mid-hand, and he reeled from her cruelty. "Cora!"

"Jim," she mocked.

He stood and seized her hand. "I'm sorry."

"If you say so." Cora shook her hand away from his. She meant to stomp off that instant, but fury overcame her good sense. Green eyes glowing with indignation, she said, "I thought what we had on Christmas Eve was pure and beautiful and maybe we could have that again. But you've spoiled things by dragging in other people and crowding out the love. Your parade of lovers, Robert, all of them. You've made things complicated by placing demands on me, by asking me to change my life at the snap of your fingers, while you pretend that your skirt-chasing is meaningless."

"Jesus. I said I'm sorry, Cora. Other girls don't mean anything to me. I guess I'm conventional. I can't handle the idea of Helston being with you."

"Then we're at an impasse. I'm not ready to break the engagement just to meet your 'terms'."

"I love you and I won't compromise," Jim said stiffly. "You're right, Cora. You'd better go."

****

Without a word, she left. He sat for a long while, staring at her vacant chair. Eventually, the loneliness of the kitchen felt suffocating, like being caught under the ice or fighting pneumonia. Jim dreaded talking to anyone. He couldn't face Gran's sympathy, Tom's humor, Mama's fretting, or a do-gooder snoop happening by. Dad had made himself scarce, thank God. Jim had to get out of the house. Escape. Still lethargic, he donned his jacket and cap, poured oil into the lantern, and lit the wick. Off he trudged, tired and demoralized, feet heavy as stone.

As he approached the barn, the familiar odors of hay and straw, manure, and the pungency of animals comforted him. Buttercup usually pushed against her stall door and whinnied before he even entered the barn, but he didn't hear her. Had the sound of his footsteps changed because of being sick?

Tom had kept everything in fine order. The floor of the barn was swept, the pens had fresh bedding, and the animals were healthy, fed, and watered. Daisy had been milked. But where was Buttercup? Jim peered into her stall. Empty. Her curry comb, filled with horsehair, and her hoof pick had been left on a ledge where they didn't belong, her blanket had been tossed into the corner of the stall, and her bridle was missing from the tack hook. Tom wouldn't ride her, especially not at night. Jim went to the paddock in case she had been forgotten outside. No Buttercup.

Damn. Sickness burned in his throat. He was too tired to walk to the field, too winded to whistle for her in the night. He sat on an overturned crate, put his hands on his knees, and chased his breath. There had to be a logical explanation for Buttercup's disappearance. Tom wouldn't have taken her. He would have told Mama or Gran if she were sick or lame. Usually no one else besides Mama and Dad came into the barn. A horse thief wouldn't brush the mare's coat and clean her hooves before stealing her away.

Dad. He'd taken her. He'd steal a crippled man's cane to pay off a gambling debt if the collector threatened violence. The temptation of a valuable mare was too much for him. Jim could write the script. *They're only keeping her as collateral, son. I'll win her back. Don't worry. The pay-off will be worth it.* Jim couldn't chance a walk into town in his condition and finding Buttercup wasn't an errand for Mama or Gran. He could only wait. As soon as Dad stumbled home, he'd find out who bought Buttercup and get her back.

As he mustered the strength to walk back to the house, he heard the clomp of hooves on the icy flagstone outside the barn. The door swung open. Buttercup. With a loose rein she led the sloppy disgrace who claimed to be his father through the doorway.

After a few seconds of concerted focusing, the older man slurred, "It's Jim! You're up and about again. Won't your Mama be pleased."

Jim scanned Buttercup for signs of abuse as she clopped toward him, whinnying, wild-eyed, and impatient. "That's it, girl. I'm here." Ignoring his father, he took hold of her bridle and hugged his equine pal. "A carrot for you tonight."

"She doesn't deserve it. Won't be ridden even bareback. Damned fool horse." His father swayed, then leaned against the wall of the pigsty. "Oh, she looks sound enough, but she's mad, and the buyer wouldn't take her. Guess I gotta find some other sucker."

Jim looked sideways at his father as he removed the bridle and turned Buttercup into her stall. There wouldn't be another buyer. Jim would see to that. "Who was tonight's sucker?" he asked casually.

"The newspaper guy. Helston. He heard you wouldn't need a horse anymore, and thought he'd do us a favor."

"Is that right?" Jim filled a bucket of water from the trough.

"Yup. He reneged. Horse wouldn't even let him touch'er. Just kicked and fussed."

"And you didn't ride her either?"

"Nope. Same damned problem."

"She's a wise judge of character." Jim patted Buttercup's neck. "Aren't you? So smart."

"What's that, Son?"

Jim didn't reply. He watered and fed the mare, fastened her blanket over her back, and put away the grooming tools, his fatigue erased by furious energy. Tasks completed, he latched the stall, and turned. "You still here?"

"Don't be rude, Son. I didn't raise you to speak that way."

"I'll speak how I want. Buttercup isn't for sale. If you ever touch her again, I swear I will hurt you."

"Hurt me?" The older man stepped forward and pushed Jim hard. "You can't. You're too weak. Too nice and likable. You're a girl's boy, not a man."

In an instant, years of suppressed rage coursed through Jim, and he threw a right cross, hitting his father with a sickening crack. The older man lurched and fell. Too drunk to sense pain, he spat out a tooth, tested his jaw, and rubbed the side of his face. Then he struggled to his feet, threw a wild jab, and staggered away, presumably to nurse his sore mouth in bed.

Exhaustion consuming him once more, Jim slumped down on the crate to catch his breath. Rubbing the pain from his knuckles, he looked at Buttercup, her big, black eyes shining back in the lantern light.

"We will make a new life for ourselves," he promised. "Together."

Chapter 29

For two days, Cora threw herself into work, checking on patients whom she hadn't been able to visit while occupied with Jim, cleaning the cottage, writing letters to postpone the wedding, and preparing food for Aunt Jenny's return. Neither Robert nor Jim contacted her, nary a letter, a message, or a secret visit, and Cora told herself she was relieved to have some time to think. However, whenever she was alone, she fell into a dark pit of worry. How foolish of her to think that either man would go on adoring her, pursuing her, and doting on her while she trifled and played one against the other. In prolonging her engagement with Robert, in rejecting Jim in a pique of jealousy, she'd played with fire, and she couldn't dismiss the possibility they were both turning their backs on her.

At last, at midday on Thursday, Jenny flung open the door and entered the kitchen in a gust of fresh winter air and Cora was alone no longer. Jenny set down her carpet bag and opened her arms, and Cora rushed across the room to hug her.

"So, you did miss me," said Jenny.

"Of course, I did," exclaimed Cora. "Now you must tell me all about Ivy and the orphans."

"First I'll change my dress." Jenny hung her coat, picked up her bag, and went to her room.

Cora set out a hearty lunch of soup, bread, cheddar,

sausage, and pickles, and when they were seated at the table, they resumed their conversation.

"Ivy is somewhat better," Jenny reported. "If I didn't love her so much, I'd be fascinated by her condition. The paralysis began in her extremities with clumsiness and progressed proximally until she was bedridden, flaccid, and helpless. Her speech was barely intelligible for a couple days, but that has cleared. I thank the Gods the paralysis never advanced to the point that she couldn't breathe or swallow."

"And you wrote she's improving."

"Yes. Though she's not walking or using her hands properly. Every day she gets a little better, and I have faith she'll bounce back." Jenny crumbled cheese into her soup and lifted a spoonful of the mixture to her mouth.

"Have you ever seen a case like hers?" Cora buttered a hunk of bread.

"No, though I've heard of them. The patient gets ill with something, diarrhea, pneumonia, or some such, and a few weeks later, boom, he's flattened. If he's lucky, he recovers. I expect Ivy to be lucky."

They ate in silence for a few moments. Jenny seemed lost in thought, or perhaps she was searching for words. Cora held her questions.

At last Jenny set down her spoon. "Ivy won't be strong enough to manage the orphanage for some time. What if I step in for her, until she can return to her duties?"

"You mean, move to Brucedale?"

"Yes. For weeks, or months, or even permanently."

"Well, that would be your choice, Aunt Jenny, and I'd respect it."

"You're independent now, Cora, and you could go on living here. With Dr. Blackmore on the scene, only one of us is needed in Maryville."

Cora recognized the merits of the proposal. "Have you discussed this with the staff?"

Jenny nodded. "It was their idea."

A pang of loss cast a pall over Cora's endorsement of the sensible plan. "I would miss you terribly," she said.

"Brucedale isn't far from Maryville, and you'll marry," Jenny predicted. "Having a home and livelihood of your own offers you the luxury to choose the right man, not the rich man."

Tears welled in Cora's eyes. "Oh, Aunt Jenny. I've been so stupid," she cried.

Jenny raised her eyebrows and nodded slightly, as if to say, "Go on," and then she resumed eating like she'd heard it all before and Cora's misery bored her. Cora would be cross with her aunt, but Jenny's matter-of-fact attitude gave Cora latitude to reveal everything that had happened over their eventful week apart. When at last Cora had nothing left to say, Jenny pushed her empty bowl away and spoke.

"You've learned more this week than if I'd been here hovering over you," she said mildly. "First, you learned that men can be unpredictable. Mr. Helston especially."

"You're not angry? Or disappointed in me?"

"Why would I feel that way?" Jenny shrugged. "It's an unjust, ridiculous world that demands chastity from women while granting men the freedom to make rough advances with no repercussions."

Cora wiped away an unbidden tear with her sleeve.

"I've made a hash of everything."

"Yes, though you can fix it," said Jenny. "Life is much simpler if you choose one man and behave with integrity. It isn't fair to Robert or Jim for you to make demands and excuse yourself from your own rules. You do know that, don't you, Cora?"

"Yes but—"

"No buts. Your troubles won't go away until you truly commit to one man or the other. Then you'll be in a position to negotiate with the lucky party."

"Ugh. You sound like Jim."

"Do I?" Jenny grinned. "I'm flattered. Seriously now. Choose the one with whom you can see yourself spending the rest of your life and deliver a sincere apology to the other. The sooner the better."

"Okay, but I love them both and I can imagine a future with either one."

Jenny crossed her arms, arched her brow, and gave Cora a searching look.

Cora exhaled with resignation. "I know what you're thinking."

"Do you?"

"It's true. You see it plainly. I've lost faith in Robert, but deep down I know he loves me, and he's more mature than Jim."

"Cora, you postponed your wedding for good reasons. I'm going to ask you some pointed questions. Don't tell me your answers. Just think. Think hard. Be ruthless with yourself. Ready?"

"Yes." Cora nodded and closed her eyes.

"Which man would love you as you are, whatever you wear, whatever you do?"

"Okay."

"Which man makes you laugh? Not smile politely while you wave a lace-trimmed fan before your face and titter, but really laugh."

"Go on."

"Which man would put his life on the line to rescue a child, secretly provide you with firewood, and take you to Brucedale on one of the coldest nights of the year."

Cora opened her eyes and looked sharply at Jenny. "Okay, the answers are obvious. But Robert treats me like a queen."

Jenny snorted. "In exchange for hanging off his arm like a Christmas tree ornament. I don't doubt he loves some version of you, but is it the real Cora? Final question. And I shouldn't have to ask this. Has either man given you reason to fear for your physical safety? Not when you were children. Schoolyard squabbles don't count."

"I should be practical though, shouldn't I? Jim hasn't a penny to his name. He hasn't proposed to me. He might be leading me on as he has all his other conquests. He only asked me not to marry Robert. He hasn't asked me to marry him."

"Maybe Jim's the one who's being practical. You want guarantees. You want assurance you can trust him. Most men want that too. He likely won't ask for your hand unless he's fairly certain your answer will be yes. Anyway, he has something rare, something Robert does not, and that's potential greatness. Jim is energetic, intelligent, industrious, cheerful and—here's the difference Cora—he's genuinely good. Materially, he doesn't have much. He's only twenty-three and his hands are tied behind his back with family obligation, but when the time is opportune, he'll soar."

When Cora made no comment, Jenny asked, "Who do you think of as you close your eyes to go to sleep, and first, when you wake?"

"Jim," Cora replied without hesitation. "But Aunt Jenny, he probably hates me. If you heard the way I spoke to him…"

"There you go. Guessing, assuming. Just apologize to him, Cora. You owe him that anyway."

"All right. Advice noted."

"Cora! Don't rely on Jim to fix this rift. Do the decent thing."

"I will. I'll apologize."

"That's better. Your father would've preferred Jim over Robert, you know."

"Let's not drag Father's hypothetical opinion into this, Aunt Jenny. Now tell me, how are the children?"

Jenny smiled. "Now that's a wonderful question. While we wash the dishes, I'll tell you all about our thriving, clever, lovable little monsters. Oops. Wanderers."

****

Jim read the *Trumpet* in his room. Although healthier, he had to pace himself and rest before afternoon chores. Moira Kelly had dropped off the paper so he could read the Beck family's open letter of gratitude to their hero on page three. However, the article that caught Jim's attention was the front-page hagiography of Dr. August Blackmore, more interesting for its presence than its content. Subtle revenge on Cora by her aggrieved fiancé?

Jim heard a knock on his door. "Yes?"

"It's me. Gran."

"Come in." He swung his long legs over the side of

his bed and sat up as Gran poked her head round the door. She never came into his room, at least not when he was in it. Well, maybe to tidy and whatnot.

"Have a minute?" she asked.

"Yes." All the time in the world.

Instead of taking the chair at his table, Gran plunked her fat bottom next to him on the bed, as she had for bedtime stories and prayers years before.

"You seem sad, Jimmy. I thought I'd check on you. In case there's anything I can do."

"I'm okay," he sighed.

"Well then, I'll leave you be." Gran started to stand up. "Since you're okay."

"No. Wait. I'm not okay."

Gran sat down again and looked fondly at her grandson.

He continued. "It's obvious I'm stuck, Gran."

"Ach. Not so obvious to me," she smiled and patted Jim's knee.

"But I am. I've lost ground that I'll never regain. I thought I'd be back at McGill by now, but I can't save enough for tuition. I hoped Cora would change her mind on Robert Helston, but I can't give her the life he can, especially if I can't go back to law school. Even if I could go, I don't think I should leave you and Mama."

"Whoa. Slow down. One problem at a time, lad."

"But they're all bound up together in one nasty ball of wax called my life."

"Hmm. Self-pity. That's the trouble with self-pity. It's a ball of wax and not much use for anything besides sealing things up."

Jim stared out the window, vaguely watching a squirrel scurry to its nest in the top of the apple tree. The tiny animal was oblivious to the problems of people. "Dad tried to sell Buttercup." He sensed Gran stiffen next to him. "He's out of control, and Mama's too sick to manage him and the farm without me."

"Maybe having to manage the farm is just what she needs, Jimmy. She did it when you were away before with help from the O'Mallory boys. Her trouble is heartache, an unhappy marriage. If she had a God-given purpose and some grit under her wheels, she'd get on better."

"But what about Dad?"

"Now that's a puzzle. Even as a wee lad, your dad was a wild one and he grew into a 'blethering, blustering, drunken, blellum'. I still haven't figured out your father after forty-five years. But he's my son, Jimmy. Not yours. As I see it, you have no duty to behave as if you're his father, harsh as that seems."

"I couldn't just pick up and go."

"Why not? Grandpa and I left Scotland, and we did well for ourselves, and may the Lord strike me dumb for bragging. You can go wherever you fancy—Montreal, New York City, west to the prairies, Timbuktu—and take Cora with you. It isn't carved upon a stone tablet that the farm should belong to the Sinclair family forever."

Jim said nothing. He gazed through the window seeing nothing.

Gran said gently, "That's the real trouble, isn't it? It's Cora."

"Yes," he said, voice barely louder than a whisper.

"Ach, she's a firecracker, that one. Cross my heart, I didn't eavesdrop on purpose, but I couldn't help but hear snatches of your row from my room. Seems to me you're used to having your way, and you were surprised when the 'other party' drove a hard bargain."

Jim looked sideways at Gran and asked sheepishly, "Snatches or the whole thing, Gran?"

Gran's dark eyes met his with angelic innocence. "I only heard what the Lord meant for me to hear, and I'll thank you for agreeing. As I see it, the two of you have the same trouble, a high level of self-regard, some folks call that 'pride', and a stubborn streak. That's not a criticism, Jimmy. Being that way serves you both well most of the time."

"I'm not proud or—"

"Yes, you are," Gran interrupted. "Bear with me, lad. You took a big risk the other day, but you didn't see it through. Cora bears half the blame; I'll grant you that."

"Exactly what didn't I see through, Gran? I told her I loved her. I've never told any other girl that."

"Aye. Cora's the one and you tried to tell her so. Now look at yourself from Cora's side. What does she see?"

Jim frowned. "An impoverished farmer with poor prospects."

"For a clever lad, you're awfully daft. I doubt Cora cares overmuch about money. The Pattons are salt of the earth themselves. Think."

"I don't know."

"Here's a hint. She loves you too, Jimmy, but something is holding her back. She felt it briefly at Christmas, and then she withdrew from you and there's a reason for it. She told you it plainly."

Jim gazed through the window again, recalling their lives from childhood to present…their schoolyard battles, adolescent misunderstandings, and the tumult of the last six months from the tornado to his brush with death. The answer came to him in a single word. "Trust."

"Aye. That's the trouble." Gran patted Jim's knee. "Alas, it seems that Mr. Helston got to her somehow, though Cora doesn't really love him. She looked like a lamb lost in the wilderness when the minister read the banns. She's having second thoughts where he's concerned."

"How do I convince her she's safe with me? That she can trust me? She probably won't even talk to me, Gran. I sent her away."

The old woman shrugged. "I guess you'll have to seek her forgiveness and show her she *can* trust you, not just tell her."

She stood, tousled Jim's hair as if he were a little boy and left the room.

Chapter 30

Cora walked up the lane and spotted Jim before he saw her. He swung his axe and split a log in three blows, then set another log in its place. He was getting stronger, but he still looked tired judging by his posture. Before the pneumonia he'd probably have managed the task with one swing of his axe. The large animals stood in the field adjacent to the barn. Buttercup sensed Cora's presence before Jim did, for she tossed her great head and whinnied.

Jim turned, saw Cora, and leaned his axe against the wood pile. He walked toward her.

She couldn't read his expression right away. A frown would warn her that her visit was unwelcome. She straightened her shoulders to take her medicine, however bitter. Trying to make amends with someone she'd wronged was not a mistake even if he rejected her apology. Her heart pounded as he approached. His pace quickened as he neared. By his stride, he might send her away. How awful for this to be the way their short friendship ended.

Now she saw his face clearly. He was smiling. She thought she'd collapse with relief, but she didn't. Instead, she smiled back.

"Cora." That was all he said. He opened his arms, she went to him, and he held her.

She sank into the warmth of his chest, into the

musky scent of him and the lightness of his kiss on the crown of her head. She was forgiven. Words were not necessary to know this. For a time, they held each other, drinking in each other's being, reveling in each other's joy that they were bridging their rift.

When she was quite certain she wouldn't cry, she spoke. "I'm sorry, Jim. I'm so sorry that I hurt you."

"I'm sorry I hurt you too," he said. "You know that I love you."

"I love you too."

"Do you have time to, um, negotiate?" he grinned.

Cora laughed through the tears she'd tried to hold back. "Yes, Mr. Sinclair. But only if you're offering an exclusive deal."

"I am, Miss Patton. My office is in the hayloft. If that's okay."

"It is."

Jim put his arm around Cora's shoulder, and they walked together.

Sunbeams shone through the gaps in the planks and filled the upper story of the barn in an ephemeral, mystical, subdued light. Cora looked up at the man she loved with all her heart, looked into his dark eyes. He hadn't shaved that morning, for his strong, square jaw was covered in stubble and Cora thought him even more handsome for it. Gently, he pulled her down into the straw, and they were together once more, body with body, soul with soul.

Cora expected Jim to kiss her, but he didn't, not right away. He gazed at her and playfully twined a lock of her hair in his finger. How warm she felt cradled in Jim's arm, how secure and happy in his embrace.

He kissed her lightly on the lips, once, and then he

asked, "Will you marry me?"

"Yes," said Cora. "Yes, in principle."

"In principle?" Jim laughed.

"Yes. You must be willing to establish an equal partnership and the partnership must be absolutely exclusive, from this moment forward."

"Those are easy terms, Cora. I consent to them without reservation."

Now Jim did kiss her. Lips slightly parted, their mouths met, and carefully, tenderly played together. At first the kiss was soft and warm and sweet. Jim took the kiss deeper, and Cora followed, lips exploring, tongues circling, caressing, mouths seeking each other's essence. An urgent desire to know all of him overwhelmed her, so exquisite was his kiss. She felt as if she were falling into a passionate madness. It was he who broke away.

"I have one more condition to impose on our deal," he said quietly, his tender gaze upon her once more.

Cora nodded. "Okay."

"We consummate our love on the day of our wedding." He reacted to her surprise by elaborating. "Cora, I don't want to place you at risk. Helston will try to ruin you. We can't take any chances that might tarnish you in scandal. I realize you probably know all the tricks to…you know…"

"Avoid pregnancy?"

"Yes. But I want us to have the strongest foundation possible for our marriage. I want to honor you as a husband should honor his wife. I want nothing more than to make love to you now, this very minute, but I think we should wait."

"You've put a lot of thought into this," said Cora.

"I have." He kissed her again, then continued. "Let's

marry as soon as we can. No banns. No formal engagement. We can elope. As soon as you break your engagement to Helston."

"Now who's being impulsive?" Cora asked. "Though I do like the idea. I wanted to break the engagement this morning, but the staff at the *Trumpet* told me Robert's away for a few days."

Jim propped himself up on his elbow. "I think he already sees the writing on the wall, Cora. Things are liable to get ugly when he's back."

"I don't think so. After his broken heart heals, he'll marry someone else."

"Perhaps, but let's be vigilant all the same."

"Okay."

Jim fell into a pensive silence. Cora sensed there was something unspoken between them that had to be addressed. "What is it?" she asked. "I can tell something is bothering you."

"Not bothering, exactly," he replied. "I'm just curious. When did you change your mind about me? I mean, I've always known I love you, but you hated me for a long time."

Cora turned to face him. "I didn't hate you. I was afraid of you. When we were in school, wherever you went, chaos reigned."

"I was a brat."

"Yes. And that unnerved me. Now I see that you were very clever, and you yearned to be free. You were a caged animal. In time, as you matured and turned from boy to man, you made up your own rules, better rules than most people's, and you follow them. Reckless Jimmy turned into self-disciplined, decent Jim."

"That's quite the analysis."

"But it's accurate, isn't it?"

"I guess," Jim hedged. "When did the seesaw drop my way?"

Cora smiled. "That happened in stages. Many small things added up. The night you took me to Brucedale was the tipping point. Then, when you were sick—"

"Not the hero thing," Jim frowned.

"No, not that, though that didn't hurt your cause. It was something that seems mundane, but it was significant to me. I saw the firewood by your stove, and I realized that you had filled our wood box last fall without taking credit. Robert misled me. He allowed me to believe he had done it. Then last week, Robert and I were together—"

"Don't tell me anything about what you did together. I don't want to know."

"Very well. Anyway, I very casually asked him about the wood. He inadvertently revealed the truth. In that instant, I knew I couldn't trust him. So many things came together and I felt he was sly. At the same time, even when I was with him, all I could think of was you. I wished you were with me, not him. I hurried back to your place, and you were struggling, and I was so afraid, Jim. So afraid I'd lose you. Afraid the world would lose you."

"I'm here."

"Yes, you are."

Jim kissed Cora one more time, a leisurely, joyful kiss. Then he stretched and sat up. "If only the chores would do themselves," he said wistfully. "I'd lie here with you all afternoon."

"I'll help you," Cora offered eagerly. "Teach me how to farm, partner."

"I don't know. The work is awfully heavy and you're kind of small."

"Jimmy Sinclair, do not underestimate me. I insist that you let me help you."

Jim shrugged and laughed. "All right, Miss Polka Dot. I accept."

****

Jim walked Cora home despite her protestations that it wasn't necessary in safe, friendly Maryville. When they arrived at the cottage, Jenny was cooking a supper of fried fish and potatoes. "Oscar Landry was ice fishing over at the lake range and dropped off fresh perch. There's way too much for two," she said, and Jim agreed to stay.

Upon hearing their news, Jenny found a bottle of elderberry wine in the pantry, and they had an impromptu engagement party. It was a happy occasion and merriment was expected, yet Jim was struck by Cora and Jenny's cheerful arguments, by their teasing and banter, and by the joyful coziness of their home, so different from his own, and he told them so.

"You and Cora will be just as happy in your household." Jenny raised her glass, her second, and toasted their engagement with a long, uncannily perceptive speech that embarrassed them both and ended in more laughter. Then she asked about their plans.

"We haven't made any yet," answered Cora, and with that admission Jenny drilled them on their hopes and dreams, from wedding and honeymoon to children and vocation. With Cora at his side, Jim welcomed the future for the first time in months. He could surmount any hurdle with this woman as his wife.

He left the cottage after the sun set, carrying a

lantern Jenny lent him to see his way in the moonless, clear night. Orion and his starry dogs shone in the southern sky. Generations of men and women had fallen in love, lived, and died under these constellations, and many more men and women would follow. Set in the vastness of time, Cora and he were ordinary people, and they would be forgotten. Someday, their children would be forgotten. Still, they would seek their destiny within the order of the universe, timeless and infinite, and though their humble lives were finite, Jim was overwhelmed with gratitude for the privilege of being alive.

As soon as Cora broke her engagement with Helston, Jim would speak with Reverend Cameron. Until then, their secret must be kept. Jim would go with Cora to the *Trumpet* office and wait for her while she spoke to Helston.

She criticized Jim for being dramatically over-protective, but she had no idea what Helston might do. Helston was a man who didn't lose. He possessed things and people with cunning greed. Cora was about to wound him, humiliate him, and he would retaliate like an injured wolf. Jim granted that Helston was probably too sophisticated to resort to violence. His revenge would appear in print or across a desk, but a scorned man was unpredictable. Cora and he had to be prepared.

Jim walked up the lane to the barn to check on the livestock before turning in for the night. Buttercup greeted him with a stamp of her hoof and a snort, and he picked up a piece of turnip that had rolled under the bottom slat of the pigsty, brushed it off, and gave it to her with an affectionate rub on her long nose. If the night weren't so dark, he'd take her for a run.

"Tomorrow, Buttercup," he promised. "Tomorrow we'll gallop across the fields and plan our future."

Chapter 31

Cora hadn't received a single letter from Robert while he was away, not even a note when he returned. When she met Jim in front of the *Trumpet* office, she speculated that Robert might break the engagement.

"I don't think so, Cora," said Jim. "I think he's giving you the cold shoulder to bring you to heel."

"Oh, I dislike that expression. I'm not a dog," said Cora, brow furled.

"But by ignoring you, he means to train you, so it's apt."

Cora looked up at Jim. "You shouldn't come in. Just wait here, okay?"

"Right here. And if you feel unsafe in any way, just scream."

"Scream? I don't scream; I shout, Jim, but I'm sure that won't be necessary. He's not a monster."

Cora squared her shoulders, stiffened her spine, and took a deep breath. "Here goes. I'll see you shortly," she muttered.

"Leave his door open," Jim called as she entered the building. He didn't see Cora's eyes roll.

After exchanging pleasantries with the staff, Cora knocked. Her mouth was dry, her stomach queasy as she entered Robert's office. He was hard at work, pen in hand, piles of paper littering his desk.

"Cora." He smiled and rose from his chair when he

saw her, then, reading her face, he sat again and gestured toward the chair by his desk.

"Good morning, Robert. Do you have a minute?" she asked as she took her seat. She wanted to blurt out the reason for her visit and bolt from the office, but she had a duty to break the engagement as gracefully and humanely as she could. She looked at the man whom she might have married. His blue eyes were bloodshot and ringed with a gray weariness. Though his wavy hair was well barbered and combed and he wore a freshly pressed shirt, there was a sad dishevelment about him. He already knew.

"Of course," he replied. "I always have time for you."

She should get right to the point. He looked so vulnerable. "How was your trip?" she asked.

"Fine. I managed to haggle a lower price on ink and paper, and I saw the plans for a spur line that should be profitable. I'm sorry I didn't have time to write."

"That's okay. You're busy," said Cora. "Um, I have some difficult news."

Robert leaned back in his chair, as if difficult news were a matter of routine, and he nodded.

"I've decided to break our engagement," she said.

"All right. May I ask why?"

No argument, no pleading for her to rethink the matter. Cora had to credit him. Robert comported himself impeccably.

She gave the answer she'd rehearsed. "We want different things, Robert. You want an obedient, doting wife by your side, and I want to continue working. You like the finer things in life, and I'm small-town and provincial. We haven't connected on a spiritual level.

We're too different and we'd make each other miserable."

Robert's face was like steel, though he spoke softly. "All this is coming out of the blue, Cora. These supposed incompatibilities, they seem contrived. If you'd told me sooner that our differences troubled you, we could have worked through them."

"I'm sorry," she said weakly. She felt as if the office walls were closing in, the air thick with despair. Robert hid his pain under a calm façade, yet it was palpable.

"Is there someone else?" he asked.

Cora focused on the desk before her. She didn't dare meet his eyes. "Yes."

"Who is it?"

"Does it matter?"

"I'd like to know."

She had to end this excruciating conversation. The room was spinning, and Robert's sadness was transforming into a bitter rage. "Jim Sinclair." He'd find out anyway.

"Please go."

Two ice cold words of dismissal. Cora nodded and hastened away.

On the street, she inhaled the bracing winter air. Jim looked at her with a kindness she didn't deserve.

"Are you okay?" he asked, taking her arm.

Numb with shame, she nodded. "He took it well. On the surface. I'm afraid I hurt him very badly."

"You had no choice."

Cora looked up at Jim to discern whether he recognized the monstrosity of what she'd done.

Expression and voice earnest, he said, "Try not to look back. Only look forward."

"I'll try."

They walked down Main Street toward St. Andrew's in silence. Cora said, "I need some time alone, Jim. In the church."

Jim bestowed a sympathetic smile upon her. "Will I see you later?"

"Yes. I'll go to your place in the afternoon and help you with chores."

"Later then." Jim squeezed her hand and strode away.

Cora ascended the steps to the front doors of the church and the haunting stillness of the nave. She would sit with her sins, pray for forgiveness, and, hopefully, find a glimmer of grace and light.

****

As he turned the corner at the far pasture, Jim spotted the Brocketts' cutter with a man waiting in it by the front door of the house. Adeline was paying a visit. He pictured the tableau with uncanny accuracy: Adeline, Mama, and Gran seated in the parlor with teacups in hand, dust motes lifting from seldom used furniture and dancing in the midday light streaming from the tall south window.

He could hide in the barn, but he'd already waved to the Brocketts' hired man in the cutter and, anyway, he wasn't a coward. Quietly he entered the house by the kitchen door, drank a glass of water to quell the sudden dryness of his mouth, and unconsciously checked that his shirt was tucked.

Three pairs of eyes were upon him as he entered the parlor with a tight smile pasted on his face. Mama looked relieved to see him, Gran looked both amused and concerned, and Adeline looked achingly hopeful. She gazed up at him with pretty, long-lashed brown eyes, sunlight playing on her stylishly arranged, dark hair.

"Well, speak of the very devil himself," exclaimed Gran. "Only now we were discussing your miraculous recovery, Jimmy."

"So that's why my ears were burning." Jim stopped just inside the doorway. "Hello, Adeline." He hoped he didn't sound too stiff, too unfriendly.

Mama rose from her chair and nudged it toward him. "Sit, sit, lad, and Miss Brockett and you can have a proper visit. There's plenty more tea in the pot and a cup in the cabinet."

In mere seconds, Gran followed Mama out of the room, and he was alone with Adeline.

As he seated himself at a distance bordering on rude, she said, "You look quite well."

A safe opening gambit. She sat still in her silk frock, her hands folded demurely on her lap, but there was a tension about her mouth and a squareness in her shoulders that suggested a suppressed nervousness.

"I feel well," said Jim. "I have to pace myself, but you may tell your father that I should be strong enough to return to the mill in a week or two."

"Never mind the mill, Jim. We were all so worried about you. I was worried about you."

Yet she hadn't come before today. And he hadn't missed her. They both knew it.

"Thank you for the grapefruit," he said. "It was very sweet."

"The gesture or the fruit?"

"Both. Thank you."

"You're welcome." Adeline paused, then tested, "We're quite alone."

"So we are," said Jim. "But Mama and Gran are in the house. Look, Adeline—"

She tried to beguile him with round eyes, to tempt him by parting her soft, pink lips, by opening her hand in a graceful invitation and reaching for him. Three weeks ago, she would have succeeded.

"Adeline. The accident has changed me. I hold you in high regard and, if you wish it, I will always be your friend."

"Oh no." Her breath caught. "No—"

"I don't want to hurt you."

"But you will," she said quietly, tears flooding her eyes.

"Yes, I'm afraid so."

"You've found someone," she guessed.

"Yes." His voice was barely louder than a whisper.

"Is it Cora Patton?"

"Yes. We're engaged. You're the first friend I've told. We haven't announced it yet. We won't for some time, I expect."

"That's my Jim. Keeping his sordid secrets." Adeline's voice was reedy with pain and accusation.

It was unwise to defend himself. He should accept her blame and end the visit, but he couldn't help himself. "To be fair, Adeline, I never made any promises to you. I never led you on. We had many a laugh together. But all along I told you how I felt about Cora, and you told me again and again that you'd marry a rich man."

"Don't you see, Jim? I meant you."

Not fair. She hadn't. Jim shook his head in bewilderment.

Adeline looked at him quizzically, appeared to make a calculation, and steadied herself. "Father can make you a rich man," she said evenly. "That's what I meant. If you were my fiancé, he'd pay your way through law school and help set us up."

In the shadow of Adeline's desperation, Jim could only feel sorrow for her and the inevitable loss of her friendship.

She leaned forward and placed her hand on the tea table, palm up, fingers curled to beckon his hand. "Cora can't offer you any of that."

"She doesn't have to."

"Fine. Sow your wild oats with Cora. Be your beastly, wild self. But consider who's worthy of you and who can make something of you."

"Adeline, I'm sorry." He shook his head in refusal.

"You're making a big mistake, Jim. With me at your side, your future is secure. Cora comes with baggage. Broken people pull at her apron day and night. She has an aunt who's mad as a hatter. And I can't imagine Cora allows you to do with her what you do with me. She's ever so serious, boring, and straight."

"Did. What we *did*, Adeline. It's over."

The only sound in the small room was Adeline's plaintive weeping. Jim felt sick with remorse. Comforting her with soothing words and a gentle touch would only prolong the cruelty of his rejection yet he had to help her so she could leave with her pride intact. He looked at the dark-haired, dark-eyed beauty sitting opposite him and considered her predicament. Surely rage was easier to endure than grief. He spoke with sly insolence.

"We had a few laughs, Adeline, but you should know you weren't the only one who provided me with that." How had Cora inaccurately put it? "You were a bead on my string."

"A bead on your string? You dare to call me that!" Adeline's tear-filled eyes lit in fury. "Jim Sinclair, you'll rue this day for the rest of your life!" Abruptly, she stood, slapped his face with all the strength she could muster, snatched up her cape, and marched out of the parlor, through the front door, and away.

Jim's left cheek stung. A welt rose where the ring on Adeline's second finger had made swift contact. He deserved that and more. If she'd made to slap his right cheek too, he'd have let her. For a time, he slouched in the straight-backed chair with his arms folded and his legs extended and crossed at the ankle. He stared at the dust motes suspended in the air. Neither Gran nor Mama bothered him, thank God.

He'd lost a dear friend in Adeline Brockett, and that hurt far, far more than a slap on the face ever would.

Chapter 32

The ever-turning stones of Maryville's rumor mill issued several versions of the biggest scandal of the winter. Few foresaw the shocking cancellation of the Helston wedding. Sightings of Cora Patton and Jim Sinclair laughing and carrying on together in the very month she should have been wed to Mr. Helston only added grist to the mill. Wherever Cora went, people turned to stare at her, and snatches of murmured gossip assaulted her ears. She was infamous.

"Why can't people mind their own business?" Cora complained as she hung laundry on the line near the stove. "It's nasty for Jim and me, but it must be excruciating for Robert."

"Oh contraire," replied Jenny. "In a week or two, Mr. Robert Helston will be counting his lucky stars for he has become Maryville's most eligible bachelor."

"Widower," corrected Cora.

"In practical terms, 'bachelor'. Until his engagement to you, he was a widower, too grief-stricken over Eliza for remarriage. Everything has changed. Eliza's death, your betrayal. Well, what red-blooded Maryville maiden won't want to succor his undeserved wounds and save him from the black hole of despair that you and Jim have thrown him into? And Mr. Helston is rich. He's a fully formed, highly desirable *bachelor* now."

"Aunt Jenny! Shame on you! You sound just like those moralizing busybodies in the Temperance Union."

Jenny winked. "I take my pleasure wherever I may find it. Observing all the knicker twisting that you and Jim have caused is rather entertaining. Anyway, Cora, I'm trying to reassure you. Don't worry about Robert. Readership of the *Trumpet* has undoubtedly risen, and after the dust of scandal settles, he'll discover he's better off without you."

"Somehow, everything you say is cold comfort."

"Is it? Shucks, Cora. I'm sorry," Jenny said sarcastically.

Cora turned her attention to stretching the stockings over the line so they'd dry evenly.

Jenny spoke again, this time kindly. "Don't waste a single moment on worry. Gossip is like egg salad at a summer picnic. It gets old quickly. You and Jim will be yesterday's news come spring."

"That's better," said Cora.

Seeming to tire of philosophizing on human nature, Jenny stretched in her chair. "I've decided to catch an afternoon train to Brucedale tomorrow. That way, I can dawdle in the morning and still arrive at the orphanage in daylight."

"Your clothes should be dry for packing by morning," said Cora. "I'll go with you to the station and see you off."

"Cora, you'll do no such thing. If I can't carry my bag, I've packed too much. And tomorrow you ought to visit that new family, over by the O'Mallorys. Both Kate and Father Finney are concerned. The children look malnourished and sickly, and Kate says the mother is five months pregnant and very weak. Sullivan. That's their name."

"Should I visit today?"

Jenny shook her head. "The parish is providing them with extra food. Tomorrow morning should be fine. You've already been out and back to the east side of town today. You'll wear your feet out if you don't give them rest."

"Whatever will I do when I don't have you here to manage me?" Cora asked rhetorically.

"I think the verb you want is 'boss', isn't it?" laughed Jenny. "I'm sorry, Cora. Sometimes I forget you're all grown up. Now, to happier matters. Did Jim manage to set a date with Reverend Cameron? I know you don't want a fuss, but I'll come back from Brucedale for your wedding."

Cora put the surplus clothes pins in the basket and set the laundry things in the corner. "Not yet." She seated herself at the table. "We've run into a snag. I was meaning to talk to you about that."

"A snag, eh?" Jenny didn't look worried or surprised.

"Reverend Cameron is refusing to marry us without reading the banns. In fact, Jim thinks he's reluctant to marry us at all."

"I expected that."

"What? Aunt Jenny! How can he be so obstinate? We've taken good care of his family whenever they've needed us. The Sinclairs and the Pattons helped build the very church Reverend Cameron preaches in. He's our minister."

"Now he's Robert Helston's minister too. Have you forgotten the gorgeous and very expensive stained-glass window of St. Andrew with his cross that Mr. Helston commissioned in January?"

"What's money to blood, sweat, and tears?" argued Cora.

"You might ask the minister that," Jenny sniffed. "He that pays the piper…"

"Calls the tune," Cora finished.

"Money is probably the big reason," Jenny continued. "Mr. Helston has a lot of power, his newspaper, his investments. When you announced your engagement to him, he became the largest donor to St. Andrew's, and if he doesn't get his way, he'll cancel his support."

"You said, 'big reason.' That implies there's another reason."

"A reason in the same vein. I've noticed that Mr. Helston wields power from behind a curtain. He pulls strings and all the town's puppets dance as he wishes, and he takes advantage. I'll bet he paid a friendly yet intimidating visit to Reverend Cameron soon after you broke the engagement, and he won't return to St. George's until he thinks you're thoroughly miserable."

"I hope you're wrong, Aunt Jenny." Cora sighed with exasperation. Though the minister's rejection of Jim's request for expediency made sense, it felt like a slap in the face.

Jenny said, "Fortunately, to any problem there's usually a solution hiding in plain sight for those who care to find it."

Cora raised a curious brow.

Jenny continued. "The orphanage chaplain is Presbyterian. You remember Reverend Ross from Christmas? Shall I ask him if he would marry you?"

"Do you think he would, Aunt Jenny?"

"Yes, I think so. In fact, I'd be surprised if he didn't agree to it. He took quite a shining to you and Jim…and Buttercup."

"Will you ask him, please?"

Jenny nodded. "One more thing, Cora. Consider me a tiny bird, twittering in your ear. Not intruding or giving unwanted advice. Just a wee chickadee singing unobtrusively."

"Okay." Cora doubted Jenny's birdsong would be at all unobtrusive.

"You ought to follow your dreams. Both of you. You each have a vocation, a calling, that you should heed. Maryville is thriving and there's talk of building a hospital. I've written a letter to put forth my ideas to the men on the committee who recruited Dr. Blackmore. Pay attention, Cora, because change is afoot. Change with opportunity riding on its coattails."

"Change? Opportunity? Why must you be so cryptic, Aunt Jenny?"

Jenny adopted a comically confused expression. "Because I scarcely know what is happening one day to the next myself. All I know is that times such as these favor people who take calculated risks. Jim's grandmother agrees with me."

"You talked to Mrs. Sinclair?"

"Older people have friends too, Cora. Naturally we talk."

"Somehow I suddenly feel quite exposed," Cora laughed as she rose from the table to knead the dough that Jenny had left to rise in the sunny window near the sink.

Chapter 33

The next day, Cora and Jim lazed in each other's arms in the hayloft after completing afternoon chores.

"We could be relaxing on actual furniture," said Cora. "Aunt Jenny left this morning, and we'd have the cottage to ourselves."

"I like it here, Cora. It's peaceful and private in our own little nest." Jim tickled Cora's neck with a piece of straw. "And we're invisible to the prying eyes of curtain twitchers and muckrakers."

"If we go about our lives as we wish, people will tire of minding our business."

Jim gave Cora a funny look of disbelief and Cora batted the straw away.

"Anyway, since when do you care what other people think?" she asked.

"Usually I don't, but I don't want you subjected to any nonsense." Jim stared off into middle space and lowered his voice. "I received a couple of vinegar valentines in the mail."

Cora frowned. "They're distasteful, but surely they're a harmless joke."

"Not these," said Jim. "They weren't the humorous kind that you buy at Beck's. They were handwritten because no valentine maker would ever write anything so vile."

"What did they say?"

"Cora, you don't want to know. I'll only say they accused me of ungentlemanly conduct of a criminal nature, and they threatened to expose 'my dark secrets', whatever that means."

"Dark secrets," repeated Cora.

"Dark and depraved secrets. I won't let it bother me."

"Except it does bother you."

"Yeah."

"Did the writer sign them?"

"No. They had handwritten verses of clumsy poetry and I can't tell who the author is. Could've been a man or a woman, reasonably well-educated as there were no spelling mistakes, and the handwriting was plain, nondescript."

"Maybe I could tell who wrote them," Cora suggested.

"Too late. I burned them. Anyway, you don't want to read that garbage."

"I suppose burning them was best. I'll send you a valentine to cancel the hate."

Jim interlaced his fingers with Cora's. "No need. Just be with me."

They cuddled in silence until Cora spoke again. "Aunt Jenny says she'll ask the orphanage chaplain to marry us."

"Reverend Ross?"

"The very one."

"That's great, Cora! If he says yes, all we'll need is a marriage license. How soon do you think he can do the ceremony?"

"I don't know. Aunt Jenny will write and let us

know."

Jim slipped his hand under Cora's cape and cupped her breast. "Good. The sooner the better, because I don't know how long I can hold out, lying here with you and not doing anything."

"That, my dear Jim, is your choice," Cora said coquettishly. "Besides, what's this?" She placed her hand over his. "This feels too nice to be nothing."

"A tease, Miss Polka Dot. That's all."

Cora shook her head. "As I said, your choice." She didn't mention his hardness pressed against her thigh.

They kissed playfully as dusk gradually set in and the barn darkened.

"I'll walk you home," Jim whispered in Cora's ear.

"It's that time, isn't it," Cora agreed, sitting up.

As they dusted each other off, Cora asked, "Have you put anymore thought into where you'd like to live after we're married?"

"We could set up here in the hayloft."

Cora ignored the silly joke. "Aunt Jenny says we can live in the cottage. She won't be there anyway, and she thinks it's better if newlyweds live on their own, without in-laws. On the other hand, the farmhouse is handier for you."

"I agree with Jenny. Definitely not the farm. I can ride Buttercup back and forth from the cottage if walking is a bother. You know where I really want to go, though."

"Montreal. To school."

"Yes. As soon as we've saved enough. Maryville could use an honest lawyer to fill Charles Tucker's shoes."

"Honest and competent," said Cora.

"Whether I'm ever competent or not is for others to

decide. I can only claim honesty."

After they climbed down from the loft, Jim secured the door and they walked down the lane, hand in hand.

Cora said, "We may have to live apart for a while. I can't abandon my patients. The ones who are struggling with money. I'll need to find someone to fill in for me if I'm away."

"What about Dr. Blackmore?"

"I won't deign to respond to that suggestion, Jim, as you're well aware of his character. I've been thinking of Kate O'Mallory. She has a lot of experience. She's cared for people from birth to death, people suffering from all manner of illness, and she was a deft hand when you were sick. Also, Kate's literate and that's crucial. If I trained her in the basics and she read Aunt Jenny's books, she could handle simple cases when I'm not here. I'd even let her borrow my *Gray's*."

"I wish you could go to medical school," said Jim. "Then you'd receive respect and credit for what you do and you'd give Blackmore a run for his money."

"Thanks," said Cora. "Anyway, even if they admitted women to medical school, we couldn't afford two tuitions, so we can put that out of our minds."

As they turned from the lane to the road, neither spoke of what both were thinking because it felt greedy to think it. If Jim could wrest ownership of the farm from his father before it became a gargantuan chip on a poker table, they could seek their fortunes by means of its equity. As Jenny had oft intimated, it would be a reasoned risk, not a gamble. Selling the empty lot Cora inherited from her father would go some way to securing their future, but it wouldn't be enough. They walked on, now arm in arm, savoring their closeness before they separated for the night. The urgent matter of money would be their second item of business after they married.

****

Jim had only been to the Shamrock and Thistle once since his recovery, and he missed the careless banter of the tavern's patrons, the mingled odors of tobacco smoke and sweat, and the bittersweetness of Kelly's ale. The friendliest tavern in Maryille tended to be busiest on clear nights such as this. A gibbous moon rose in the east, and men could walk home without tripping over hazards that were hidden on darker nights, if they weren't too soused. The warm glow from the tavern windows attracted Jim like a moth to a lantern, and when he pushed through the doors, he was glad to see Tom and Kelly at the bar.

Kelly smiled broadly and pulled a tankard of ale from the keg as Jim made his way to his usual spot next to Tom.

"This one's on the house." Kelly pushed the tankard across the bar to Jim.

"Thank you, Kelly," said Jim. "You gave me a free one last week, so there isn't any—"

"If you don't want it, I'll take it," Tom broke in. "I deserve free beer too, for today I heroically and bravely saved a cat from a laundry mangle." He raised his chin proudly. "Jenkins' son came over to play and claimed he wanted to see if the cat would flatten. Poor kitty has a tail that looks like a calico spatula, but I rescued her from worse."

Jim and Kelly toasted Tom's heroism and his blarney.

Tom shrugged. "You hear lots of unbelievable stuff,

on the streets and in the *Trumpet*. My story meets the standard."

"I reckon it does," said Kelly. "But no free beer for you. I'd go bankrupt."

"No harm in trying." Tom took a swig of his ale and looked impishly at Jim. "I'm surprised to see you here. I thought you'd be hiding in a cave or going about town with a sack over your head to disguise your identity."

"I have nothing to be ashamed of. Neither does Cora."

"Oh, I agree. But whoever wrote the article in today's *Trumpet* thinks otherwise."

"Huh?"

"Kelly. Do you have a copy of today's paper for this immoral, predatory bounder?"

"I do." Kelly rummaged under the counter and presented Jim with a rumpled copy. "Mind the *Trumpet*'s highest use is as a birdcage liner, but you may have it, Jim—if you dare."

"Looks like this copy has had a lot of pre-birdcage use," Jim muttered as he scanned the paper for the pertinent article. There it was.

Fathers of Maryville Be Warned. Your Daughters are in Danger

By Staff

Alas, it has come to the attention of Trumpet staff that a certain young man, recently hailed a hero for rescuing a boy from Brockett's millpond, has a dark side to his character. A courageous maiden recently confessed to Maryville's highly respected physician, Dr. August Blackmore, that the young man had taken liberties by force in the early morning of January 1st. Fortunately, the girl's mother interrupted the attack and the girl's modesty was preserved. We shudder to think what might have happened if he had not been halted by the matron's timely entrance on the scene.

Since this event has come to light, other young ladies, who shall remain nameless to protect their innocence, have made similar allegations. A despicable pattern has emerged wherein the young man uses pretty talk and flattery to gain the young lady's trust, contrives to find her alone, and attempts to have his way. No young lady, including the daughters of Maryville's leading families, is safe from his wily predation. Indeed, it appears that the young man targets the daughters of prosperous families over those of humble origins.

Naturally, the maidens are distraught, and the Trumpet will not add to their discomfort by revealing their names or turning the matter over to authorities. However, we implore all fathers and guardians to protect their daughters from this rapacious young man. Heightened precautions are warranted until he is thoroughly deterred from his despicable ways. The Trumpet staff regret the truism that many mortals have a dark side which is only revealed when their victims stand up and bravely say, "Enough!"

"Jesus. What the hell." Jim ripped the paper in half and ripped it in half again.

"Your bird cage liner is only good for starting fires now," quipped Tom.

Kelly shook his head at Tom to warn him from further joking, and Tom returned a small shrug.

Jim sensed the eyes of the other patrons upon him, stares of prurient curiosity and ridicule. Men were fascinated by another man's disgrace, and they got to observe his firsthand.

"What the hell should I do? What if Cora reads this?"

"I reckon you shouldn't do anything," said Kelly as he refilled a tankard. "It'll blow over. Some juvenile delinquents will tip a bunch of privies, or a band of cattle thieves will come through, and you'll be yesterday's news."

Tom raised a brow dubiously. "I dunno, Kelly. Seems this article isn't really 'news'. It's a personal attack and the intent is malicious."

"'Isn't *really* news', Tom? It isn't news at all. It's a fucking, steaming shit pile of lies," Jim fumed.

"You and I know that. The 'innocent maidens' know that. Hell, even the writer knows that. But does the man in the street know it?" Tom asked.

Jim looked around the smoke-filled room at the working-class men and farmers drinking in clusters and decided they did not. How could they? They weren't in the room when he politely declined Betsy's invitation to join her on her chaise lounge. When Adeline fumbled for his fly. When Helen's older sister Diana, fresh home from her European tour, invited him into her bedroom on a Sunday morning while the family worshipped at St. George's.

"The timing is damn suspicious, ain't it," said Kelly. "The writer could'a brought you down a peg any old time. Old Helston's heart is aching bad and he's retaliating."

"As usual, Kelly has stated the obvious," said Tom. "The question is, how far will Helston go?"

Jim's mind flew to a furious Mr. Meyer, pen hovering over documents at the Commercial Bank, to a livid Mr. Brockett, pulling at his gray beard and refusing employment at the mill, to an enraged Mayor Jones considering if he should expropriate the Sinclairs' land for a song to build the hospital Blackmore dreamed of. Yet the most troubling question of all was of Cora. How would she feel? Helston had only to push over a key domino to ruin Jim's future in Maryville and he'd done it.

As if reading Jim's mind, Tom asked, "You're solid with Cora?"

He nodded. They were solid. "She'll be pretty upset when she finds out about it, but we'll be okay," Jim said.

Awash in worry, he drank his ale. He had to stop Helston. Make him retract his lies, print an apology, and promise on his knees never to slander the Sinclair name again.

Kelly said, "I'd watch my back for a bit if I were you. Men who lack confidence in themselves and their wives can be mighty dangerous. There'll be folks who imagine all sorts."

"I will," said Jim.

"What are you going to do?" Tom looked pointedly at Jim's fisted hands.

"I'm going to finish my ale and walk home and go to bed," said Jim.

"Mind you're alone," winked Tom. "Don't want to provoke any scandal."

Chapter 34

Jim no longer cared to project an image of newfound moral rectitude. After morning chores, he took Buttercup for a run, and they wound up at the Pattons' cottage. He tethered the mare to a tree in a sunny place in the garden so she could warm her back, then knocked on the kitchen door and entered. Cora greeted Jim as if she didn't know about the slanderous article, returning his affection as ever. Red-cheeked from the cold, she'd just returned to the cottage from a visit with Father Finney and Kate to discuss what might be done for the Sullivan family.

Cora picked up the teapot. "Tea?"

"Sure. Thank you," said Jim.

She gestured to a chair to bid him sit. "The poor children bounce from town to town. Mr. Sullivan picks up work as he's able, but he's simple and they can't seem to get a toehold anywhere. He came over as a boy from that awful famine and now, thirty years on, he has a shack full of children and an exhausted wife with nary a penny in his pocket. I'd hate to see the children wind up in an orphanage only because their parents are destitute."

Cora spooned leaves into the teapot and filled it with water from the stove kettle, speaking as she worked. "Seeing the hollow, goopy eyes of the children, hearing their croupy coughs, their poor careworn mother. Well, it puts our troubles into perspective, doesn't it? You know what I'm talking about, or you wouldn't be here.

Not with me unchaperoned and you with a farm to run."
Sarcasm edged her voice.

"That newspaper article," said Jim.

"Yes. Kate and Father Finney warned me. You're
notorious."

"And so are you by association."

"Jim, I'm quite unlike you in one way. I don't have
a wide circle of friends. I'm respected rather than liked
and I care little about what other people think of me.
Robert's drivel hurts me because it hurts you. His readers
are being subjected to the ravings of a broken-hearted
man. Broken-hearted because of me. I think it's best if
we ignore that ridiculous article and live our lives as
happily as we can."

"Thank God you don't believe any of it." Jim smiled
with relief.

"Believe it? An ounce of it is true, isn't it? The other
fifteen ounces of the pound are utter shite."

Jim noticed a slight narrowing of Cora's eyes, a
clench in her jaw that hinted at pain. "Cora." He reached
across the table for her hand, but she didn't take it,
pouring the tea into mugs instead. "All of it is bullshit,"
he declared. "The whole pound. One hundred percent."

Her eyes watered, but she didn't cry. Instead, she
looked away.

"How have I treated you? Not when we were kids,
but since you lost your father?" Jim asked.

"With kindness," replied Cora.

"Have I given you any reason to doubt my sincerity?
To doubt that I love only you?"

"No, Jim, you haven't. But we've both been cavalier
with other people's feelings and now we pay the price."

Absently, Jim lifted his mug and blew over it. He

took a sip and burned his tongue.

Cora continued. "My first instinct is to go on as if nothing has happened. When I'm troubled, I busy myself with work and most problems vanish of their own accord. I concede that you're right, though. I didn't realize Robert would stoop to this ugliness. I thought he was a better man than this."

"He won't stop until he wins. However he defines winning," said Jim.

"Maybe I should talk to him," said Cora.

"What? No. Please don't. You won't make it better." Jim extended his open hand and this time, after a brief hesitation, she accepted it and met his eyes.

"Then I suppose we shall just ignore him. Until his bitterness and anger burn away," she said.

"Cora, you're a very intelligent woman but a mediocre judge of character."

"Says the lawyer."

"Yes. Says the future lawyer who happens to be a shrewd judge of character. Will you allow me to fix this? So we can marry without the cloud of scandal over our heads?"

"Okay," Cora agreed slowly. "What are you going to do?"

"That, my dear Miss Polka Dot, is the proprietary knowledge of a law student. I can't tell you that. You'll just have to trust me."

****

After tea with Cora, Jim went directly to Helston's office to confront him, but he wasn't there.

"He's in Toronto on urgent business," said Willy.

"That's convenient," said Jim. "Do you know when he'll be back?"

"In a few days." As if to curtail any possibility of violence, Willy added, "I didn't write that piece, Sinclair. The one you're here about."

When Jim said nothing, only stood immovably, Willy stammered, "If you must know, he stays at the Colonial Hotel when he's in the city."

"Thank you, Willy," said Jim. "I didn't have to know, but now that I do, I'll put the information to use. And if Helston should receive an urgent telegram from you today, I'll be back to deal with you."

Jim rode Buttercup to the O'Mallory farm, had a brief word with Tom, then stabled the mare in the barn and walked home. Tom would do chores on the Sinclair farm until Jim returned. Jim washed, put on clean clothes, told Gran he was headed out for the night, and boarded the afternoon train. He arrived in Toronto at about a quarter to four.

There were more people in Union Station than all of Maryville and everyone was in a rush. Smartly dressed ladies and gentlemen, impatient children pulling on adult hands, porters carrying trunks and shoeshines polishing boots—each person took his place in the mass theatrical scene. Jim carved his way through the crowd to the street and asked an urchin the way to the Colonial Hotel.

"Why, tis right up that way. Two blocks," said the boy.

"Thanks."

Jim tossed a coin in the air, and the boy caught it, examined it, and grinned.

"For another one of these, I'll carry your bag all the way there," the boy said as he pocketed the coin.

Jim displayed his unburdened hands palms up, and said, "No need," thanked the boy again, and strode away.

The Colonial was posh and though he'd worn his best clothes, he barely passed as acceptably attired to enter the warmth of the lobby and take a seat. At four o'clock in the afternoon, it was the hour of coming and going, and Helston would either return to his room to refresh himself after a day of business or head out for drinks. Jim considered asking the desk clerk for Helston's room number but decided against it. Better to follow and ambush Helston on the street. Jim picked up a *Globe* newspaper discarded on a table and pretended to read it.

He didn't wait long. Wearing a dandyish long frock coat, pinstriped trousers, and shiny hat and boots, Helston descended a grand staircase, left his key at the desk, and headed to the street. Jim tucked the newspaper under his arm and trailed at a distance, concealing himself in the crowds on the sidewalk. After several blocks, Helston turned onto a quiet residential street of large, smart, brick houses. At the fifth house, he knocked on the door and it swung open, the unseen occupant admitting him with haste. An unseen *female* occupant, for her ruffled, pink sleeve had been visible at the doorknob.

Jim stood behind a juniper shrub and considered what he'd witnessed. Who was Helston visiting? A lover? A cousin? A business associate?

The door swung open again and a man left. His face had the slackness of a man whose carnal whims had been satisfied. In a flash, Jim realized that he was standing in front of a bawdy house and Helston was there for entertainment.

Without thinking, Jim walked to the house, stuck the newspaper under a frozen flower urn, and knocked on the door, and again, the door swung open. A girl, rouged, painted, and elaborately coiffed, stood behind it. A flicker of suspicion passed over her face and Jim blurted, "I'm a close friend of the gentleman who just arrived."

"Oh yes," she smiled. "He's in there, taking off his hat and coat."

Jim hurried past the girl, gaining the cloak room in two long strides. "Hello, Helston," he said.

Helston turned. Recognizing Jim at once, the color drained from his face and his mouth gawped like a guppy, wordless, soundless.

"Sir! Sir," said the girl by the door. "You haven't been properly introduced and—"

"You're right. How rude of me." Jim extended his hand. "Jim Sinclair. And you're?"

The girl looked at Helston who had frozen like a deer, stunned and silent. Receiving no direction, she shook Jim's hand and said, "Anastasia."

"How do you do?" Jim smiled at the girl to show he meant no harm. He looked into the parlor and saw three other girls clothed in low cut flounces, faces also painted. Then he spoke to Helston. "Have a moment for a meeting? Before…you know…"

Without a word, Helston donned his coat and hat, and they left the house, Jim thanking Anastasia as he closed the door.

"Fancy a drink?" Jim asked Helston.

Face recovering color, Helston shook his head. "No, I think not. What's your bottom line, Sinclair?"

"A full retraction of your article in the *Trumpet* by Friday, a telegram to Cameron to inform him that you only wish for Cora's happiness and that you withdraw your objection to our marriage, and a promise to cease making libelous claims or telling any more lies about any member of the Patton or Sinclair families."

"And if I don't?"

"I'll tell Cora about Anastasia and the other girls inside that house. And I may drop by the police station. The girls don't look happy in their occupation."

Helston's expression contorted into fury, but outmaneuvered, he merely nodded his assent to Jim's terms.

"You're getting off easy," said Jim.

Heston regained his composure. Voice like iron, he said, "You'd never blackmail me, Sinclair. You haven't the guts. In fact, I don't have to agree to terms at all. I don't care what Cora thinks of me. She's damaged goods and I'm done with her. The girls know me. They have no foibles when money's at stake. It's a simple matter for them to allege that you're a patron too. Anastasia has a colleague in Montreal."

"Fine. Have it your way," said Jim.

In the sliver of a second, he grabbed Helston by his lapels and threw him into the shrubs as if he were a sack of beets. When Helston started to get up, Jim kicked him hard, and Helston was down again. It was too mild a rebuke for a man who would dare call Cora, 'damaged goods'.

"If you want to settle this matter with fists, I'm happy to oblige," said Jim.

Helston shook his head.

"You're agreeing to my terms?"

Helston nodded.

"Very well. You may get up."

As Helston struggled to his feet, Jim said, "I'd shake on our deal, but your hand is so flabby and limp, I fear

I'd crush it."

As Helston picked up his hat, Jim turned and walked away though alert to movement behind him. Time would tell if Jim had succeeded in neutralizing the man's poisonous pen and verbal venom. To say Helston couldn't be trusted was a gross understatement.

Chapter 35

Much to Cora's delighted surprise, a tersely worded, emphatic retraction of all allegations against Jim appeared in the *Trumpet,* and though Jim and she remained compelling subjects of gossip, the accusatory stares and salacious chatter diminished to a tolerable level. As the icy grip of deep winter eased, Cora decided it was high time she called on Mrs. Tucker to extend her condolences and she was received in Mrs. Tucker's informal sitting room with a cordial welcome and a well-brewed cup of tea.

"What a terrible time we've both had," exclaimed Mrs. Tucker—'Beatrice'—as she insisted Cora call her now. "I only wish I could've been a better friend to you when you lost your father last August. And now, even after the way Charles treated you, here you are being a friend to me."

"Mr. Tucker was very sick, and he was desperate," Cora said gently. "He had to grab any rope he could if he hoped to hang on. The one I gave him was failing. I don't hold that against his memory."

"But Dr. Blackmore didn't help him. Not one bit. If you weren't to be married when Charles took his bad turn, I would have sent for you or your aunt."

"I couldn't have saved him either, Beatrice."

"But you knew he was dying, and he'd have had a better end. Dr. Blackmore convinced Charles he'd get better on his medicine. He gave him false hope. It may as well have been a quack's medicine from the mythical fountain of youth for all the good it did. Then Dr. Blackmore insisted Charles stop the drink, like that." Beatrice snapped her fingers. "Not a single drop should he have and two days later, Charles was in fits. I trickled some brandy into his mouth, but he couldn't swallow it. He choked and brought up blood. He had a terrible end, Cora. Charles did not die in peace."

"You were with him, Beatrice. All along and through the end. You did your best and gave him all the love a wife can give a husband. Even though he suffered, Mr. Tucker must have felt that."

Beatrice closed her eyes for a moment and nodded slowly. Then with pained, dry eyes, she regarded Cora and said solemnly, "Yes. I think he found comfort in my presence. Despite his faults he was a good husband. I miss the old buzzard terribly."

It occurred to Cora that Beatrice must have run out of tears for her late husband, having shed so many during their marriage and the chaos of his wretched death.

Beatrice sighed. "And now, I go on without him. Sometimes I go into his office, sit at his desk, and try to imagine his world." She straightened in her chair and her face brightened. "Forgive me my pride, Cora, but over the years I've learned a thing or two from Charles. I do believe I'd make a half-decent lawyer. If there were female lawyers."

Sensing Beatrice had more to say, Cora only smiled her encouragement.

Beatrice waved her hand over the small tower of thick books on her sitting room table. "I'm studying up on 'medical malpractice'. Did you know you can sue a doctor if he's negligent in his care?"

"If you can prove it," Cora answered mildly.

"It gets me thinking about that Dr. Blackmore, though I wouldn't dare think of suing. For one thing, I'm not a lawyer, far from it, and for another, to have one's day in court would dredge up all manner of horribleness." Beatrice shook her head. "No. I study for my interest only. Speaking of lawyers, and students of law—"

Predicting the turn in conversation, Cora blushed.

"I heard that young Jim Sinclair is your new beau."

"He's more than my beau. We're to be married in the spring." How strange and wonderful it felt to say it openly.

"If you don't mind me saying, you two make a fine match."

"Thank you," Cora said shyly.

"I'm not ready to give away Charles' things yet, but please tell Jim that he may have the run of Charles' library when he sets up practice."

"If he sets up practice."

"If?"

"Jim has all but taken over the farm because, well, his father—"

A wave of shame washed over Cora, shame for her future father-in-law, and she winced slightly.

At once, Beatrice noticed and responded. "I believe I have an inkling of what the Sinclairs must cope with. It's very trying for the family and for you." She squeezed Cora's hand.

"It is," said Cora. "Very trying." How odd that she was visiting to offer sympathy yet receiving it instead. Perhaps commiseration was doing them both a world of good.

"You will do well to remember, Cora, that responsibility for James senior's behavior belongs to James senior and no other. As you join your new family, don't pick up burdens that aren't yours to carry."

"I'll try not to," said Cora.

"Good. Morag hasn't learned that lesson and it's destroying her," Beatrice said in a warning tone. "Even with old Mrs. Sinclair and Jim about the house, hers is a lonely lot. Now that I have more time, I must pay her a visit."

"I'm sure she'd appreciate it."

Beatrice smoothed the fabric of her skirt over her lap. "Now, tell me about your wedding plans, my dear."

"Since the retraction of the allegations against Jim in the *Trumpet*—"

"Ridiculous and slanderous." Beatrice rolled her eyes. "Simply slanderous, they were."

"Reverend Cameron has agreed to marry us right after Easter."

"Why, Easter's on the 28th of March this year. That's only a month away!"

Cora nodded happily. "We're planning for the first week of April, before the hardest work on the farm begins."

Beatrice seized Cora's hand again. "April. Imagine that! If I weren't in mourning, I'd hope for an invitation. Oh, do let me help with the food."

"It will be a small wedding," said Cora. "With light refreshments for a very few guests."

"Nonsense. People won't hear of it."

"They must. We actually planned to elope."

"Elope!"

"Well, not elope exactly," Cora explained defensively. "Aunt Jenny knows a minister in Brucedale, and she was helping us arrange everything."

"Stealing away like thieves in the night to Brucedale of all places! But why?"

"To avoid the tarnish of scandal. However, Jim's grandmother wouldn't hear of it. She said our plan was sneaky and would only, um, how did she put it? 'Put another letter in the devil's postbag'. I think she was referring to gossip."

With concealed amusement, Cora thought of Gran's ambush of Reverend Cameron on their behalf.

Beatrice said, "Old Mrs. Sinclair's right, you know, Cora. If you act as if you're guilty, people treat you that way. Mr. Helston acts the victim, but as a lawyer's widow, I know better. Don't ask me how." Beatrice pursed her lips and mimed the pulling of a string. "Charles bound me to secrecy after he caught me 'organizing' his files. Just know that you're marrying the better man by a country mile so you might as well proclaim it with a big wedding."

"But they're so expensive," Cora protested.

"Nonsense," countered Beatrice. "The more people you invite, the more people will donate to your future. Most folks are good, deep down, and they want good people like you and Jim to succeed."

"I don't know…"

"Perhaps I'm self-interested, but I think Jim simply must finish his law degree, or I won't have anyone to use all these books." Beatrice scowled comically as she glanced over the table, then slowly shook her head. "No, a small wedding won't do."

Cora only laughed noncommittally and sought

Beatrice's advice on the best way to force flowers to bloom when snow yet lay upon the ground and the green shoots of spring were weeks from emerging.

Chapter 36

A week later, as news spread of his engagement, Jim was summoned to the Commercial Bank. Square and intimidating in a boxy suit, Mr. Meyer stood and extended his hand with uncharacteristic warmth.

After they shook, Meyer said, "Sit. Sit. I should've asked you in sooner, Jim. I've been remiss."

"Not at all, Mr. Meyer." Jim settled onto a hard wooden chair opposite the older man at his desk.

"First off, congratulations on your engagement. You have a fine girl in Cora. Betsy's thrilled to bits for both of you and expects an invitation to your wedding."

"Betsy's very kind," Jim said guardedly.

"Yes, kind but impetuous, I'm afraid. Before I get to the proposal I alluded to in my letter, I need to share something, um, rather embarrassing. Nevertheless, it must be confronted." Mr. Meyer picked up a pen and spun it like a tiny baton in his sausage fingers.

"Okay." Jim hid his curiosity under an impassive expression.

Mr. Meyer continued fidgeting with his pen. Beads of sweat broke over his brow, and his face flushed crimson despite the coolness of the room.

"Um, you probably recall that disparaging editorial that appeared in the *Trumpet* last month. Concerning certain allegations," said Meyer.

"If we're thinking of the same article, I can tell you

its author didn't allege. He lied," said Jim.

"True. So true," Meyer concurred. "May I have your word that you will hold what I'm about to tell you in strictest confidence?"

"Of course," replied Jim.

Mr. Meyer's words poured forth in a tumble. "My darling, rash, wildly jealous Betsy made one of the, um, allegations about you to Dr. Blackmore and then she repeated it to me upon Blackmore's urging. Please understand, I should have known better, but we both believed her and before you could say 'poppycock,' a meeting was convened, and the daughters of Maryville's leading families were provoked into taletelling. I believe they were quite willing to cut you down to size when they discovered that Cora had captured your heart. Hell hath no fury…"

"Jesus," muttered Jim.

"Now Betsy isn't a bad girl. She deliberately besmirched your name, no question about it, but she did it because she fancied you and she was jealous. Betsy knew better than to lie, though, and she came to me after the editorial came out and confessed what she'd done. She was beside herself with shame. We would've come to you to apologize forthwith, but Helston rectified the injustice of his own accord. He's sharp enough to realize when the accuracy of his journalism has been compromised and he wrote the retraction and apology without hearing of our, um, admission."

Jim sat in stunned silence for a moment, watching Meyer torture his pen, piecing together the events of the previous month. Finally, he said, "I'm curious, Mr. Meyer. Why tell me this? You didn't have to tell me about Betsy's mistake as doing so now doesn't affect

Cora and me."

"Betsy insisted. She's too sheepish to apologize herself, though she's promised me that she will eventually. She asked me to do it for her and I'm afraid she's rather spoiled. Jim, if you're ever blessed with a daughter, you'll understand."

"I accept her apology. Please tell her so for me."

"Thank you. We won't speak of this again?"

"No sir. And you may tell Betsy that the matter is concluded. No hard feelings."

"Thank you. I had a hunch you'd understand." Mr. Meyer put the pen on his blotter, leaned back in his chair, and said, "Now to business. Dr. Blackmore has asked my permission to seek Betsy's hand in marriage, and although they've only known each other for a few weeks, I've granted it. He'll pop the question in due course and Betsy will be over the moon with happiness when he does."

"Congratulations to them," said Jim.

"There's a wrinkle, however. Blackmore's offer comes with certain, um, strings." Meyer paused and scratched his head, nervous once more. "Naturally Betsy's mother adores her daughter, and she couldn't imagine a future without her girl nearby."

"Naturally," Jim repeated sympathetically as he followed Meyer's strange meandering.

"Well, it's a conundrum for the ages. Blackmore is a proud physician who wishes to elevate his profession and how it's practiced, yet he finds himself in an obscure rural town. He's Oxford educated, but he has occasion to treat patients on kitchen tables in farmhouses. That's fine for some practitioners, but it's simply not his way."

Jim's mind leapt to Cora and her territorial

skirmishes with Blackmore. Best hear Meyer out before launching a defense of country medicine on her behalf.

"Cora works so hard," Meyer said, as if reading Jim's thoughts.

"She does," agreed Jim.

"In fact, I'd venture that she and Blackmore share the burden of caring for the citizens of Maryville more or less equally."

"More or less." Jim stopped himself from mentioning that, in general, Blackmore saw to the wealthy and Cora to the poor.

"And you'd agree that, as medical people, their goals are identical," said Meyer.

"If not identical, then similar," said Jim.

"I'll come to my point," Meyer said gravely. "Blackmore insists on having a hospital built. Bribery, blackmail, leverage, call it what you will, but either the citizens of Maryville muster the wherewithal to provide him with one, or he'll move to a town with a hospital and take Betsy with him. Or not marry her at all. Either outcome is intolerable to Betsy's mother and me. Maryville must have a hospital."

"I see."

"Good. I don't have to explain myself." Meyer looked relieved.

"No, you don't, Mr. Meyer. I believe I understand," said Jim. "Dr. Blackmore wants a hospital. Betsy wants to marry Dr. Blackmore. You and Mrs. Meyer want them to reside in Maryville."

"And this is where you come in," said Meyer. "You and Cora."

Jim nodded, bidding the older man elaborate.

"Patton Memorial Hospital. We could build it on the

empty lot where Dr. Patton lived and practiced medicine until August last year. That is, if you and Cora agree. The Town of Maryville will pay fair market value for the lot."

"It's an intriguing idea, but Cora must decide."

"Fine, fine. Perfectly reasonable. Get her consent and we can move forward." Meyer shook his hammy fist in the air. "Progress, Jim. That's what we'll have!"

Assuming the meeting was ending, Jim sat forward. "Also, I should mention..."

Jim settled back and looked attentively at Meyer.

"Miss Jenny Patton wrote to Mr. Jones, Mr. Brockett, and me. Like Dr. Blackmore, she recognizes the need for a modern hospital. She's remarkably sharp, forward-thinking. It's so unusual to find such qualities in the weaker sex."

Meyer regarded Jim for a moment, then cleared his throat and continued. "Miss Patton has made some unorthodox suggestions, and I've been thinking about how to proceed. We'd have to form a board and plan meticulously before any shovels break ground."

"Suggestions such as?"

"The first is that ladies sit on the hospital board and all committees alongside men and that the advice of mothers and nurses be sought in all decision-making."

"That's a sensible suggestion," said Jim.

"Do you think so? I think Miss Patton is very bold in making it. Your Cora could have considerable influence on the project." Meyer took a heavy breath, as if oppressed by outspoken women. "Miss Patton also suggests that no one who requires care be turned away from the hospital for lack of ability to pay. The well-off would subsidize the poor."

Pure Patton, Jim thought as Meyer continued.

"Her third suggestion, one I endorse whole-heartedly, is that the Commercial Bank, in cooperation with the town, cover the capital cost of the hospital by issuing bonds to the community and offering a low interest loan to the hospital board. That's prudent. A brand-new hospital will attract investment to the town and the bank will reap its reward down the road. However, much depends on the provision of a site, an ample, conveniently located lot such as Dr. Patton's old place. Cora's land." Meyer picked up his pen and again fiddled with it. "You'll put our best foot forward when you speak to Cora?"

"I'm certain she'll agree to your request. I'll speak to her," said Jim. "May I ask a favor of you, Mr. Meyer?"

"Depends what it is," shrugged Meyer.

"Could the Commercial Bank stop extending credit to my father? You're aware of our financial challenges. I'm trying to gain control of the farm."

"Jim, I won't loan any more money to your father, but the farm isn't in your name and your father is free to borrow elsewhere. How you rectify that chink in your armor is up to you."

"Mr. Meyer, I don't want the farm to slip from my grasp if I'm away and my back is turned. Dad would never let me buy him out, let alone sign the farm over to me. He wants my labor but not my management. Do you have any advice?"

"Perhaps." Meyer frowned and scratched his head again. "To your knowledge, has your father taken out other loans? Besides the mortgage?"

"To my knowledge, none worth the paper they're written on."

Only loans carrying penalties of a punishingly

physical nature, thought Jim, recalling his father's missing finger.

"Hmm, well then," said Meyer. "I do have one idea. It's tricky, or bald-faced trickery if you will, though perfectly legal. You could form a company, fundraise, sell shares. Anything's possible if you approach the right men. And then you loan money to your father yourself with the farm as collateral so if—when—he defaults, the farm belongs to you. Of course, you must square things here first. But I'm creative when I see benefit, and I'd back you."

"Thank you," Jim smiled gratefully.

"Drop in when you have an answer for me, Jim. See that Cora understands the lay of the land. The hospital, your future, the farm. We can work something out, I'm sure," Meyer said gruffly.

Jim thanked Meyer again and promised a swift reply as they stood and shook hands to end the meeting.

Jim emerged from the bank in a mood of sunny optimism. Although he lacked a mentor in his father, he had only to observe the pragmatic tactics of his elders as they negotiated matters of money and power, and he would learn as much in Maryville as his McGill professors taught him. Whether motivated by greedy self-interest as was Helston, or humanitarianism as were Gran and Jenny, or a mixture of both, as were Brockett, Jones, and Meyer, his elders were fonts of knowledge. One could glean information on pitfalls and traps by watching a foe with wary attention while seeking the wisdom of friends.

Jim couldn't wait to share the news of the day with Cora.

****

Later that day, Cora found Jim washing sap buckets and hardware in a sunny, sheltered area next to the barn. The forest was too muddy for the winter work of harvesting lumber, and drifts of snow would patch the fields for some time yet. In the lull of early March, tapping the maple trees and boiling sap into syrup was their only pressing task on the farm. They had the luxury of time.

"Aren't your hands freezing?" Cora asked.

Jim straightened and smiled. "You'll warm them. I'm almost finished anyway."

Cora helped him lay the clean equipment on a blanket in the sunshine to dry.

"It's early yet, Cora," he said. "Let's leave the chores for now. Anyway, I have some news."

Cora peered up into Jim's eyes. "Good news?"

"The best. But I'm not saying anymore till we're in the office."

As they settled into the straw together, Cora said, "Well?"

"Well."

"Your news?"

"Right. I don't know where to begin."

"Begin at the beginning," pleaded Cora. "Only please tell me this good news."

"Great news," Jim corrected, and at last, as Cora snuggled into his arms, he told her of his visit to Mr. Meyer, Jenny's ideas for a hospital, and the bank manager's advice on how to wrest control of the farm from his father.

Cora was silent as she pondered the implications of what he'd told her. That very morning, Jim had forged a path toward a future of prosperity and purpose for them both, and naturally she was pleased. However, matters of importance were decided without her knowledge, let alone input. Jim and Aunt Jenny acted as if her consent in all matters were a given, and she supposed it was, but still—

"You don't seem very happy." Jim combed a loose lock of her hair with his fingers.

"I'm happy. Of course I am," Cora protested. "But I thought we'd agreed that we'd make decisions together. And Aunt Jenny's no better. She told me she had ideas for a hospital, but she didn't give me any details. We'll sell the lot for a hospital, but I might have been consulted sooner. And you should have included me in the meeting."

"Hold on, Cora. Meyer summoned me, not us. You know what he's like."

"Not really."

"You do. His daughter's your friend."

"Okay, but you should have at least told me you were meeting him."

"You're right. I'm sorry. I should have told you."

"That's better."

Now can we please be happy together?"

"I don't know. I'll decide that myself."

"You're being sarcastic."

"I'm carving out a tiny nook of power for myself. That's all."

"Think of the power you'll have when you're on the board of Patton Memorial Hospital. That's what Meyer wants to call the hospital. Your chair between Helston's and Blackmore's, holding them to account…"

"The first order of business will be changing the name of the hospital."

"You don't like 'Patton Memorial Hospital'?"

"I hate it." Cora made a face.

"Strong words," Jim laughed.

Tiring of the argument and feeling guilty for her reaction to Jim's news, Cora said, "Wrestling match?"

"Okay. You're on. But don't be too hard on me."

"And you don't let me win too easily," said Cora.

"I never let you win. You always beat me fair and square."

"Now you're lying, Jim, and, hey! Not fair!"

Before Cora had finished her sentence, Jim had pinned her down, but his grip on her wrists was ridiculously loose and she had only to twist her hands away to free her arms.

"We didn't say, 'ready, set, go'," said Cora.

"All's fair in love and war and this is both."

Cora pouted and looked away. Just as Jim suggested they start over, she yanked her wrists free, and the battle was on, Jim giving Cora the upper hand, then seizing his advantage to challenge her. Now they rolled around in the straw, Cora fighting with all her might, Jim pretending to be overcome and laughing all the while. The mock fight ended with a breathless Cora astride the trunk of her supine foe, victoriously pumping her fist in the air.

"I surrender," Jim grinned. "What will you claim as your prize?"

"This." Cora resettled herself over Jim's thighs and pressed her fingertip against the bulge under his fly.

He groaned. "You can't have it. Not yet."

Cora laughed and quick as a flash of lightning, he was over her, face an inch from hers. "I have a better idea." Jim kissed her, more deeply, more hungrily than ever. Their lips came together in a pliant exploration as Cora sought the faint taste of coffee in his mouth. To be kissed in this way was utterly intoxicating. Then Cora lay still and let herself be loved.

Jim unbuttoned her bodice, cupped her breast in his hand, and bowing his head, took her taut nipple in his mouth, sucking and teasing with such care that she gasped with pleasure. Now he lay over her, his body pressed against her, her thighs yielding to him. He didn't take her other breast. Instead, he licked and kissed and teased her with his mouth, across her ribcage and belly until he arrived at her waist. He pushed her skirt up, eased her underclothes off, and settled himself between her legs.

Jim's tongue slid over her clitoris and into her folds, softly at first, then with a firm pressure, caressing her in rhythm. With each of stroke of his tongue, Cora inched closer to ecstasy. She was falling into a thrilling madness with no end. A ripple of joy welled from her womanhood and washed over her entire being in relentless, repeated waves. Jim held her thighs in his warm, rough hands and buried his tongue in a place most tender. Cora moaned, a deep, animalistic moan, for her mind left her as climax took her body and soul and left her spent.

She rested, muscles limp, sexual hunger sated. Gently, Jim fixed her clothing, laid beside her, and held her. Cora felt him hard against her and she slid her hand there to offer pleasure in return. However, Jim covered her hand with his and moved it away.

He said, "Not today, Cora. Today is for you," and he kissed her softly once more.

Chapter 37

Jenny arranged Cora's hair for the wedding. Though Cora sat as still as she could, Jenny scolded her niece for wiggling as she wove satin ribbon into her thick auburn tresses.

"However you pin it, my hair will come loose anyway. It has a mind of its own," Cora complained.

"Like the girl it belongs to," said Jenny. "Such beautiful hair, yet willful and fiery."

Cora let Jenny's comment pass.

"Your mother and father would be so proud of you. And overjoyed to have Jim as their son-in-law," said Jenny. "It's times like this I miss them most. Well, I shall have to be happy for them."

"I miss Father terribly," said Cora. "And I suppose Mother too, though I recall so little about her. It's funny, I have no specific memories of her. Only a vague feeling of security when I conjure her in my mind."

"You inherited her hair." Jenny tugged her comb through a tangle.

"Ow!"

"Sorry."

"I'm glad you came back for the wedding, Aunt Jenny. Though I may be bald when you're through with me."

"Alas, I'll have to return this evening. I wish I could've come sooner, but Ivy is still too weak to be without help."

"Poor Ivy," murmured Cora.

"At least her voracious appetite has returned," said Jenny. "She made me promise to bring back a slice of wedding cake for under her pillow, and a detailed description of the whole ceremony."

"She hasn't given up on dreaming of 'the one'?" asked Cora.

Jenny sniffed. "Of course, she has. Men and romance are the furthest thing from her mind. We're stuck with each other and quite content, but she has a sweet tooth. To Ivy, a piece of fruitcake, even mushed up with squishy marzipan from following that old superstition, is a treat."

"Do you think you'll ever come home to Maryville?" asked Cora. "To live with us?"

"No one can predict the future, Cora, but I doubt it. The cottage is yours now and you're all grown up. I'm not needed here. On the other hand, I am needed there. I don't believe in notions such as destiny, but if there were such a thing, I do believe I was meant to care for the orphans, by Ivy's side."

"And if Jim and I should be blessed with children and we need you?"

"Ha! I'd be a nuisance. Oh, I'll return for a spell, but you have Jim's family and Kate and Moira who's right next door. You won't want for help." Jenny stopped fussing with the comb, stepped back, and circled round Cora to admire her work. "Finished. You're radiant. Go see yourself in the looking glass."

Cora rose and went to the hallway, then returned to the kitchen as proudly as she might. "You missed your calling, Aunt Jenny. Hairdresser to society debutantes and brides."

Jenny waved the comment away and picked up Cora's gown. "It's almost one o'clock. You'd better get dressed."

"Old bracelet, new stockings, borrowed gown, blue ribbon," Cora said as she took the garment from Jenny.

"It was 'ever so kind' of Betsy to loan the gown to you, along with that extra tight corset and tall shoes so it fits. Ivory taffeta trimmed in blue is perfect for a spring wedding."

"I must say, I'm happy she'll be at the wedding. I've noticed a dramatic change in Betsy recently. Rather suddenly, she's no longer selfish, no longer self-centered. She's more mature," said Cora.

"And she's expecting to attend a wedding this afternoon, so for heaven's sake, get dressed. We mustn't keep old Mr. MacTavish waiting for you at the door."

As if to underscore Jenny's command, the grandfather clock struck the hour, and Cora hastened to prepare for her walk down the aisle of St. Andrew's and into her future.

****

Kelly closed the tavern for the afternoon so Moira and he could attend the wedding. The ceremony would begin in an hour. While the women prepared refreshments in the St. Andrew's church hall, the men assembled in boisterous conviviality at the Shamrock and Thistle to celebrate the groom. Jim was overwhelmed with happiness yet so humbled by the occasion that he looked as if he were about to face a firing squad. If his friends wondered if he were having doubts, they didn't say so. They only teased him with toasts and advice, some heartfelt, some comedic, some maudlin, and some unfit for the ears of the fairer sex.

In an eternity and an instant, it was time to embark on the two-block journey to the church. Walking backward ahead of the mob, Tom conducted an enthusiastic, off-key choir of men singing "For He's a Jolly Good Fellow" all the way to the church. Well-wishers filed up the stairs, through the narthex, and into the nave, taking their seats in the pews. Jim walked down the aisle, the very route Cora would take in a few short minutes and stood before the communion table with Tom at his side.

As Mrs. MacTavish played a prelude on the organ, Jim was swept up in memory. Once upon a time, he'd proudly helped his grandfather and the other men build this church, fetching tools and whitewashing plaster as best as a young boy could. He also remembered the departed. Doc Patton dozing beside Jenny, Grandpa fidgeting beside Gran, and little cousin Rosie, perched on the pew swinging her short legs. She was taken by scarlet fever at the age of six.

He remembered seeking shelter in the narthex with Cora on the day of the tornado, how he'd teased her to stave off fear and then stood by in silent witness when she discovered her father had perished. And he remembered Helston's smarmy smile as his marriage banns were read.

There was Dad, slipping into a pew at the rear of the church and lifting his hand in a low-key wave. Jim waved back. Now the women entered the nave from behind the altar, Mama and Gran among them. Yellow forsythia, daffodils, and narcissus, forced in warm water for the occasion and held in place with silver and blue ribbons, captured the joyful atmosphere of the building.

Even the sun shone cheerfully upon the stained-glass windows, filling the room with colorful light.

A hush descended over the assembled as Reverend Cameron followed the women into the nave. He sidled up to Jim and Tom.

"Are you ready?" he asked Jim.

"Yes. I'm ready," Jim declared.

A moment later, Jenny peeked through the doors from the narthex and signaled Mrs. MacTavish who struck up a stately march. All at once, everyone rose and stood transfixed as Cora entered the nave on the arm of ninety-two-year-old Iain MacTavish, patriarch of the congregation, standing in for her father, and with Jenny as her maid. As the bride and her entourage slowly proceeded to the altar, Jim's eyes watered, and Tom discreetly passed him a handkerchief. Jim's heart burst with love. Anything was possible with Cora by his side. They need only clasp each other's hands, profess their commitment to each other before their community, make their vows before God, and they would begin their lives anew as Mr. and Mrs. Sinclair.

The bride's party joined the groom and his best man at the front of the church. Cora turned to old Mr. MacTavish. After he handed his cane to Jenny, he turned to Cora. With hands twisted by a lifetime of toil, he lifted Cora's veil, and he bestowed upon her the blessing of an elder's toothless grin for a favored child.

When Cora turned to face her groom, Jim felt he couldn't breathe. How beautiful she was. Her crown of copper hair, her creamy skin dusted with freckles, her arched brows and her intelligent green eyes peering deeply into his, her lips the color of rose petals and parted in an adventurous smile. Cora's sumptuous gown held her curves in confident sensuality, and if Jim was permitted the indelicacy, he would have swept her into his arms and kissed her at once.

Instead, Reverend Cameron asked, "Shall we begin?"

Cora and Jim joined hands and in unison replied, "Yes."

*****

The Sinclair wedding wasn't covered in the *Trumpet*. No society columnist conveyed its touching poignancy, grace, and beauty to the curious. Only the people in attendance were fortunate to witness the joining in holy matrimony of the two young people, of a man and a woman who were a study in complementary opposites, a match so right it was as if God had arranged it Himself.

Easter was only behind them and the timing of the nuptials within the year of Doctor John Patton's death demanded restraint in the celebration that followed the ceremony. Nevertheless, Reverend Cameron averted his eyes when Tom spiked the punch with rum and Kelly popped the corks on bottles of champagne. On the other hand, no Calvinist restraint was shown in the trestle table of food, and though dancing would not be countenanced, gluttony was tacitly permitted. Everyone indulged in the feast, everyone that is, except the bride and groom who were too in love with each other to have any appetite for food or drink.

And so, as soon as they could graciously exit the party, Jim caught his wife's attention with a subtle smile and a nod toward the door. From across the room, Cora smiled back at her husband, expressed her gratitude to the women with whom she was conversing, and made a beeline to his side. After Jim helped Cora into her coat, they stepped into the glow of a fine, early spring evening, and began their life as one, so entranced with each other that they were oblivious to the send-off cheers of their friends and family.

****

"I wish I were carrying you off in a fancy coach," Jim said wistfully as he offered Cora's his arm. He led her to a back street, an alternative route to Main Street and away from prying stares.

"Things like that don't matter." Cora tucked her hand into the inside of Jim's elbow. "I'm the luckiest girl in the world, however we travel."

"In one year from now, Buttercup will pull a carriage and I'll be practicing law," Jim predicted.

"You'll be a lawyer, Jim, but I don't think you'll ever harness Buttercup," said Cora. "Any other predictions?"

"Yes. We'll be expecting a baby."

Laughing, Cora punched Jim's shoulder. "You're joking, right? We have to establish ourselves first."

"I'm not teasing, my dear wife. I've said it repeatedly. I don't want to wait for us to have children. Neither of us has brothers or sisters. Our families are just plain small."

"Small and uncomplicated."

"Wouldn't you rather have a family like the O'Mallorys though? A big, messy crowd of us. Enough for a hockey match on the pond. For a three-story pyramid with the smallest kids on the top."

"Let's start with one or two to test your mettle as a father."

"Fine, but let's not delay."

Cora slowed her pace and looked up at Jim. "You're serious."

"Yes. Very serious. You told me yourself that Kate is a competent, capable assistant, and you can manage a busy home and your midwifery duties with her help."

"Yes, I suppose I did say that."

"And with the money from the sale of your lot, Jenny's gift of her cottage, and Tom's offer to help Mama while I finish at McGill in exchange for partnership in the farm—well—"

"What are we waiting for?" Cora said, following his line of reason.

"We're taking a small risk, but in a year or two, when I've got control of the farm and I've hung up my shingle and I start taking clients, we'll be secure financially."

"Well, Mr. Sinclair." Cora squeezed Jim's arm affectionately. "In that case, hadn't we better get busy?"

The slush of early spring was freezing into ice as Cora and Jim walked up their street. In daytime, the sap ran in the sun-warmed trunks of the maples and filled buckets for the sugar shack to the song of redwing blackbirds building their nests in the wetlands. At dusk the temperature plummeted, a dark silence descended over the land, the sap ceased flowing in the maples, and it was winter once more. In the days and nights of early spring, the mood of town and country was one of tempered optimism, for despite the promise of brighter days, the trials of the winter months still cast shadows of difficulty.

Cora and Jim understood this. They didn't have to say it out loud. The timing of their wedding portended a married life of unfurling, unlimited possibility, yet together they would have to overcome obstacles and challenges to live and thrive as one.

Cora held tightly to Jim's arm for balance as she picked her way along the uneven, slippery laneway in tottery high heels. Sensing the threat to Cora's ankles, Jim scooped his bride into his arms and carried her to the door as she laughed with delight. Practicality was for tomorrow. This night was reserved for exuberant, passionate discovery.

Chapter 38

Jim carried Cora over the threshold of the front door and into their matrimonial home. He gently set her down in the hallway next to crates of Jenny's clothes, books, and sundry items which lined the wall, ready for shipment to the orphanage.

"Jenny doesn't have to move out," said Jim, casting his eyes over the crates. "She should keep her home here and come and go as she pleases. There's space enough for three."

"I told her that, Jim, but she insists she wants to live permanently in Brucedale and equally insistent that we accept the cottage as our wedding gift." Cora stepped out of her pinching shoes. "She said she wants to be a mother to the motherless and stay by Ivy's side, always and forever."

"I believe I have a glimmer of understanding." Jim stepped back and took a long look at his bride in the dim light. "Cora Sinclair, you are beautiful, but you're far shorter than the girl I married this afternoon."

Cora laughed. "Maybe I'm not the real Cora."

"I suppose I'll have to investigate." Jim took Cora into his arms and kissed her once, briefly. "Your lips feel like Cora's," he murmured.

Then he kissed her again. He kissed her in the way she'd longed to be kissed all afternoon. With lips parted, their mouths came together and moved in an erotic dance. This time, their kiss would not end in a frustrating separation. They would begin with this kiss and fall into rapturous lovemaking until they were sated and bound together for eternity.

Cora led Jim to her bedroom, *their* bedroom, a simple, yet comfortable room. The furniture was spare, well made, and sensible, the space clean and well ordered, yet the bed was blanketed in a soft luxuriousness that would be the envy of any princess. As they entered the room, Cora again felt as if she were trapped in a dress that was wrong for her. Thank goodness she'd never have to wear it again. The gown of ivory taffeta with blue satin flounces and ribbons confined her to the status of a pretty ornament, yet with Jim she was far more than a wife to decorate his arm. When he unbuttoned the borrowed gown, she felt as if she were shedding pretense and deception forever. As the tight-fitting bodice and skirt fell away, a soaring sense of freedom lifted her soul.

Jim untied the strings of her corset, softly nuzzling her face as he worked. In turn, she unfastened the buttons of his shirt and trousers. Their clothes slipped away, and they stood naked before the other, each enthralled by the sight of the other's body in the shadows of the room. How manly Jim was. A shock of black hair fell over his forehead and his eyes held her in loving intensity. His mouth was serious, his square chin already darkened with stubble.

Cora reached up and placed her hands on his broad, strong shoulders. Jim pulled the ribbon from Cora's hair and her auburn curls spilled over her shoulders and down her back. He gazed upon her form. By the widening of his eyes and his tender smile, Cora knew he was entranced by the roundness of her breasts, the curve of her waist, the swell of her hips and her thighs. She should be shy, yet she wasn't. To be admired in this way by the man she loved with her whole heart was a liberation.

She gazed at the whole of him in return and traced her finger from his shoulder over his collar bone to his chest. She remembered his body from when he was her patient, but now she would know him as a wife knew her husband. She would explore every hair, every sinew of muscle, every inch of his masculinity.

His chest and trunk were rippled with muscle, his smooth skin enhanced with dark curls. She ran her finger around one small, brown, manly nipple, then followed the pattern of his hair to the center of his chest, down his flat belly, to the base of his long hardness. Cora ran her hand over his shaft. He was powerfully erect. There was no turning back.

In an instant, Jim swept her onto the bed and teased her with his mouth—earlobe, neck, breasts, nipples, nuzzling and licking and sucking. Cora's skin sizzled at each point of contact. She had never felt so desperately alive. Her womanhood and pelvis throbbed with carnal heat. His hand sought her, and he stroked but he didn't linger, for he found that she was ready for him.

Jim eased her legs apart, moved over her, and met her eyes again. "It shouldn't hurt, Cora," he said softly. "Maybe a small hurt at first, but if it doesn't feel right for you, I'll stop."

Cora nodded, nervous, excited, eager to know him in the depths of her being. "I'm ready," she whispered, her breath rising.

As he mounted her, she felt an aching fullness at her entrance. He moved slowly, tenderly, and slightly more deeply with each caressing thrust, watching her face all the while to be sure of her pleasure and seeking consent before he penetrated further. At first, she felt a piercing discomfort; it was unavoidable, yet she also had an urgent craving, a gnawing need that could only be satisfied with the melding of their bodies and the touch of him deep within her. This need commanded her to angle her hips to receive his weight and strength as he carefully rocked her in a soaring passion.

So novel were the sensations that even with Jim's patient lovemaking, Cora couldn't find her way to the edge. He seemed to sense this, for he unleashed his power in a few fast thrusts until his every muscle tightened, and he groaned with release. Without a word, he slid down her body and licked her until she cried out in the climax of her own ecstasy. Waves of urgent joy swept over her whole being, welling up, subsiding, and leaving her spent and fulfilled.

Afterward, Jim lay beside her, playing with her hair and gazing at her with the deepest love she had ever known, a soft quilt enclosing them and holding them as one.

Hesitantly, Cora said, "I'm sorry I couldn't go along with you when—"

"It was our first time, and you were nervous," replied Jim. "I hope I didn't hurt you."

Cora shook her head and smiled up at Jim. "I'm glad you made us wait. It was worth it."

****

Jim woke in the night with Cora's back curled against his front, her wild hair tickling his face. Moonlight reflected off the curve of her blanket-covered hip. Though he could barely hear her breathing, the rise and fall of her shoulder indicated she was deeply asleep. So was his left arm, for at present, it was tucked under her head in place of a pillow. He dared not wake her. She lost so many nights to duty, she deserved to have undisturbed rest even if his shoulder ached and his fingers felt numb. Still, if he could turn his arm just a little, it would relieve the pressure.

She stirred, muttered unintelligibly, arched her back slightly, and settled back to sleep.

Better. Shoulder aligned, circulation restored. Now he was wide awake. He inhaled Cora's essence, the floral fragrance of her soap, the erotically charged scent of her body, the smell of sex lingering in the room, and he was bewitched. The very smell of her stiffened him. If he should stroke her hair with his fingers and softly kiss her ear…no. She needed her sleep.

Jim would place Cora's needs over his own. Always. Forever. He would provide for her, protect her, be true to her, and love her. If he could stabilize their financial footing by sorting out the business of the farm and finishing the final year of his law degree, they'd have a solid foundation to start a family. Jim had watched Cora with children often enough to know she'd be a doting mother. They would share something that he had never had. A happy family.

He'd married a virgin. Many girls pretended to be inexperienced when they weren't, but ever-unconventional Cora did the opposite. He'd been surprised by her innocence on that afternoon in the hayloft, after their 'wrestling match' when she allowed him to explore her body. Her facade of worldly awareness crumbled before his eyes when he discovered that she was naïve. He wouldn't embarrass her by mentioning it.

Cora's breathing quickened and she shifted. Was she waking? Her rear pressed against him. If he angled just so, he could slip in close, seek the heat of her...he wouldn't enter her...only lie close.

"Cora," he whispered.

"Hmm..." The mumble of a drowsy woman. "Jim." She arched her back again, this time consciously. "Yes."

He ran his free hand over her hip, down the contour of her thigh, and held her there as he buried himself between her legs.

"Oh," she moaned.

She broke away and turned over to face him, and he drew her knee up and entered her, thrusting gently until he was fully engaged in her flesh. She angled herself, pressing back to receive him.

"Yes...oh...Jim...yes." A throaty, guttural permission to take her without restraint.

Locked together, they rolled as one, and she bore the weight of his primitive need. Over and over, he gave, and she received, faster and harder until he felt he'd explode. He couldn't stop from pushing through to his ultimate pleasure and with a husky, primal groan, he released his seed deep within her.

Tired now, he rolled onto his back. He couldn't read her expression in the darkness, but he knew he'd been selfish. Jim eased his hand to the heat between her legs to return her love, but Cora gripped his wrist and took his hand in hers.

"But you're not satisfied," he said.

"It was enough for me," she said. "You got what you craved, right?"

"Yeah."

"Well, that makes me happy." She cuddled against him. "Besides, we're married. We can give and receive from each other as we please for the rest of our lives."

Jim held Cora, her head resting on the crook of his shoulder, and he played with her hair. After a spell of contented silence, he said, "Next time, I'll give you exactly what you want."

"Hmm," said Cora. "What do you have in mind?"

"Whatever your pleasure," answered Jim. "Only teach me how to please you."

She stretched and snuggled even closer in wordless reply, and they both yawned and drifted back to sleep.

****

Cora left Jim to doze in bed while she started a fire for breakfast and fed the chickens. How one's perspective changed when one was newly married and in love. In the weeks after Father died, she'd have tackled her chores with grief-stricken numbness, completing tasks without noticing the magic of the morning. Now in early spring, the sun rose cheerfully and fattened the buds on the plum and willow trees as it lit the world in rosy hues. Light glinted on kernels and seeds as Cora scattered a scoop of feed in a wide arc. The chickens eagerly clucked and scratched as if she were serving them a gourmet meal. A vee of geese returning from the south honked overhead, a train whistle sounded, and a dog barked. Morning in Maryville was as raucous as a band parade.

Cora gathered a half dozen eggs from the nest boxes into her apron and went inside. The stove was heating nicely. Soon the burner would be hot enough for frying so she unwrapped a hunk of bacon and cut it thickly, then took an onion from the string bag and sliced it too. She'd feed Jim well. A man with his build needed a lot of food. As she put the frypan on the stove to warm, she sensed his presence behind her.

"I'll need to bell you like a cat if you sneak up on me like that." She smiled and worked without turning.

"I'm only appreciating your attitude toward work." Jim wrapped his arms around her waist and lifted her. "It moves so enticingly under that plain gray dress."

"What would you rather I wear?" Cora squirmed out of his hug.

"Nothing at all." Jim kissed the top of her head. "But if you must wear a dress, the one you have on is perfect. When you move, I imagine you underneath it without the hindrance of corset or bustle."

Cora spooned a dollop of bacon fat onto the pan and turned to challenge him. However, her irritation withered when she saw his lopsided grin and the love in his eyes. "I'm not a fashion plate," she said defensively.

"No," Jim agreed. "You're Miss Polka Dot, beautiful yet practical. I wouldn't change anything about you, even if you let me."

A loud knock on the front door interrupted their negotiation. Cora held up her spatula and said, "Could you get that?"

"Do we have to?"

"Yes, we do. Someone might need—"

Jim didn't wait for a scolding. He was already halfway down the hall. When he returned, he said, "It's Jenkins. At the station. He was clearing ice from the eaves and fell off his ladder. They tried to get Blackmore, but he's busy with an appendix operation."

Cora was already untying her apron. "Do you know how to cook?"

"Not very well."

"Then this morning you can practice, and I'll be back as quickly as I can."

Cora handed Jim the spatula, donned her cape and bonnet, grabbed her satchel, and hurried out the door. She ignored Jim's frown of resignation as she hastened to tend to what turned out to be the non-urgent case of Jenkin's sprained ankles, bruised tailbone, and wounded ego.

Chapter 39

After setting some cheese to drain, Cora dried her hands and collected the afternoon mail from the mat at the front door. She shuffled through envelopes of various sizes as she returned to the kitchen. An invitation to tea from Beatrice, an appeal for donations for a house of refuge, a plain white envelope from McGill. Cora wanted to tear it open at once, but it wasn't addressed to her. Surely the addressee wouldn't want to wait till supper to read his letter. He'd want to read it right away!

Cora put the letter in her pocket and hurried through the kitchen door into a warm May afternoon. All the world was aglow. The letter had to contain good news. How could it be otherwise when the lilac and lily-of-the-valley released their heady fragrance, the leaves of the trees unfurled in the sunshine, and ducks nested in the rushes by the creek. Jim was freeing an ox from a yoke and harness for the reward of the pasture as Cora walked up the lane. He sheltered his eyes from the sun with his hand and smiled.

Waving the letter in the air, she broke into a jog. "McGill!" she panted excitedly. "Jim! It's from McGill!"

At once, Jim accepted the envelope and sliced it open with his dirty thumbnail. Cora knew better than to suggest he wash his hands at the pump. Instead, she studied her husband's face as he withdrew a sheet of snow-white paper and read. His eyes lit with relief, thank

God, and his face broke into a broad smile.

"The dean has decreed that I'm welcome back in August," Jim announced. "He's sending a reading list so I can make up for lost time."

"That's wonderful," Cora exclaimed. She made a mental note to speak with Beatrice about her library when they had tea.

"They didn't have to accommodate me, Cora. I was concerned when we hadn't heard."

Concerned? All month, since he'd sent his letter requesting readmission, he'd been in knots with worry, though outwardly he went about his days in cheerful optimism.

"We shouldn't be idle in good weather, but I can't concentrate on work." Jim gathered Cora into his arms and swung her in the air. "Let's take a walk in the woodlot, by the pond."

"We'll gather fiddleheads for supper," suggested Cora. "And then you won't have to admit to being idle."

Cora found a clean bucket and two utility knives in the barn while Jim washed his hands, and they set off, arm in arm, to the cool of the forest at the back of the farm, on an adventure as gleefully romantic as an afternoon in Tuscany. The damp air remained blessedly free of the black flies and mosquitoes that would attack anyone who entered the woodlot come June.

In a short time, the glades gave up two meals' worth of fiddleheads, and Cora and Jim paused to rest in a grove of cedar. In similar comfort to the hayloft, they discussed Jim's return to law school from every which angle, as people who receive welcome news are wont to do.

After a spell, Jim rolled onto his side to face Cora.

"I went to Beck's this morning to pick up a sack of alfalfa seed," he said in a low voice.

Hardly earth-shattering news for his serious tone, thought Cora.

"I saw a fine black gelding and—"

Cora guessed, "He was pulling Robert's carriage?"

"Yes. With Adeline Brockett in it. Her arm was tucked under Helston's just so." Jim demonstrated Adeline's demure grasp on Cora's arm.

"Well, I suppose this news absolves us of our sins against them. I hope they'll be as happy as we are." Cora turned to Jim.

"Do you mean it?"

"I do," she said, for it was the truth.

Limbs entwined, they listened to the rustle of leaves in the trees and the croak of an early rising peeper. After a spell, Jim said, "I would rather Helston and Adeline lived elsewhere. Anywhere but Maryville."

"Alas, they don't. And if—"

"When—"

Jim had read her mind. "*When* they marry," Cora continued, "we must show them all the grace we can muster."

"But he's dangerous, Cora."

"Exactly. You subdue a dragon with kindness."

Jim shook his head. "No, Miss Polka-dot. If you feed a dragon with kindness, you embolden him. I feel badly for Adeline. She has no idea who he is."

Cora felt a flash of envy at the mention of her name. "Adeline will be fine," she said more sharply than she'd intended.

"Whoa, Cora. Adeline deserves to be happy, and he'll make her miserable."

"She's strong enough to handle Robert. Maybe even strong enough to improve him."

"Perhaps," Jim said vaguely.

A hazy dimness engulfed the woods as clouds gathered and hid the sun. They lapsed into lazy contemplation as more peepers joined in chorus with the first. Cora looked up at her husband and felt a stirring in her soul. Why, oh why couldn't she be as generous as he was? Why did she have to be so petty? Jim was right about Robert and right about Adeline Brockett. She didn't deserve to be unhappy. Neither did Dr. Blackmore or the Jones sisters or anyone else Cora unjustly resented, even after they'd changed.

Jim cradled her cheek in his hand. And then he kissed her. This time, she would be the generous one. She would love him as he had loved her. She broke his kiss and nudged him onto his back.

First his shirt and then his fly. He lay back and watched her, his mouth slack, his breath rising, as she unbuttoned his clothing. Then she took him into her hands and stroked his shaft. Kneeling between his legs she took him into her mouth, circling with her tongue, gripping him in her warm hands. He would come quickly. Except he chose not to.

"Cora," he gasped. "Ride me."

She would. She ached to take him deep inside. Underclothes cast aside, she straddled him, her skirt hiding their naked loins as they merged. Cora shifted her pelvis and admitted him, allowing him to slide as high within her as she decided. At first, she teased, but she couldn't contain her own longing for him, and they fell into a fast rhythm, his manhood finding greater depth than ever before.

They looked intently at each other as they took their pleasure. Jim's dark eyes were serene yet focused. She saw by the set of his jaw that he was struggling to hold himself back. "I'm sorry," he groaned as he slipped his hands over her hips to hold her. "I…I can't stop."

Cora felt she would split apart in ecstasy. He quivered within her as she rode him as deeply as she could, and then she tumbled with him into the greatest pleasure she had ever known. Her own cry silenced his apology, and he held her hips with his powerful hands to support her as their urgency shattered into orgasm.

Spent, they fell into each other's arms and rested in silence. Their bodies smelled of sweat and sex and earth. Cora nuzzled Jim's neck. She'd remember this afternoon forever, and the salty taste of his skin was a detail worthy of memory. How like a man to drift off to sleep after a coupling like that. Yet sleep he did. "I love you," she whispered. As she drifted into a delicious torpor herself, she wondered if she was already pregnant.

Perhaps it was foolhardy to not take precautions with responsibility ever-looming and Jim away in the fall. However, he often wished aloud for a child, and he would welcome their baby whenever fate dictated. As she dozed, Cora's limbs relaxed, and she was semi-aware of a trickle of seed warming her inner thigh. Everything would be okay. Together they'd raise their son or daughter with the happiness of parents who loved each other very much.

Epilogue

In the heat of a midafternoon Sunday, the songbirds took refuge in the trees, leaving the creek to dragonflies and whirligig beetles. Downriver, a heron stood in a pool and stalked his dinner. Cora was grateful to sit quietly under a willow bough and watch the majestic creature while Jim taught Johnny how to fish.

A rivulet of perspiration trickled between Cora's shoulder blades. Funny how she'd forgotten the awfulness of morning sickness—all day sickness—until it set in. She'd felt just as wretched with Johnny three years ago, but this too would pass. Cora leaned against the ridged trunk of the willow, took a sip of ginger beer to settle her stomach, and closed her eyes.

A splash, little boy laughter, and Jim's voice. "Hold on tight! We've caught something." Cora quickly opened her eyes to watch Johnny catch his first fish. His straw hat had fallen off and he was barefoot and shirtless, but he was tanned and brown as a nut like his daddy, so Cora made herself not mind. Johnny let go of the rod and clapped his small hands while Jim pulled in the line. A sunfish, round and shiny, danced in the air and landed on the muddy bank. Father and son bent over the fish and Jim released it. "Too small for our dinner," he explained. For a moment, Cora forgot her nausea as she took in the scene of Johnny's wonder, Jim's patience, and their contented male companionship.

As they cast their line again, Cora caught sight of Betsy and August Blackmore on the opposite bank, he pink-faced in a black suit, she round-bellied in a mauve maternity dress, a matching parasol balanced on her shoulder.

"Cora! Jim!" Betsy hollered and waved.

Though the pair were several yards distant, Cora saw August's scowl, their exchange of words, and a slump in Betsy's posture. How dare he. Betsy only meant to reach out to old friends.

"Come on over!" Cora called back. "We have ginger beer!" And plenty of leftover food.

Betsy shouted back, "We're coming!" and headed to the bridge with her husband trailing. Good for her. Cora rose to straighten the picnic blanket and make space for company.

Minutes later, Betsy was sprawled on the blanket with Cora, and August was perched on a creek-side boulder with a bottle of ginger beer in hand. After commiserating on the discomforts of pregnancy, Cora and Betsy gossiped lazily, fixing on the topic of Mr. and Mrs. Robert Helston.

"I heard they're moving to the States," said Betsy.

"Chicago," added Cora. "Since that devastating fire, the city's in a building frenzy and Robert probably wants a slice of the pie."

"And an escape from angry investors and rabid lawyers here in Ontario. Daddy and August don't tell me anything, but they look ever so cross when anyone mentions Mr. Helston."

Cora thought of Jim finding the Helston file in the Tuckers' library and seeking justice, but she decided to let the 'rabid lawyer' comment drop. "How does Adeline feel about moving?" she asked.

"About moving? You mean 'fleeing'?" corrected Betsy. She shrugged. "Adeline claims she's thrilled, but I think she hoped for New York City and not bleak, dusty Chicago. By the way, I heard your Aunt Jenny is coming back to Maryville to help at the hospital when it opens."

Cora smiled and sighed in a resigned way. "I wish that were true, but she's devoted to the orphanage and Ivy and she's very happy in Brucedale. They've fifty-seven children now. Fifty-seven! And I'm fully occupied with one." Cora looked fondly at Johnny, who was showing an open jar of dew worms to a grim-faced Dr. Blackmore.

Betsy's gaze followed Cora's. "You have other responsibilities besides a son. August says he's glad you're on the hospital board, Cora. And he's relieved that Jim wrested control of the finances from Robert Helston." Betsy imitated her husband's pompous bluster in a convincing English accent. "James Sinclair has a steady hand on the tiller and his wife is an obedient helpmeet with a feminine instinct, an intuition if you will, for making a hospital a modern place of healing."

"August should credit the basic common sense of Florence Nightingale," laughed Cora. "Aunt Jenny sent me her book, *Notes on Hospitals*, and I refer to it often."

Jim caught Cora's eye and tipped his head toward August who was mopping his blond brow with a handkerchief and wilting into a livid crimson.

"Would you boys like some watermelon?" Cora offered.

Presently, all five of the party were gathered on the blanket with slices of melon in hand. Johnny squealed with glee as Jim blew seeds all the way to the creek.

Although Betsy, Cora, and Johnny were game, August declined Jim's invitation to join the seed spitting contest that followed.

****

If grain prices held and the weather remained favorable, they'd have enough money from the fall harvest and the legal practice to build an addition on the farmhouse. Cora would want a porch and a summer kitchen. With dormers, new porches on front and side, and an extension at the back, the house would hold Gran, Mama, and a growing family comfortably. They hadn't heard from Dad since he vanished for the prairies and the farm needed a man. Jim rolled up the architect's sketches, pushed them into a cubby, and stretched. Enough. It was getting dark. He'd show Cora the plans in the light of day.

Careful not to bang the screen door lest he wake Johnny, Jim joined Cora on the porch swing. Fireflies darted over the garden in fleeting bursts of light. He slid his arm around Cora's shoulders, and she snuggled in close with her feet tucked under her skirt, her knitting abandoned to the basket.

"Feeling better?" Jim asked.

"Yes, for now," Cora replied.

"You mean, this sickness. It comes and goes?"

"Yes," she smiled weakly. "It's worse in the morning, but I feel queasy all day."

"Maybe it's something you're eating, though Johnny and I are well, and we eat all the same things as you do."

"No, you're quite right, Jim. I don't think the cause is food. It's something inside."

Inside. Oh God. A tumor? Cancer? This sounded

serious. Think. Think. "Cora, I know you have all your books and everything, but have you spoken to Jenny or August about this?"

"No. Only Betsy because she figured out—"

"Betsy! But she's useless!" What a terrible thing to say. "I mean, she used to be silly, and although she's more sensible now, I don't think she'd have any idea how to diagnose and treat you."

"Actually, Jim, she understood my situation completely."

Okay. Nausea. All the time. Something inside. Crediting Betsy in an off-kilter way. Cora *had* seemed off. Sluggish. Quiet. He mustn't be alarmed, he mustn't panic. Better to ask more questions and consult August himself. He'd heard Cora speak to patients often enough. "When did you start feeling unwell?" he ventured.

"About a month ago."

"You've been sick a whole month and you didn't say anything?"

"I didn't want to concern you right away."

"But you and Johnny, you're my top 'concerns'. You know that. You should have told me." She was sick and he was hurt that she'd kept it secret. Still, he mustn't scold. Arms about her, he met her eyes and this time, he spoke gently. "This could be serious, Cora. I love you and I can't imagine what Johnny and I would do if anything ever happened to you."

"Jim. Just listen." Cora peered up at him, shy-eyed yet smiling. "I'm not ill. The nausea will resolve of its own accord. And in about seven months." She patted her belly.

"A baby. A baby?!"

"Yes. A brother or sister for Johnny. Probably in

early February."

"That's fantastic!" Jim kissed Cora's forehead, and then he kissed her mouth, but too enthusiastically. He had to be careful. She'd be delicate in her state.

"You're happy?" laughed Cora.

"Very happy. And so lucky." He laughed in return, then held her snugly again. "Cora, do you remember the day of the tornado, when we sheltered together at St. Andrew's?"

"Remember? I'll never forget it."

"Together, in the storm, we were still school kids with each other. Then after—"

"Father."

"Yes. You were alone and vulnerable, but you were also strong and proud. When you lost your dad and your home, you didn't buckle. You straightened your back and stepped into the future. I realized that if I were to have any chance with you, I had to grow up too. To try to be the equal of your father, even if he set an impossible standard."

Cora grasped his hand and squeezed it. "Jim, you are the equal of Father. He would be so proud to have you as his son-in-law and the father of his grandchildren."

"Thank you, Cora. I know you love me, but hearing those words means more to me than I can say."

Sheet lightning lit the sky. The air was still and there was no thunder. They were together in a love and gratitude beyond words. This time, Jim would stay by Cora's side as their family grew. This time, he wouldn't leave her for even a single day.

A word about the author…

Renata North is a registered nurse who writes when most people are sleeping. She lives in Stratford, Ontario, Canada with her husband who is also a nurse.